Also by Jennifer L. Schiff

A Shell of a Problem

Something Fishy

In the Market for Murder

Bye Bye Birdy

A Sanibel Island Mystery

Jennifer Lonoff Schiff

Shovel
& Pail
Press

BYE BYE BIRDY: A SANIBEL ISLAND MYSTERY
by Jennifer Lonoff Schiff

Book Four in the Sanibel Island Mystery series

http://www.SanibelIslandMysteries.com

© 2019 by Jennifer Lonoff Schiff

Cover design by Kristin Bryant

Formatting by Polgarus Studio

ISBN: 978-0-578-46401-5

Library of Congress Control Number: 2019901742

Everyone likes birds. What wild creature is more accessible to our eyes and ears, as close to us and everyone in the world, as universal as a bird?
— David Attenborough

Sometimes I think that the point of birdwatching is not the actual seeing of the birds, but the cultivation of patience. Of course, each time we set out, there's a certain amount of expectation we'll see something, maybe even a species we've never seen before, and that it will fill us with light. But even if we don't see anything remarkable—and sometimes that happens—we come home filled with light anyway.
— Lynn Thomson,
Birding with Yeats: A Mother's Memoir

PROLOGUE

Guin sat at her desk, staring out the window, wondering for the dozenth time if she had made the right decision, about so many things. Should she have offered more money for the house? Should she have gone off to Asia with Ris? Should she have told Ginny to assign someone else the profile of noted birder/wildlife photographer Bertram "Birdy" McMurtry, the Indiana Jones of ornithologists?

She sighed and turned back to her monitor. Well, it was too late now. Someone had outbid her on the Simms house, where she had found that dead body. The house had gone from being unsellable to one of the most looked at properties on Sanibel, thanks to Guin's reporting on—and solving of—the murder. After much hemming and hawing, Guin had put in an offer on the place, only to discover herself outbid.

Now she just prayed the condo she was renting, which the owner had just put up for sale, didn't sell too quickly. Though the owner had told Guin she would give her at least 30 days' notice before she had to move.

There was always Ris's place in Fort Myers Beach. She had lost track of how many times he had asked her to move in with him.

Her mind flashed back to their dinner a couple of months before at the Beach House. She had been sure, from the Champagne and the way Ris was acting, that he was going to propose. And she had been terrified. Fortunately, the proposal had to do with travel, not marriage.

Ris, aka Dr. Harrison Hartwick, a professor of marine biology at Florida Gulf Coast University and a much in-demand lecturer, who also happened to have been voted one of the sexiest men in Southwest Florida, was taking a sabbatical from his teaching position. He had received a generous grant to lecture and conduct research (i.e., search for shells and study marine biology and ecology) in and around Southeast Asia and Australia.

Ris had asked Guin to join him, offering to pay her travel expenses, but she had turned him down. She looked at the black cat asleep in her lap.

"Who turns down an all-expenses paid trip to Asia and Australia?" she said to the sleeping animal.

She sighed again and looked at her monitor, attempting to read, for the umpteenth time, the latest blog post on Birdy McMurtry's website. But her mind kept going back to Ris, who had left a few days before.

When he had asked her why she wouldn't come with him, she had told him she was worried about losing her job at the *Sanibel-Captiva Sun-Times*, and not having a place to live when she got back. He had told her that he doubted the paper could easily replace her and had said she could always get freelance work. He had also told her she was welcome to come live with him in Fort Myers Beach.

They had gone back and forth for weeks, until she had finally agreed to meet up with him in Australia just before Valentine's Day, which happened to be their one-year anniversary. And then he had left, the week after New Year's, and her condo was about to hit the market. And she had stupidly agreed to interview Birdy McMurtry, even though she knew next to nothing about birds. True, she did own a field guide to the birds of the Southeast, coincidentally by Birdy McMurtry. But she was far from a birding expert. And Guin had questioned her boss, Ginny Prescott, as to why Ginny wanted *her* to do the story when there were dozens of far more knowledgeable bird watchers on the island.

But Ginny had told Guin it was precisely Guin's lack of birding knowledge and natural inquisitiveness that made her the perfect person to do the interview. As a novice bird watcher herself, Guin wouldn't talk down to readers, and she would ask more questions than someone more experienced would. Though Guin suspected Ginny had an ulterior motive for assigning her the story, a more personal one.

Ginny knew Guin had been blue since the house fell through and Ris had gone off to Asia. And Guin suspected that Ginny had assigned her to the story in hopes that Mr. McMurtry, who was single and a dead ringer for a forty-something Harrison Ford, would be a pleasant distraction. Though Guin had made it clear to Ginny that she and Ris had not broken up, and that she had no interest in hooking up with anyone. To which Ginny had just smiled that cat-ate-the-canary smile of hers.

"Focus, Guin!" Guin said aloud, startling Fauna, her black cat.

Guin had been staring out her window again, watching a flock of ibis make their way across the golf course. Now she returned to her computer monitor and reread Birdy's latest blog post. She needed to be prepared if she didn't want to sound like an idiot when she accompanied him through the J. N. "Ding" Darling National Wildlife Refuge the next morning.

She finished reading the post, then clicked on the embedded video. At the sound of birds tweeting and chirping, Fauna woke up and jumped onto Guin's desk, animatedly chirping at the birds on the screen, which brought a smile to Guin's face.

She finished watching the video, which Birdy had shot on his recent trip to Patagonia, then read a few more posts. As she was reading about Birdy's experience eating the Patagonian specialty *Cordero al Palo*, spit-roasted lamb that's cooked over an open fire until the outside is crispy and the meat falls off the bone, her stomach started to growl.

She looked at the clock on her monitor. It read 6:00.

"Guess I should go get something to eat," she said to Fauna. "Got to be sharp for the big interview tomorrow."

She got up and headed to her kitchen, the black cat trotting after her.

CHAPTER 1

Guin had set her alarm for 6:30, even though she rarely slept past then. Ever since moving to Sanibel nearly a year and a half before, she had become a morning person, waking up with the sun. But she had been up a bit later than usual the night before, usual being 10, doing more research, and she didn't want to be late for her private tour of Ding Darling with Birdy McMurtry. And no way was she going to do a big interview without having a mug of coffee and a little something to eat beforehand.

So as soon as the alarm went off, she got out of bed, much to the consternation of Flora and Fauna, her two cats, and headed to the bathroom. Her morning ablutions taken care of, she went into her closet to pick out something suitable to wear.

It was mid-January, and it had been unseasonably cool for Sanibel, which meant it was in the low 60s. So Guin opted for a pair of chinos, a white polo shirt, and a navy-blue hoodie.

"Now coffee," she announced.

She headed down the hall to the kitchen, the two cats following her. As soon as she turned on the lights, Fauna started to meow.

"Hold on," Guin admonished her. "I will feed you in a minute."

Guin's other cat, Flora, a multicolored feline who rarely spoke, sat in the middle of the kitchen, giving Guin a beseeching look.

"Fine. I'll give you guys some food and water."

Guin walked over to the pantry, Fauna practically tripping her en route. She opened the door and grabbed the bag of cat food, then poured a little bit into the two cat bowls. Then she picked up the water bowl and refilled it.

"There!" she said, placing the water bowl on the floor. "Now can I make myself some coffee?"

The cats did not reply. They were too busy stuffing themselves.

"Eat slower, so you don't throw up," she cautioned them.

But the cats ignored her and continued to inhale their food.

Guin sighed. Then she walked over to the cabinet where she kept her coffee. She reached in and retrieved the container of freshly ground beans and placed two heaping scoops in her French press. Then she heated up some water in her electric kettle and poured it into the glass carafe as soon as it had boiled. Five minutes later, her coffee was ready.

She poured the coffee into her favorite mug and lowered her face to inhale the aroma. Was there anything better than the smell of freshly brewed coffee? If there was, Guin hadn't smelled it. Though the smell of the sea was a close second. Followed by chocolate.

She took a sip of her coffee and sighed with pleasure. Then she grabbed a protein bar out of the cabinet and took a bite.

"Oops, time to go!" she said a few minutes later, seeing that it was a little after seven.

She downed the last sip of coffee, rinsed out her mug, then went to brush her teeth.

As she brushed, she stared at her reflection. Her curly, strawberry blonde hair was being its usual unruly self. She rinsed out her mouth, then held her hair up in a ponytail.

Up or down? she wondered, turning her head from side to side.

She grabbed a ponytail holder from the drawer and pulled her hair back. Then she applied some sunblock.

She eyed her reflection again, then opened the drawer where she kept her makeup. She applied a little mascara and some lip gloss.

"Good enough," she said, staring into the mirror.

She left the bathroom and headed to her desk. She gathered her phone, her microcassette recorder, her notepad, and a pen, then grabbed her messenger bag and placed everything in it. She walked down the hall and took her keys off the peg where she kept them, took one last look in her bag, to make sure she hadn't forgotten anything, called out a goodbye to the cats, and left.

Guin arrived at Ding Darling at 7:25 and parked her purple Mini Cooper in the visitor lot. She then made her way to the Education Center, where she would be meeting Birdy.

She climbed the stairs and immediately spied him, speaking to a ranger.

"Mr. McMurtry," said Guin, walking up to him and extending her hand. "I'm Guinivere Jones, with the *Sanibel-Captiva Sun-Times*."

Birdy smiled at her.

"A pleasure to meet you, Ms. Jones. And please, call me Birdy."

Guin noticed he was still holding her hand. It felt warm.

"Yes, well, I'm looking forward to our tour of Ding Darling," she said, removing her hand from his grip.

"Have you been to the refuge before?" asked the ranger, who wore a pin announcing his name was Bob.

"Oh yes, many times," Guin replied.

"Well, you haven't been here with me," said Birdy, giving her a self-confident grin.

"Shall we?" asked Ranger Bob. "I've a special vehicle to take us around. It's just over there," he said, pointing towards the parking lot.

"Excellent!" said Birdy. "After you, Ms. Jones."

They headed down the steps and toward what looked like a large covered golf cart.

"Mr. McMurtry," said the ranger, indicating for him to sit up front.

"I'm going to sit in back with Ms. Jones," he replied, with a smile. "It'll be easier for her to ask me questions that way."

"Whatever you say, Mr. McMurtry," said the ranger.

Birdy took a seat in the back and gestured for Guin to sit next to him, which she did, albeit a bit hesitantly. Something about him put Guin on her guard.

"You can put your bags in front, if you like," said the ranger, indicating the empty seat.

"I'm good," Birdy replied.

"Me too," said Guin.

"You two set?" asked the ranger.

"Ready when you are," replied Birdy.

The ranger started the cart and they headed off to Wildlife Drive.

As they made their way to the first stop, Birdy told Guin all about his trip to Patagonia.

Guin had just read about it on his blog, but she let him go on.

"You should have seen the Chilean flamingos!" said

Birdy, enthusiastically. "Such gorgeous birds. A bit like your roseate spoonbills, only bigger, with large black beaks. You should see them in flight. Their flocks are quite large. Like a pink rainbow streaking across the sky."

Guin opened her mouth to comment, but Birdy cut her off.

"Stop!" he commanded.

Guin wasn't sure if he was talking to her or to the ranger.

Ranger Bob stopped the cart.

Birdy grabbed his camera bag and raced over to the water as Guin and the ranger watched. There were a bunch of birds, diving for fish.

Birdy turned toward them.

"You two coming?"

Guin and the ranger got out and followed.

"That's a double-breasted cormorant, yes?" said Guin, pointing to a black bird whose wings were extended.

"Good eye, Guin! People often confuse cormorants with anhingas," Birdy replied. "They do look quite similar, to the untrained eye. But if you look closely, you will notice that anhingas have a straight, almost spear-like beak whereas the double-breasted cormorant has a curved beak."

Guin actually knew that but kept silent.

"And did you know that the name *anhinga* means 'water turkey'?" Birdy continued.

"I did not know that," said Guin.

Birdy smiled at her. It was a nice smile, but it didn't compare to Ris's. Guin sighed inwardly. Had she been foolish not to go off to Asia with Ris? Well, too late now.

They stood by the water for several minutes as Birdy took photos and narrated what he was shooting and Guin took notes. Then they got back in the golf cart and headed to their next stop.

As they drove, Guin asked Birdy questions, about what

led him to study birds, if he had any favorites, and where he planned to travel next.

He answered each question enthusiastically, often going off on tangents, which made Guin glad she had brought her microcassette recorder with her, to supplement her notes. At the rate he was expounding, she would run out of tapes before the tour was over. More reason for her to get one of those digital recorders or an app for her phone. But old habits died hard.

By the time they arrived back at the Education Center, over two hours later, after having seen yellow-capped night herons, tri-colored herons, little blue herons, a flock of white pelicans, and several roseate spoonbills, Guin's head was spinning and her hand had cramped from all the note-taking. She had more than enough information to write an article, several articles, and had taken over a dozen photos of Birdy and the various birds they had seen to include with the piece.

Birdy was a bit long-winded, but he clearly knew his stuff. Every time they spotted a new bird, Birdy would immediately identify it and tell Guin some fascinating fact about it, which she would quickly write down.

They got out of the cart and Guin thanked Ranger Bob for taking them around the refuge.

"Happy to do it," he replied. "I learned a few things myself."

"And thank you, Mr. McMurtry," Guin said, turning to Birdy. "I learned a lot today. Will you be staying on Sanibel for a few days? I may have some additional questions as I type up my notes."

"Yes. I'm doing back-to-back private tours tomorrow, to raise money for the Ding Darling Wildlife Society. Then I'll be staying on through the weekend. I'm crashing with some old friends here on Sanibel."

He paused.

"Say, my friends are having a little get together in my honor this Saturday. Why don't you come? That way if you have any questions, you can ask me in person."

"That's very nice of you, Mr. McMurtry, but are you sure it's okay? I wouldn't want to intrude."

"Nonsense!" said Birdy. "And please, call me Birdy. My friends do."

"Thank you... Birdy," she said.

She fished in her bag for her card case.

"Here's my card," she said, handing one to him. "Please text or email me the information about the party."

He took the card and pocketed it.

"And what's the best way to contact you?" Guin asked.

"I'll give you my mobile number."

She reached into her bag and pulled out her phone.

"Go ahead."

He recited his number and Guin entered it into her contact list, repeating it back to make sure she had entered it correctly.

"Well, I'm sure you must be busy, and I should get going," Guin said.

"Before you go, do you know where I could get a good strong cup of coffee around here?"

"The Sanibel Bean has pretty good coffee," Guin replied. And there's always Bailey's."

Birdy sighed.

"They're okay, but I was hoping there was someplace with really good coffee. You know, freshly made, and strong. Americans tend to like their coffee on the weaker side."

Guin raised an eyebrow. She had never heard anyone complain about the coffee at the Sanibel Bean or Bailey's. Though it was true that most places didn't serve the kind of dark, bold coffee she preferred, and you never knew how fresh it was.

"Well," she said slowly. "I make a pretty good mug of coffee, that is, if you like it really strong."

"The bolder, the better," said Birdy, grinning.

Guin could see where this was going and felt unable to stop herself.

"Would you like to come over to my place? I could make us a fresh pot. Though I have a ton of work to do," she added quickly, hoping he would turn her down.

"That would be delightful, Guin. Do you live near here?"

"Not too far," said Guin, mentally kicking herself. Why did she have to open her big mouth? "You want to follow me? I'm just down the road."

"I'll just get my car. Where are you parked?"

"I'm the purple Mini, over there," she said, pointing.

Birdy grinned.

"It suits you. I have the red Jeep," he said, pointing.

Guin wasn't the least bit surprised.

"I'll wait for you at the exit," she told him.

Guin walked over to the Mini, silently cursing herself for inviting Birdy back to her place. She had no desire to entertain anyone and had work to do. Those tapes wouldn't transcribe themselves.

She got in her car and took a deep breath, exhaling slowly. Hopefully he wouldn't stay long. She started the engine and slowly drove to the exit. She stopped there and waited for Birdy's red Jeep. As soon as she spied him, she made her way out of Ding Darling toward the condo.

CHAPTER 2

"What a lovely place you have here, Guin," Birdy said, walking around. "And what friendly cats."

Flora and Fauna had both immediately cottoned onto Birdy and were rubbing themselves against his legs. He had stopped to pet them and Guin could hear them purring.

Guin looked out from the kitchen, where she was brewing a big pot of coffee. The French press only made a mugful, so she had gotten down her old coffee machine.

"They like you. Maybe they smell bird," she said.

Birdy chuckled.

"As long as they don't try to eat me. Cats are a major nuisance in some parts of the world. They've been known to destroy whole bird populations."

"So I've heard," said Guin. "I don't think these two would know what to do with an actual bird, though. They're strictly indoor cats."

"You'd be surprised," said Birdy, continuing to pet each cat.

"Coffee's ready," Guin called a couple minutes later.

Birdy straightened up and headed toward the kitchen, much to the cats' dismay.

"Smells heavenly," he said, taking an exaggerated sniff.

Guin had to agree.

"Do you take anything in your coffee?"

"No. Black is fine. If it's good coffee, it doesn't require anything."

Guin totally agreed with him.

"Shall I get you a to-go mug? You can give it back to me Saturday."

Guin hoped he would take the hint and leave.

"You trying to get rid of me, Ms. Jones?"

He was grinning at her, and Guin felt her cheeks turning pink.

"I do have an awful lot of work to do, and you must be very busy yourself."

"Never too busy for a good cup of coffee with an attractive woman," he said, continuing to smile at her.

And I could have been in Cambodia with Ris, Guin thought to herself. She shook off the thought and poured some coffee into her extra to-go mug.

"Here you go," she said, handing Birdy the mug.

"Thank you," he said, taking it.

He took a sip and closed his eyes.

"Heavenly."

He opened his eyes.

"Are you married, Guin?"

The question startled Guin.

"No. Why?"

"Would you marry me? I've been looking all my life for a woman who knew how to make a good strong cup of coffee."

"You must not have been looking that hard," Guin replied.

"You would be surprised," he said.

"Well, I'm afraid I'm already taken," she told him.

"A shame."

Birdy looked at his watch, one of those smart watches that monitored your heart rate, reminded you to work out, and displayed messages, in addition to telling the time.

"Well, it seems I actually do need to get going."

He took another sip of coffee and sighed with pleasure.

"Thank you for the coffee," he said, handing her back the mug. "I'll text you the details about Saturday."

Guin saw him to the door.

"Can you find your way back to San-Cap Road?" she asked.

"Even without a GPS," he said, smiling at her.

He took her hand.

"Until Saturday."

"Until Saturday," Guin replied.

He released her hand and headed out the door.

Guin closed the door behind him and exhaled. She hadn't even realized she had been holding her breath. What had she gotten herself into?

Guin spent the rest of the day transcribing her interview with Birdy and typing her notes, taking short breaks for food and to relieve herself. She knew that Birdy liked to talk, but she didn't realize how much until she had spent over six hours typing nearly every word he had said. She had decided to leave certain things out, like the incident with the tango dancer in Buenos Aires, to save a bit of time. But still.

She got up to stretch a little after 4:30 and took her phone out of the drawer she kept it in when she was working. There were several messages from her best friend, Shelly, wanting to know if Guin wanted to go for a walk or do something that afternoon.

Instead of texting her back, Guin decided to call her.

"Hey!" said Shelly, answering after a few rings. "I was about to call missing persons."

"Hey yourself," said Guin. "What's up? You still want to

get together? I've been working and wasn't checking my phone."

"Yes!" she replied. "Steve is out of town on business, and the house feels empty."

"You missing the kids?"

Shelly and her husband Steve had two adult children: the older one worked at Disney and the younger one was in college. They had both been home over Christmas and New Year's but had gone back to their respective lives after the holidays.

"Totally. I need noise! I need activity!"

Guin laughed.

"Well, I'm not sure I can help you with that."

"You up for going to happy hour?" Shelly asked. "I don't feel like cooking tonight."

Guin didn't usually attend happy hours. She wasn't much of a drinker, and, unlike Shelly, she preferred quiet. But she could tell her friend needed to get out of the house.

"Sure. Where were you thinking?"

"There's always Doc Ford's," said Shelly. "Actually, let's go to Cip's Place. I haven't been there in a while."

"Fine. What time?"

"How about 5:30? Does that work?"

"Perfect. See you soon."

Guin arrived at Cip's Place at 5:40. She had debated what to wear and then had encountered traffic, mainly day trippers heading back off island. (Traffic was a big issue during the season, which ran from January through mid-April.)

She spied Shelly by the bar, chatting with someone. Oh God, it was Marty Nesbitt. Marty ran one of the more popular shelling groups on Facebook and thought Guin had a crush on him. How he had gotten that idea, Guin didn't know. Marty was a widower in his sixties, balding, with a ponytail. He also had a penchant for wearing Hawaiian shirts. She suspected he was also a bit deaf, which would explain why he had a tendency to talk over people.

Guin forced a smile on her face and headed over to the bar.

"Hey, Shell, Marty."

"Guin!" said Shelly, giving her friend a big smile. "I was just discussing the Shell Show with Marty."

"Yup. I was just telling Shelly here she'd better watch out. I'm working on my entry for the Artistic division. It's going to knock the judges' socks off."

Guin continued to force herself to smile.

"Looks like you've got some competition, Shell. So, can you reveal what you're working on, Marty?" Guin asked. Not that she really cared.

He grinned.

"Nope. It's a surprise. Won't even tell Tilda. She's my new squeeze. Take a look," he said, pulling out his phone.

He passed the phone to Guin. There was a photo of Marty with a petite Asian woman. Guin smiled, then passed the phone back to Marty.

"Very nice," said Guin.

Marty grinned.

"Can I get you something to drink?" the bartender asked Guin.

"Yes, please!" said Guin, sounding a bit desperate.

The bartender smiled at her.

"What'll it be?"

"She'll have a margarita, no salt," said Shelly.

The bartender looked over at Guin.

"Sure, why not?" said Guin.

Margaritas and beer were her typical happy hour beverages of choice.

The bartender went to fix her drink and Guin tried to

telepathically tell Shelly she wanted to get a table.

A minute later he returned with Guin's margarita. She took a sip.

"Mmm… that's good. Thank you. Could I also see a happy hour menu?"

"Sure," he said. "Be right back."

"Marty," said Shelly, sweetly. "Would you excuse me and Guin? We have some catching up to do."

"Of course, of course," said Marty. "I should be heading home anyway. Me and Tilda are going dancing later," he said, waggling his bushy eyebrows.

Guin nearly choked on her drink.

"I hope you two have a lovely time."

Marty took Guin's hand, startling Guin, who held on tight to her drink with her other hand.

"*Enchanté*, Guinivere," he said, lifting her hand to his lips and kissing it. "Until we meet again."

He looked up at her, waggled his eyebrows again, and then released her hand.

"Here are a couple of menus," said the bartender.

"Thanks," said Shelly, grabbing them. She had been watching the scene and trying not to laugh.

"Well, see you around, Marty," Guin said, holding up her hand and giving Shelly and the bartender a pleading look.

"There's a free table over there," said the bartender, indicating an open table by the window, just a few feet away.

They quickly headed over to it.

"Oh my God," said Guin, after they had sat down. "What on earth were you doing chatting with Marty?"

"Like I had a choice?" replied Shelly. "He was sitting by himself at the bar, and I felt bad for him."

"You're a good soul," said Guin.

"Well, you were late, and what was I supposed to do, ignore him?"

Part of Guin wanted to shout "Yes!" but she restrained herself.

"You ladies know what you'd like to eat?" asked the bartender.

"Give us a minute," said Shelly, smiling up at him.

"Sure thing," he said. "Just give a wave when you're ready."

"So, what do you think of him?" asked Shelly. She was staring at the bartender, who was tall and well built and looked to be in his late twenties or early thirties.

"Not bad," Guin replied, following Shelly's gaze. "But isn't he a bit young for you? And what about Steve?"

"Hey, I'm married, not dead. Besides, there's no law against looking," Shelly sniffed, watching as the bartender mixed a drink, his biceps flexing. She sighed.

"Pick out what you want to eat," said Guin. "I'm starving."

Their order decided, Guin signaled to the bartender, who came over a minute later.

"What'll it be, ladies?"

"I'll have the rigatoni Bolognese," said Guin.

"And I'll have the baby back ribs," said Shelly, glancing at the bartender's torso.

Guin rolled her eyes.

"Anything else?" asked the bartender.

"Just some water, for now, and maybe some bread," Guin replied.

"Coming right up," said the bartender, giving them a smile.

Shelly sighed.

"I'll give you that he's cute," said Guin. "So, when's Steve getting back?"

"Tomorrow," said Shelly.

"Well, control yourself," said Guin. "Everything okay at home?"

"Oh, everything's fine," said Shelly. "I'm just feeling old, and Steve's new gig has him traveling a lot."

"Ah," said Guin. "What's he doing again?"

"Consulting," replied Shelly. "And before you ask, I don't know what about exactly. Every time he explains, my eyes kind of glaze over."

Guin gave her a look.

"I know. I'm a bad wife."

They continued to chat. Shelly asked Guin about what she was currently working on that had her so busy, and Guin asked Shelly about her kids and how her new items were selling. Shelly made jewelry that she sold on Etsy and at some of the local art shows.

"Here you go, ladies," said the bartender, depositing their food on the table. "Can I get you anything else?"

"I'll have another one of these," Shelly said, smiling and holding up her nearly empty glass.

"Coming right up," said the bartender, smiling back at her.

Shelly watched as he made his way back to the bar.

"Just look at that derriere," she sighed.

Guin ignored her, focusing on her food instead.

"So, what's Birdy McMurtry like?" Shelly asked a few minutes later, after she had eaten a few of her ribs. "Is he as cute as he looks on the back of his books?"

"Since when have you been into bird watching?" asked Guin. She had never really paid much attention to the photo on the back of Birdy's books.

"Honey, you can't live on Sanibel for years and not know a thing or two about birds. Besides, I like birds," she said, continuing to work on her ribs.

Guin ate her rigatoni.

"Well?" asked Shelly.

"I guess. I was too busy taking notes."

Shelly glanced at her friend.

"You missing Ris?"

"Is it that obvious?" Guin said.

Shelly placed a hand on top of Guin's.

"Here you go," said the bartender, placing Shelly's drink in front of her and removing her old one.

"Thanks," said Shelly.

She took a sip, then she and Guin ate a little more of their food.

"So, whatcha got planned this weekend?" Shelly asked a few minutes later.

"I'm supposed to go to this cocktail party for Birdy Saturday."

"Oh?" said Shelly, interested. "Where's the party?"

"Not sure," said Guin. "He said he'd text me the details."

"So, you gave him your number?"

"How else was he supposed to text me details?" said Guin, annoyed at Shelly's implication.

"Down girl. I come in peace."

"Sorry," said Guin. "I haven't been sleeping so well, and I guess I'm a bit grouchy."

"What you need is to get laid," said Shelly, taking another sip of her drink.

Guin pulled Shelly's drink away from her.

"That's enough booze for you."

"Hey!" said Shelly, pulling it back.

Guin looked at her watch.

"I should get going."

"You pissed at me?"

"No," Guin sighed. "I just have more work to do. Birdy's only on the island for a few days, and I want to make sure I have everything I need from him before he flies off to his next destination. Ginny's hot to get this profile ASAP."

"Okay. Well..." Shelly took another sip of her drink.

"Have fun at the party. And ask him for a signed photo."

"Seriously?" said Guin.

"Yeah, he's famous. And cute."

She smiled at Guin, but Guin didn't smile back.

She signaled to the bartender.

The bartender saw her and came over.

"Check, please," said Guin.

He reached into his back pocket, pulled out a pad, and placed the check on the table, smiling at Shelly as he did so.

"Hey, Rafe, over here," someone called from the bar.

"I'll be back in a minute," said the bartender.

Shelly watched as Rafe headed back to the bar, then picked up the check.

"I got this," she said.

"You sure?" asked Guin. "At least let me leave the tip."

"Fine," said Shelly.

They put some money on the table and left, Shelly waving goodbye to Rafe on their way out.

"We going shelling this weekend?" Shelly asked Guin in the parking lot.

"If I have time," said Guin. "Can I let you know tomorrow?"

"Sure," said Shelly. "Text me."

"Will do," said Guin. "You sure you're okay to drive?"

"I'm fine," said Shelly.

Guin eyed her.

"Really."

"Okay," said Guin. "I'll text you as soon as I'm up."

They said their goodbyes and Guin headed to her car. She wasn't lying when she told Shelly she had work to do. At least now, thanks to all that rigatoni, she had the energy to do it. That is, if it didn't make her fall asleep.

CHAPTER 3

"What?" asked Guin, peevishly, glaring at Fauna, who was pawing her head. "What time is it?"

Guin looked over at the clock next to her bed. It was just past six.

"Go away," she said, swatting at the feline.

Guin had been up late the night before and had been hoping to sleep until at least seven. But Fauna and Flora had other ideas.

"If I feed you, will you leave me alone?" she asked the cat.

Fauna (at least she assumed it was Fauna) immediately stopped pawing her face and meowed instead.

"Fine. Let's go," she said, dragging herself out of her bed.

She trudged down the hall to the kitchen and flicked on the lights. The two cats had followed and were now looking up at her.

She made her way to the pantry and grabbed a can of cat food.

"Special treat," she said, dividing the contents into the two cat bowls.

The cats immediately made a beeline for the food.

Guin glanced at the clock on the microwave. Part of her wanted to go back to bed, but she doubted she'd be able to fall back to sleep. She walked over to the glass sliders that separated the living area from the lanai and opened the vertical blinds. It was still dark out, but the sun would be rising soon.

She walked back into the bedroom, turned on her phone, and checked the weather. It was supposed to be a nice morning.

"May as well go to the beach," she said aloud.

She debated whether to text Shelly. She knew Shelly was feeling lonely, but Guin had just seen her and felt like being alone. She put down her phone and went to get dressed.

As it was still early, Guin had decided to drive to the beach along West Gulf Drive. West Gulf Drive was a residential area, and you needed a resident sticker to park at the handful of beach access points there. Fortunately, Guin had one on her car, and she had no problem finding a spot by Beach Access #4, next to Mitchell's Sandcastles, a low-key cottage resort right on the Gulf.

She sprayed herself with the can of insect repellant she kept in the driver's side door, to fend off the noseeums that plagued shell seekers, put on her fanny pack, tucked her phone into her back pocket, and locked the car. A few minutes later, she was standing near the shoreline, watching as the sky started to lighten and turn a pinkish hue.

Sunrise was her favorite time of day. She loved standing on the beach, watching the sky go from midnight blue to turquoise and pink as the sun rose over the horizon. She closed her eyes and breathed in through her nose, raising her arms above her head. Then she opened her eyes and exhaled slowly, breathing out through her mouth.

There were a handful of people already on the beach, no doubt looking for shells. Guin just hoped they had left some for her.

She was lost in thought, looking down along the wrack line, when she heard her name.

"Hey Guin! Guinny! Wait up!"

She turned to see her friend Lenny making his way toward her.

"Nice shirt," Guin said, eyeing his Shellinator tee. "Be the cone," she read. "Does that mean you're going to poison me?" (Cone snails, as serious shellers knew, were venomous, and some could be quite deadly. Though the empty shells were harmless.)

Lenny chuckled.

"How you doing, kiddo?"

"I'm okay," said Guin. "A little sleep deprived, but good. You?"

"Can't complain. Actually, I can, but I'll spare you."

"That's okay," said Guin. "You always listen to me. Only fair I listen to you."

"Nah," said Lenny. "Just the usual woes of an old man."

"You know I don't think of you as old, Len."

Lenny, full name Leonard Isaacs, was a former middle school science teacher from New York City who had retired to Sanibel. Like Guin, he shared a love of the New York Mets and shells and was a Shell Ambassador, a designation given to those who took a day-long course at the Bailey-Matthews National Shell Museum and passed a shell identification test. He was also a member of several local shelling groups and loved to share his knowledge of mollusks and marine life with those new to Sanibel and shelling.

"Yeah, well, I'll spare you my aching lumbago."

Guin smiled.

"So, what's new with you, kid? Find any more dead bodies?"

Guin grimaced. Since moving to Sanibel she had found

two dead bodies, both murder victims, and had been intimately involved in another murder case.

"Thankfully, no. No dead bodies so far this year. And I hope it remains that way."

They continued their walk down the beach, looking for shells, smiling at or greeting the other early risers they passed, as was the way on Sanibel.

Suddenly Lenny stopped and bent down.

Guin watched as Lenny dug around in the sand.

"Ta da!" he said, a few minutes later, holding up a large horse conch shell he had unearthed.

"Wow!" said Guin. "I would have walked right past that."

Lenny beamed.

"I'm going to go wash it off. Be right back."

He headed down to the water and rinsed off the shell. Then he returned to Guin.

"Wish I could find something good," said Guin, a bit forlornly.

"You want it?" asked Lenny.

"Nah," said Guin. "Finders keepers. I did find that one horse conch a while back. I'll find another. What I'd really like is to find a king's crown conch, or a Scotch bonnet, or a true tulip, or a junonia."

"You will," said Lenny. "Took me several years to find my first junonia."

"Great," said Guin, unhappily.

They continued walking, picking up shells along the way. Guin did manage to find a few small horse conch shells, along with some nice lettered olives, a few apple and lace murexes, and a pretty, dark lightning whelk.

"I should be heading back," said Guin, checking the time on her phone. "I have work to do."

"Gotta hot story?" asked Lenny.

"I wouldn't call it 'hot,'" she replied. "I'm working on a piece about that ornithologist, Birdy McMurtry. He's on the island right now and has a new documentary coming out."

"Annie mentioned something about that. I think she was going on a tour with him over at Ding Darling."

"Annie" was Ann Campbell, a local real estate agent and Lenny's bridge partner, from whom Guin had nearly bought the house.

"Let me know what she thought. Better yet, could you ask her if I could interview her about the tour?" asked Guin.

"Why don't you call her yourself? You still have her number?"

"I do," said Guin. "But I think she'd be more receptive to the idea if it came from you."

In her past dealings with Ann Campbell, Guin had felt the real estate agent didn't like her very much. Possibly because Guin had found a dead body in one of her listings. But she knew Ann was fond of Lenny.

"Okay, I'll give her a call later."

"Thanks, Len."

They headed east, making small talk as they scanned the wrack line for shells. When they neared Mitchell's, they parted. Guin headed back to her car while Lenny continued to look for shells and people in need of shelling help.

It was a little after nine by the time Guin walked in the door.

She made her way to the kitchen and made herself some coffee. She inhaled the aroma, then took a sip and smiled. Heaven.

As she was standing there, her stomach let out a loud gurgle.

"Right, food," she said. "What do I want?"

She peered into the refrigerator, then into the cabinet

where she kept her cereal and granola.

"Granola it is," she announced.

She fixed herself a bowl, then took it and her mug to the dining table. As she ate, she checked her messages on her phone.

There was a text from Birdy with the address and time of the party. The address was on West Gulf Drive. Guin quickly Googled it and whistled. The place looked huge, and it was right on the beach.

She sent Birdy a quick reply, thanking him for the information.

"Looking forward to seeing you!" he typed back, adding a smiley face. "Let me know if you have any questions for me."

Guin gritted her teeth. "Will do!" she wrote back.

She hadn't begun writing the article yet. Transcribing her interview with Birdy and typing her notes had taken longer than she had thought. Hopefully, she'd have a first draft done by tomorrow, before the party, so she'd know if she needed any more information from him.

She continued to check her messages. There was a text from Shelly, saying hi, and one from her brother, Lance, saying he had big news.

She quickly wrote back to Shelly, saying hi back and that she would text her later. Then she texted her brother.

"What's the big news?" Guin wrote. "You want to give me a call?"

She waited to see if he would write back immediately, but he didn't. So she checked her email. There was a message from Ginny and one from Ris.

She opened the one from Ginny, with the subject line "Story ideas," first. She scanned the list of topics. When she wasn't busy trying to solve a murder, Guin covered store and restaurant openings and did human interest stories, your standard resort community fare. Which she was fine with. She loved learning about new places on Sanibel and Captiva, and the people she interviewed were always so friendly.

She closed the email without replying—she'd do that later—and opened the one from Ris. He was in Cambodia and had sent her a bunch of photos, including an adorable one of a little boy with a giant shell, which made Guin smile.

"Remind me why I didn't go with him?" she said to Fauna, who had somehow managed to sneak into Guin's lap.

"Looks great!" she wrote him back. "Miss you."

She sighed and continued to scroll through her email. She stopped at the one from her mother. She took a deep breath and opened it.

"Oh God," she said, reading it over.

Her mother had written to inform her that she would be in Naples at the end of the month, with Guin's stepfather, Philip, and Philip's sister, Lavinia, visiting Lavinia's dear friend, Harriet, who was staying with her son, Alfred, who was divorced and in finance.

Guin groaned. Her mother had included a P.S. with a link to Alfred's LinkedIn profile.

"Stop trying to fix me up!" she said to the email, then closed it.

Guin knew she would need to respond to her mother, but she would do so later, after she had composed herself. Ever since her divorce, her mother had been concerned about Guin's love life—or, more specifically, that Guin would never give her grandchildren. And at 41, it was unlikely Guin ever would. She and her ex, Arthur, had tried to have a child, but it was not in the cards. They had even been tested, but the doctor couldn't find anything wrong with either of them. And she doubted she would have a child with Ris, even though he had told her on more than one occasion that he was open to having more children. (He had college-age twins and felt badly that he hadn't spent more time with them when they were young.)

And while Lance was happily married, to his longtime partner, Owen, they had no interest in having a child. Why couldn't her mother just leave well enough alone?

She looked back down at her phone, to see if Lance had written her back. He hadn't. So she sent him another text.

"Did you know mom was coming down here?" she wrote him. "Call me."

She took a sip of her coffee, which had gone cold, and got up, dislodging Fauna.

"Sorry, kitty cat," she said to the disgruntled feline.

She rinsed her mug and her bowl in the sink and put them in the dishwasher. Then she headed into her bedroom, which doubled as her office.

"Got to write that first draft," she said aloud.

CHAPTER 4

Guin got up and stretched. She had been sitting at her computer way too long. What time was it anyway? She looked at the clock on her monitor. How did it get to be 1:10 already? Well, at least she had made a good start on the article. But she needed food.

She headed to the kitchen and fixed herself an omelet—placing the bowl with the leftover egg on the floor for Fauna to lick. When she was done eating, Guin headed back to her office, to finish writing the article. She was determined to have the first draft done by that evening, or at least a good chunk of it.

She had checked her messages while she ate. Lance had gotten back to her and had suggested they talk at five. She had written him back that that was fine and put it on her calendar, so she wouldn't forget.

As she was about to put her phone back in the drawer, it began to vibrate. She looked down to see who was trying to contact her. Shelly.

"How's it going?" she had written.

"It's going," Guin wrote back.

"You still going to that party?" Shelly asked.

"I am," Guin replied.

"Let me know how it went."

"Will do," Guin texted back.

She knew Shelly wanted to talk, but she didn't have time to chat. She turned the ringer off and placed her phone in the drawer.

At 4:50 a message flashed on her screen, reminding her that she had a call with Lance at 5. Guin smiled. Good thing she had put it on her calendar. She was so busy writing about Birdy, she had lost track of the time.

She finished the paragraph she was working on and pressed "save." Then she got out her phone and entered her brother's number. Lance picked up after a couple of rings.

"Guinivere, my long-lost sister, is it really you?"

"Ha," said Guin. "You know someone else with my cell phone number? Besides, we just talked last week."

"You can never be too sure about numbers any more. Lots of times we get calls from familiar-looking numbers that are just telemarketers. There should be a law. And it feels like ages since we last spoke. How the heck are you?"

"You first. What's the big news?"

"Well…" said Lance, taking a dramatic pause. "Not only are we opening an office in San Francisco, but we're opening up one in Paris, too. Well, sort of," he added, a beat later.

"That's fabulous, Lance. What do you mean by 'sort of'?"

"Well, the Paris thing is kind of a joint venture. This boutique firm there is looking to team up with an American agency that can help them attract an upscale alternative clientele."

"An upscale alternative clientele?" asked Guin.

Lance sighed.

"They want us to help them put the gay back in gay Paris," which he pronounced *Pa-REE*.

Guin laughed.

"I have no doubt you can help. And Paris. How exciting! I haven't been there in ages. Are you and Owen going to go over there?"

"*Mais oui*," Lance replied.

Lance ran a very successful boutique ad agency, based in Brooklyn, and his husband, Owen, ran a gallery in Chelsea. The two of them had been together forever, and Guin loved them both.

"You should come with us!"

"I'd love to," said Guin, "but I just turned down a trip to Asia and Australia with Ris, so…"

"Which I still cannot believe," Lance tutted. "I would have gone in a heartbeat."

Guin sighed and looked up at the ceiling.

"It's complicated."

"Well, we're way more fun. And Paris is much closer," said Lance, ignoring her. "I bet you can get a direct flight from Miami."

"True, but…"

"Then it's settled. You're coming."

"But you haven't even told me when you're going. What if I'm busy?"

"Seriously?" said Lance.

He had a point.

"What about San Francisco?" asked Guin.

"I have the team there ready to go. The woman who's going to run the place seems very competent. She has all the big tech guys eating out of her hand."

"So you won't be moving to San Francisco?"

"God, no," said Lance.

"Well, mom will be relieved. Did you tell her about Paris?"

"Not yet," said Lance.

"She will be green with envy," said Guin.

"Though she would never admit it."

True, thought Guin.

"So, when is Paris happening?"

"Well, we haven't signed the contract yet. But as soon as we do, I'll let you know. We probably won't fly over until March."

"All right. Keep me posted," said Guin. "Just remember, the Sanibel Shell Festival is the first weekend of the month."

"Really, you'd pass on a trip to Paris to hang out in a room full of musty shells and crazy shell people?"

She knew Lance didn't take shelling seriously, even though she had explained to him that on Sanibel it was considered a competitive sport and there were dozens of Facebook pages and blogs dedicated to shells.

When she didn't reply, he continued.

"So, what's up with you, Sis? Find any dead bodies lately?"

"Not funny, Lancelot. As a matter of fact, no. And I'd like to keep it that way. I'm currently working on a profile of this big-time ornithologist, Bertram McMurtry, though everyone calls him Birdy."

"Birdy, eh? I can just picture him now: A funny little man in a safari outfit and pith helmet, with binoculars around his neck and a big, fluffy white mustache."

Guin laughed. That's exactly how she had pictured Birdy, too.

"Actually, he looks more like Indiana Jones, or Harrison Ford as Indiana Jones."

"Oooh," said Lance. "Is he single?"

"What has that got to do with anything?" asked Guin.

"Touchy," said Lance. "How long has Harrison been gone now?"

"A week," said Guin, suddenly missing him. "He's currently in Cambodia."

"Cambodia?"

"He's making his way around Southeast Asia, giving talks and doing research. I'm going to meet up with him in Sydney over Valentine's Day."

"I've always wanted to go to Sydney," said Lance with a sigh. "Take lots of photos."

"I plan to."

"And when does lover boy return to Sanibel?"

"Not until May."

"Ouch. And you're okay with that?"

"Not like I had much of a choice," she replied. "He's on sabbatical and got some grant to go look for mollusks in the South Pacific for four months. Who was I to tell him not to go?"

"Though you could have gone with him."

"And lose my job? No way."

"If it had been me, I would have asked him, 'When should I start packing?'"

"And leave your agency for four months? Doubtful."

"Honey, if a man as fine as Ris had asked me…"

"What about Owen?" asked Guin.

"I would have taken him with me!"

Guin laughed out loud.

"I love you, Lance."

"And I love you, too, Guinivere. But seriously, you need to take more risks. Get out more. Just promise me you'll come to Paris with us in the spring."

"I'll think about it," said Guin.

Lance sighed.

"Well, it's been lovely catching up, but I really must run. You have any plans this weekend?"

"I'm going to a cocktail party. It's at some big estate over on West Gulf."

"Well, have fun."

"And you?" asked Guin.

"Oh, just the usual. We're going to some gallery opening tonight. Then we're checking out this new restaurant in Williamsburg tomorrow with some friends."

"Well, you have fun, too," said Guin.

"Always," said Lance.

"Oh, and did mother tell you she and Philip are coming down here at the end of the month?"

"She may have mentioned something," said Lance.

"I think she's going to try to set me up with that friend of Lavinia's son," moaned Guin.

"Better you than me."

"Thanks," said Guin.

"Well, I really must go, Guinivere. Chat next week?"

"Sure," said Guin.

"Love you," said Lance.

"Love you, too," said Guin.

They ended the call and Guin looked out the window. The sun was setting. She watched as the sky turned reddish-orange and sighed.

Suddenly she felt something rub against her legs. She looked down. It was Flora.

Guin bent down and stroked the pretty multicolored cat, who purred in response. A few seconds later, Fauna joined her. Guin smiled as she continued to stroke the two felines.

As she squatted there, petting the cats, her stomach began to gurgle. She straightened up and looked at the clock on her monitor. It was nearly six. She looked at her phone. There was a text from Ginny.

"You going to the party for Birdy tomorrow?"

How did she know about that? Guin wondered. She shook her head. Of course she knew about the party. Ginny knew everything happening on Sanibel and Captiva.

"Yup," Guin wrote back.

"I'll see you there then," Ginny replied.

"You're going?" Guin asked. Not that the notion was so farfetched. Ginny constantly went to parties on the islands.

"I am," Ginny typed back. "Do you want a ride?"

"I'm good," Guin wrote. "C u tomorrow."

She put down her phone and went into the bathroom. When she came out, there was a text from Shelly, asking Guin to call her as soon as she got the message. She had marked it urgent.

"What's up?" asked Guin. "Everything okay?"

"Everything is not okay," said Shelly. "Can you come over?"

"I, um..."

Guin really didn't feel like driving over to Shelly and Steve's place.

"I have food. Please?"

"All right," said Guin. "Just give me a few."

"Okay, just hurry," said Shelly.

"Does someone have a gun to your head?" asked Guin. She envisioned Shelly being held hostage. "Should I call the police?"

"No, no. Just get here just as soon as you can."

Guin ended the call and made a face. Something was definitely up, but she didn't know what. Knowing Shelly, it could be anything. As it was just Steve and Shelly, she didn't bother changing. She just grabbed her bag and her keys and headed out.

CHAPTER 5

"Guin! So glad you could make it!" said Shelly, giving her friend a big hug.

"You said it was urgent," said Guin, glancing around. She could swear she heard people talking out on the lanai.

"Is there someone else here?" asked Guin, craning her neck.

"Just a friend of Steve's," said Shelly. "Come to the kitchen with me. I'll get you a drink."

She took Guin by the arm and steered her into the kitchen.

"What'll it be?" she asked, looking into the refrigerator. "We have beer, white wine, rosé, sparkling rosé, cider…"

Guin peeked over Shelly's shoulder.

"What's for dinner?"

"Fish. Catch of the day."

"Oh?" asked Guin.

"Steve got back early and went out fishing this afternoon and brought back dinner."

"Ah," said Guin.

She heard laughter coming from the direction of the lanai.

"Did he bring home one of his fishing buddies?" asked Guin.

"As a matter of fact, he did," said Shelly, not looking at Guin.

Uh-oh, thought Guin. She did not have a good feeling.

"Shelly…" she said, in a warning tone.

Shelly tried to ignore her.

"So, beer? Cider? Wine?"

"I thought I heard the doorbell," said Steve, walking into the kitchen.

Shelly and Guin turned around. There behind him was…

"Detective O'Loughlin. How nice to see you," said Guin, forcing a smile. She should have known.

The detective gave Steve a look. Steve in turn looked at Shelly, who gave him a sheepish grin.

"We had so much fish, and Guin is all by herself…"

Steve chuckled and went over to Guin, giving her a peck on the cheek.

"Guin is welcome here anytime. Guin, I believe you are acquainted with Bill here," he said, a twinkle in his eye.

"Detective," said Guin.

"Ms. Jones," replied the detective.

The room went quiet.

Guin had barely seen or heard from the detective since she had helped him solve that murder back in November, and the detective had kissed her.

"Can I get you a beer or a glass of wine, Guin?" asked Steve, breaking the silence.

Guin looked over at Steve and the detective. They both had beers.

"I'll have a beer," she replied.

Steve reached into the fridge and pulled out a beer.

"You want a glass?"

"No thanks," said Guin.

Steve opened the bottle, then handed it to Guin.

"Cheers," he said, holding up his bottle.

"Cheers," said Guin, holding up hers and then taking a sip.

"Well, since everyone's here, why don't you put the fish

and veggies on?" said Shelly, looking at her husband.

"You guys hungry?" Steve asked them.

Guin's stomach gurgled.

"I'll take that as a 'yes,'" said Steve, smiling at her.

Guin felt her cheeks start to turn pink.

Shelly handed Steve two plates, one containing the fish, the other a green vegetable.

"Here you go," she said. "I hope you both like broccoli rabe."

"Fine by me," said Guin.

She and the detective watched as Steve made his way to the lanai.

"Shall we?" asked Shelly, taking a beer for herself.

The three of them followed Steve out back.

"So… detective…" said Guin, feeling awkward. Seeing him again—especially here—brought back feelings she had been trying to repress.

"Ms. Jones…" said the detective, staring at his beer.

"Really, to look at the two of you, you'd think you were back in middle school," said Shelly, bringing a tray of vegetables and dip, along with some shrimp and cocktail sauce, out to the lanai. "Steve, why don't you tell Guin what you were just telling me, about, you know," she said, looking over at her husband and the detective.

He looked momentarily confused.

"You know," said Shelly, "about *the shark*."

"Did you catch a shark?" asked Guin, her eyes going wide.

"*We* didn't," said Steve.

"Some guys on the boat next to us did," clarified the detective. "A hammerhead. Must have been around twelve feet."

Guin whistled.

"Wow. What did they do with it?"

"Nothing. The line broke before they could reel it in," said Steve. "But you should have seen it. I've never seen a hammerhead that big. Have you, Bill?"

"Nope," said the detective, taking a swig of his beer.

Guin waited for them to continue. When the silence got to be too much, Shelly spoke up again.

"So Guin, tell Steve about the story you're working on."

"I'm working on several stories," Guin replied, not sure what Shelly wanted her to say.

Shelly looked exasperated.

"You know," she prompted. She flapped her arms and puckered her lips.

Guin giggled as Steve and the detective looked confused.

"You mean Birdy?" asked Guin.

"Yes!" said Shelly, relieved.

Guin smiled.

"I'm doing a big piece on Birdy McMurtry, the ornithologist," she told Steve and the detective.

"Birdy?" asked Steve.

"His real name is Bertram, but everyone calls him Birdy," Guin explained.

"He does private bird watching tours and lectures here on the island once a year," added the detective. "He's very knowledgeable. Travels the world photographing birds."

Guin's jaw dropped.

"What?" he said, looking at her.

"I just didn't take you for a bird watcher."

"I'm not, but some friends insisted I go to one of his lectures a few years back," he explained. "It was surprisingly interesting. You been?"

"I just met with him over at Ding Darling."

"And?" asked Steve.

"And the man loves the sound of his own voice," Guin replied, taking a sip of her beer.

"What man doesn't?" asked Shelly.

"Hey!" said Steve.

"Present company excluded," said Shelly, smiling sweetly.

"Anyway," said Guin, "he clearly knows his stuff. I'm working on the first draft now. It's way too long, so I'm going to have to edit it down. I just have a few things I need to double check, but I'm seeing him tomorrow."

"Oh?" said Steve.

"There's a party in his honor over on West Gulf Drive tomorrow evening."

Guin glanced over at the detective, who seemed to be contemplating his beer.

"What are you going to wear?" asked Shelly.

Guin was about to answer that she wasn't sure when Steve spoke up.

"Who's hosting it?"

"John and Kathy Wilson. Do you know them?" Guin asked, looking from Steve to Shelly. "I know they're big-time donors to the Ding Darling Wildlife Society and some other local charities, but I don't really know anything else about them."

"Mrs. Wilson was a science teacher at the Sanibel school," said Steve. "Taught both our kids."

"And what did Mr. Wilson do?" asked Guin. "I assume they're both retired, yes?"

"I think it had something to do with export/import," said Steve. "Do you know, Bill?"

"Just what I've read in the paper."

Guin took another sip of her beer.

"Dinner's ready," said Steve, a few minutes later.

"What kind of fish are we having?" asked Guin, peering over at the grill.

"Grouper," Steve replied.

"Looks good," said Guin, watching as Steve slid it onto a large plate.

"Just wait until you taste it."

"Which one of you caught it?" asked Guin.

Steve tilted his head in the direction of the detective.

"Who's ready for another beer?" asked Shelly, sensing some tension in the air.

"Sure, bring us another round," said Steve, putting the broccoli rabe on a separate serving plate.

Shelly went into the kitchen and came back a minute later with four more beers. As it was a mild evening, and not too buggy, they sat outside, though Shelly lit several citronella candles, just to be safe.

The food was delicious, and Guin felt herself relaxing. Or it could have been the second beer. The detective also seemed more at ease and had them in stitches telling them about some of the so-called urgent calls the Sanibel Police Department received, like the woman who wanted the police to arrest her neighbor for mowing the grass in his underwear.

When they were finished, they all helped clear the table and kept Shelly company in the kitchen as she made a big pot of decaf and took out several pints of Queenie's homemade ice cream, along with four bowls and spoons. Steve and the detective immediately helped themselves.

"Go on," said Shelly, looking over at Guin. "A little ice cream won't kill you."

Guin watched as Steve and the detective tucked into the ice cream.

"Screw it," said Guin, taking a large spoon and scooping herself some toasted coconut and Dutch chocolate.

She put a little of both on her spoon and put the spoon in her mouth.

"Mmm..." she said, unconsciously closing her eyes. "So good."

She opened her eyes to see the detective looking at her. Her face suddenly felt warm.

"I like Love Boat myself, but Queenie's is very good," said Steve.

"And let's not forget about Joey's Custard," said Shelly.

"Do you have a favorite ice cream, Bill?" Steve asked him.

"There was a place up in Boston I liked. They made the best pistachio ice cream."

"What about here?" asked Shelly.

The detective shrugged.

They finished their ice cream and coffee, then Guin asked if she could help Shelly and Steve clean up.

"We've got this," said Steve.

"You two run along," said Shelly, looking at Guin and the detective.

Guin looked back at Shelly, imperceptibly shaking her head.

"Shall we?" asked the detective, looking over at Guin.

"Sure," she replied.

"You know your way out," said Shelly, making no move to see them to the door. "Just close the front door behind you. And let me know how the party was, Guin!"

Guin walked over to Steve and gave him a quick kiss on the cheek.

"Thanks for dinner. It was delicious," she said.

She leaned into Shelly and whispered into her ear.

"I will talk to you later, missy."

Shelly gave her an innocent look, but Guin wasn't buying it.

"You're welcome here anytime," said Steve. "Bill," he added, nodding to the detective, who was standing a little way away, waiting for Guin.

Guin walked past the detective and made her way to the

front door. The detective opened it, and Guin stepped outside. Then she watched as the detective made sure the door was properly shut, which made Guin smile.

"What?" asked the detective.

"Nothing," said Guin.

She looked around for the detective's car.

"Where's your car?"

"In the shop. I have a loaner."

Guin glanced around. There were a handful of cars parked on Shelly and Steve's block.

"Over there," said the detective, pointing to an SUV.

"Ah," said Guin.

They stood there for several seconds.

"Well, goodnight," said Guin.

"Goodnight," said the detective.

They continued to stand there for several seconds.

"It was nice seeing you again," Guin said, feeling like an idiot as she said it.

"You too," said the detective.

"Well, I should get going," said Guin.

"Can I walk you to your car?" asked the detective.

Guin smiled.

"It's just over there," she said, pointing a few feet away.

She walked to the Mini, the detective following her. She unlocked the car and was about to open the door when the detective put a hand on her arm.

"Guin…"

She froze at the use of her name. The detective never called her Guin. He always referred to her as "Ms. Jones" or "Nancy Drew," his pet name for her, though she didn't think he meant it as a compliment.

"I…" he started to say.

She turned to look at him. He was at least half a foot taller than she was and had the build of a boxer. The lights from the neighboring houses cast a soft glow over the darkened street, and Guin couldn't make out the detective's features, but she felt his tawny eyes looking down at her. She swallowed.

The detective gently moved a strawberry blonde curl from Guin's face to behind her ear. Guin held her breath. Part of her desperately wanted the detective to kiss her, like he had the last time they had dined at Shelly and Steve's. Another part of her hoped he wouldn't and felt guilty even thinking about wanting him to kiss her.

They stood there, looking at each other, the detective's hand resting gently on the side of Guin's face. She reached up and put a hand on his other arm. It felt very solid. She looked down at his arm, then back up at his face.

"Guin…" he said again, leaning forward slightly.

Guin could feel her heart beating rapidly. She opened her mouth slightly.

"Yes, detective?"

Just then a car drove past, its headlights momentarily showering them with light.

The detective glared at the car, then removed his hand from the side of Guin's face.

"Well, goodnight, Ms. Jones," he said, taking a step back. "Good seeing you."

Guin felt a wave of disappointment wash over her.

"Good seeing you, too," she said.

She turned, unlocked the car, and got in. The detective didn't move. She rolled down the window.

"Goodnight, detective," she said, trying to keep her tone neutral. "See you around."

She started the engine, and the detective backed away from the Mini. She slowly drove away, glancing in the rearview mirror, but she could no longer see the detective.

CHAPTER 6

"So what do you think I should wear to this party?" Guin asked Shelly the next afternoon, her anger of the night before having been temporarily forgotten.

Guin was standing in her walk-in closet, eyeing her wardrobe, talking to Shelly on the phone.

"How about that cute dress you picked up in Naples the other day?" suggested Shelly.

"The blue paisley one?" asked Guin.

"That's the one!" said Shelly. "It really brings out the blue in your eyes.

"I was thinking I'd wear that one," said Guin, holding it up with her free hand. "Do you think it's dressy enough, though? Or is it too dressy? I'm still not sure about the dress code here."

"I think it's perfect, Guin. You look good in whatever you wear."

"Hardly," said Guin.

"Guin, if I looked as good as you did in that dress, I would have bought one for myself," retorted Shelly.

"You look fine," Guin replied. "You should have bought that peach one you tried on."

Shelly made a disapproving noise.

The two of them had gone shopping in Naples the week before, right after Ris had left, to help cheer Guin up. Shelly had tried on several dresses along with Guin, but she didn't wind up buying any of them, claiming they made her look fat, which Guin said was ridiculous.

Guin walked into the bathroom and looked at herself in the mirror.

"So, hair up or down?" she asked, raising a handful of strawberry blonde hair above her head and then dropping it.

"Definitely down," said Shelly. "And wear that cute heart pendant—and heels."

"I was planning to," Guin replied.

"You sure you don't need a plus one?" asked Shelly.

"I'm good," said Guin, smiling.

"What time is the party?"

"It's called for six, but I'm getting there early, so I can ask Birdy a few questions. I probably won't even see him once the party gets going."

"Well, have fun," said Shelly. "And tell me all about it tomorrow. You going to go to the farmers market?"

"First thing," said Guin.

The Sanibel Island Farmers Market took place every Sunday, over by City Hall, from 8 a.m. to 1 p.m., October through May, and Guin rarely missed it.

"Maybe I'll catch you over there."

"Well, I've got to go, Shell. Got to do a bit more work, then get ready."

"Okay. Talk to you tomorrow," Shelly replied.

Guin ended the call, then walked over to her desk. She had made a list of questions to ask Birdy later, and she wanted to review them.

Guin stood outside her closet, looking in the full-length mirror.

"Not too bad," she said, eyeing herself.

She had to admit the dress was very flattering, especially with the new bra she had purchased. She had applied some foundation to cover her freckles, then added some blush, a little eyeliner, eyeshadow, mascara, and a little lipstick. And miracle of miracles, for once her hair was behaving, the curls not frizzing but gently framing her face.

She smiled at her reflection. Then frowned. Why did she care so much about looking good tonight? It wasn't like she was planning on flirting with Birdy. She hadn't heard much from Ris, but she knew he was busy, and with Asia being so many hours ahead, it was hard for them to find a good time to chat.

She sighed.

"Gotta go," she said to the cats, who were napping on the bed.

She wanted to bring her little microcassette recorder, but she felt that would look weird. So she had downloaded an app to her phone that would allow her to record her conversation with Birdy and would supposedly transcribe it, too. If it works, she thought, she would buy the premium version. Guin hated transcribing, but it was a necessary part of her job, and she couldn't afford to farm it out.

She walked into the kitchen, the cats suddenly awake and running after her. She gave them some food, then grabbed her bag and her car keys and left.

She arrived at the address on West Gulf Drive, unsure where to park, when a man dressed as a valet ran towards her. She rolled down the driver's side window.

"You here for the party?" asked the young man.

"I am," said Guin. "Where should I park?"

"I'll take care of that. Just leave your car and give me the keys."

"I can park it myself," Guin replied.

The young man smiled.

"I'm sure you can, miss, but the Wilsons are asking all guests to let us park their cars."

A young woman, dressed in similar attire to the young man, came running up to them.

"I got this," the young man told her.

She saluted him, then ran back to a set of chairs a little way away.

"I promise, we'll take good care of your car," the young man said, smiling at Guin.

"Okay," said Guin, begrudgingly.

She stepped out of the Mini, leaving the engine running. The young man wrote her license plate number down on a ticket, then gave her a receipt.

"Thank you," she said.

"Just let me or Kim know when you want your car back," said the young man.

"And your name is?" asked Guin.

"Tim."

He smiled at her. Tim and Kim. How cute, thought Guin. She smiled back at him.

"I'm Guin, Guin Jones."

"Nice to meet you, Guin," said the young man.

He got in the Mini and adjusted the seat, then slowly drove off. Guin turned and walked up the stairs to the house.

Guin rang the doorbell, which was promptly answered by a large, well-dressed man, probably in his seventies, who reminded Guin a bit of Thurston Howell III.

"Hello!" boomed the man, grinning at Guin. "You here for the party? You're a bit early, you know. Doesn't start for another half an hour."

"I know," said Guin, feeling a bit overwhelmed. "I'm here to speak with Birdy. He's expecting me."

"Oh-ho!" said the man, eyeing her appreciatively. "Birdy always did have an eye for the ladies. Come in, come in," he said, ushering Guin into the house.

Guin was glad her makeup would cover her embarrassment. No doubt her cheeks were turning pink.

"I'm not here as Birdy's date," she clarified. "I'm writing a profile of him for the paper, and I had a few things I needed to go over with him," she explained.

The man winked at her.

"I'm sure Birdy would be more than happy to 'go over' things with you. I'll just go and fetch him."

He smiled and headed down the hallway, shouting "Birdy! You've got a guest!"

Guin gritted her teeth and prayed this wouldn't take too long. The sooner she could get out of there, the better.

As she waited for Birdy to appear, she looked around. The place was huge. It must be at least 4,000 square feet, she thought. In the back of the large, open room she was standing in, which was apparently where the party was being held, judging by the tables filling up with food and the two small bars, there was a large bank of windows looking out toward the dunes and the Gulf. She glanced over at one of the bars, where a bartender was finishing his preparations. She could use a drink, but it would have to wait.

Finally, Birdy appeared. He gave her a big smile as soon as he saw her. Guin had to admit he looked quite handsome in his button-down shirt and neatly pressed slacks.

"Guinivere! So glad you could make it!" Birdy said, taking her right hand in his two much larger ones. "You look enchanting."

"Thank you, Birdy," she said, smiling, despite herself.

She looked around.

"Is there someplace private we could go for a few minutes? I have a few things I want to verify, and there's a lot going on in here," she said, eyeing the catering crew buzzing around.

"Excuse me!" said a server, carrying a plate of hors d'oeuvres, just barely missing Guin.

"Sorry!" said Guin.

"I see what you mean," said Birdy, smiling at her. "Let's go into the library. I'm sure John and Kathy won't mind."

Did all the really wealthy people on Sanibel and Captiva have libraries? Surely not. Though the last big house she had been in, up on Captiva, had a beautiful little library, modeled after a study the owner had fancied in Italy.

She followed Birdy down the hall. He opened a door to the left, flicked on a light switch, and indicated for Guin to enter. Guin paused a moment, recalling the last time she had entered an unfamiliar room in a strange house. That time there had been the dead body of a young woman on the floor.

"Is everything okay?" asked Birdy, a look of concern on his face.

Guin peered into the room. No dead bodies. At least as far as she could tell. She smiled and entered.

"Sorry. I'm just a little overwhelmed, I guess."

"The place has that effect on people," said Birdy. "Totally intimidating, until you get used to it."

"And are you used to it?" asked Guin, curious.

"Not really, but having stayed here a bunch of times, it's not quite as intimidating as it used to feel. And I love this room."

Guin took a good look around. It was a lovely room, filled floor to ceiling with books on two sides. There were also two big, comfy leather chairs, a love seat, a wooden desk with an office chair, and a big picture window, which looked out toward the Gulf.

"Shall we?" said Birdy, sitting on the love seat and indicating for Guin to sit next to him.

Guin sat in one of the leather chairs instead.

"So, how can I help you?" Birdy asked.

Guin took out her phone and opened the app she had downloaded.

"Are you okay with me recording our conversation?"

"Fire away," said Birdy.

He slid down to the end of the love seat, close to the chair Guin was sitting in, and leaned over Guin's phone.

"Guinivere Jones is a very attractive woman," he said, in a husky, low voice.

"Do you always shamelessly flirt with reporters, Mr. McMurtry?" Guin asked.

"Only the pretty ones. And please, it's Birdy."

Guin smiled, even as she clenched her teeth.

She retrieved the list of questions she had typed up and proceeded to ask them to Birdy.

"Is that it?" he asked her a little while later, after Guin had said "that should do it."

"Unless something else comes up," said Guin, immediately regretting her choice of words. "The article is mostly finished. I just wanted to verify a few things."

"Excellent. Then may I show you around the rest of the house?"

Guin was itching to see the rest of the house. It wasn't often she got the chance to see the inside of one of the beautiful mansions along West Gulf Drive. Though the idea of being alone with Birdy made her slightly uncomfortable.

"Shouldn't you be greeting guests?" Guin asked, looking at her watch and seeing it was after six.

"Plenty of time for that," said Birdy.

He stood up and extended Guin a hand, which she hesitantly took.

He led her to the door and opened it. Before leaving the library, she took one last look around. Someday, she said to herself.

"There you are, Birdy!" said the man who had answered the door, as Birdy and Guin descended the stairs a little while later. "Kathy has been looking all over for you."

He looked from Birdy to Guin and grinned.

"You two have fun?"

Guin felt her cheeks growing warm.

"I don't think we were formally introduced," said Guin, extending her hand to the man. "Guinivere Jones. I'm with the *Sanibel-Captiva Sun-Times*."

"Ginny's rag!" said the man. He took Guin's hand and shook it. "A pleasure to officially meet you, Ms. Jones. I'm John Wilson."

"I was just showing Guinivere around the place," explained Birdy.

"Good, good," said Mr. Wilson. "What do you think?" he asked, his hand sweeping around the room.

"It's very grand," said Guin.

As they stood there, more people entered.

"Birdy, go see Kathy and meet your guests," Mr. Wilson directed. "I'll see to Ms. Jones."

He turned to Guin.

"Help yourself to a drink, my dear. It's open bar."

"Thank you," replied Guin.

She was about to say, "Won't you join me?" to be polite, but Mr. Wilson was already following Birdy across the room, to where an elegantly dressed woman and some equally elegantly dressed people were standing. Guin thought about just leaving. After all, she had what she had come for. But she decided it would be politic to stay, at least for a few more minutes. She didn't want to seem rude.

She headed to one of the bars and ordered a white wine spritzer, her drink of choice at such events. As she was thanking the bartender, she heard her name being called. She turned around.

"Don't you look fetching in that dress. Is it new?"

"Hi Ginny," said Guin, smiling at her boss.

She had forgotten Ginny would be at the party.

"You just get here?"

"I did," Ginny replied.

"Is Joel here with you?" Guin asked, looking around.

Joel was Ginny's significant other. They had been together for years but had never married. They were probably common law husband and wife at this point, so why bother?

"God no. Joel hates these kinds of things."

Ginny looked around the room.

"Good crowd."

She waved to a couple she knew.

"I should go work the room," she said. "Come with me."

Guin hesitated.

"Come along, Guinivere. It will be good for you to meet some new people. If you want to be a good reporter, you need to network."

"I thought I was a good reporter," said Guin, a bit irked. Just the other day, Ginny had referred to Guin as her "star reporter."

Ginny gave her a look.

"No need to pout, Guinivere. Now come along. I'll be there right beside you."

Guin allowed herself to be led across the room, to where Birdy was chatting with a bunch of people.

"You really do look fabulous tonight," Ginny whispered.

"Thanks," said Guin.

She didn't feel particularly fabulous that moment, mostly nervous.

"Kathy, darling!" said Ginny, embracing their hostess.

"Virginia! So glad you could make it."

They exchanged kisses.

"Good to see you, Virginia," said Mr. Wilson. "You're looking well. Joel here?"

"No, he's at home, reading."

Mr. Wilson snorted.

"Well, I'm glad you weren't too busy to come," he replied.

He looked over at Guin and gave her a big smile.

"We already met your reporter here. Got here early to ask Birdy a few questions."

"And?" said Ginny, looking over at Guin.

"Mission accomplished."

"Excellent. Have the profile in my inbox Monday," said Ginny.

"She's a slave driver, that one," said Mr. Wilson, conspiratorially to Guin.

"I don't think we've been introduced," said Kathy Wilson, extending a hand to Guin and smiling. "I'm Kathy Wilson."

Guin smiled back.

"Guinivere Jones," she said, shaking Mrs. Wilson's outstretched hand.

Mrs. Wilson then proceeded to introduce Guin to the rest of the group, all Sanibel residents or snow birds and avid bird watchers.

They made small talk for several minutes. Then Guin noticed a group of musicians setting up in the corner of the room. Mrs. Wilson followed her gaze.

"We hired this marvelous Latin jazz group out of Naples. A party's not really a party unless there's music," she said, addressing the group. "Don't you think?"

The guests nodded in agreement.

"And as Birdy just got back from South America, I thought a little Latin jazz would be appropriate."

Again, more nods.

Guin excused herself a few minutes later to go to the ladies' room. When she returned, the musicians were playing "The Girl from Ipanema," one of Guin's favorites. She stood against the wall, listening, swaying in time to the music.

"May I have this dance?" whispered a male voice in her ear.

Birdy.

Guin hesitated. There was a single couple dancing to the music in front of the band. Everyone else was either chatting amongst themselves or standing around, listening to the music.

"Come on," he insisted, pulling Guin toward the dancing couple.

Next thing Guin knew, he had his arms around her and was leading her around the dance floor. She just prayed she didn't step on his feet, or worse.

The band immediately launched into another tune when they were done, and Birdy continued to whirl her around. Several minutes and another song later, feeling a bit lightheaded, she told Birdy she could really use some food, and he escorted her off the dance floor. She was surprised to see that a small crowd had gathered.

"Bravo!" called Mr. Wilson. "Well done, Birdy. You, too, Ms. Jones."

Birdy smiled at his host. Then he took Guin's hand and kissed it.

"Encore!" someone shouted, as the musicians started up again.

Guin smiled politely, and Birdy started to lead her back to the dance floor.

"Food," Guin firmly told Birdy, pulling him back.

"Of course," he said.

He escorted her to one of the buffet tables and handed her a plate.

"Help yourself," he said.

As they were picking out food, a couple came up to Birdy and began asking him questions.

"Would you excuse me?" he said to Guin.

"Of course," she replied.

He went off with the couple while Guin finished loading up her plate. She scanned the room, found a table far from the dance floor, and took a seat.

"Is this seat reserved?" came a familiar voice.

Guin looked up to see her boss standing above her.

"It's all yours," said Guin.

Ginny sat.

"Well?"

"Well what?" said Guin, trying not to talk with her mouth full.

"You having a good time with Birdy?" asked Ginny.

Guin recognized that look.

"It's strictly professional, Ginny."

"Uh-huh," said her boss.

"Fine. Believe whatever you want."

She shoved a forkful of food into her mouth.

They sat there for several minutes, Ginny feeding her little tidbits about the various guests while Guin ate her food. Ginny knew everyone there, or so it seemed, and had something amusing or scandalous to say about nearly everyone in attendance.

"Feeling better?" she asked, when Guin had finished what was on her plate.

"Yes," replied Guin.

"Good. Well, I should go mingle," said Ginny, getting

up. "Remember to thank the Wilsons before you leave. And grab something from the dessert table."

"Will do," said Guin.

Ginny knew Guin had a sweet tooth, and Guin had watched as the caterer laid out all sorts of tempting treats on the dessert table. She headed over, watching as Ginny made her way toward a group of people Guin didn't know.

Everything looked so good, she thought, staring at the little delicacies on display before her. Would it be crass to wrap a couple of chocolate-covered strawberries in a napkin and shove them in her purse?

She had just picked one up when she heard a familiar male voice right behind her.

"That does look awfully tempting."

Guin turned to see Birdy standing behind her, smiling. She felt herself blushing.

"Go ahead, don't let me stop you," he said.

Oh, what the hell, thought Guin.

She looked directly at him and ate the chocolate-covered strawberry in two bites.

"Here, have another one," said Birdy, dangling a chocolate-covered strawberry above her mouth.

"I'll take it to go," said Guin, plucking it out of his hands and quickly wrapping it in a napkin. "Thanks again for answering my questions, and for the tour."

She stepped away from the table and scanned the room for the Wilsons.

"Leaving?" he asked. "So soon?"

"I've already stayed longer than I planned," she replied, continuing to scan the room.

She finally spotted the Wilsons, who were chatting with a group of people.

"Don't worry about them," said Birdy. "I'll tell them you got an urgent call and had to run."

Guin was tempted.

"Come on. I'll escort you out."

Guin looked back at the Wilsons, who were absorbed in conversation.

"Okay," she said.

Birdy stood outside with Guin as she waited for the valet to bring her car around.

"Let me know if you have any more questions, or if there's anything I can help you with," he said, as Tim pulled up in the Mini. "I'm here until Monday morning. Then I'm off to Australia and New Guinea."

The mention of Australia made Guin think of Ris. She would text him as soon as she got home and arrange for them to do a video call.

"Dang it!" said Birdy, slapping his neck. "The insects are in fine form tonight. Should have put on bug spray."

Guin, who considered herself a magnet for bugs, was surprised she hadn't gotten bitten.

"Well, thanks again," said Guin extending her hand.

"My pleasure," said Birdy, taking it.

"I'll send you a copy of the article when it's online," said Guin. "The print version won't be out until after you've gone."

"I'd like that," said Birdy.

Guin tipped the valet, then got in her car. Birdy waved to her as she drove off.

As she drove along West Gulf Drive, she breathed a sigh of relief.

"I'm glad that's done with," she said, then turned on the radio.

CHAPTER 7

The next morning, Guin arrived at the farmers market promptly at 8. She parked in her usual spot, over by the Sanibel Historical Museum and Village, grabbed her bags and her cart from the back seat, and headed over. She paused as she walked past the police department. She glanced up, wondering if the detective was on duty this morning. Most likely he was out fishing. Like so many men she knew on the island, and some women, too, he liked nothing better than to go fishing on his days off, or whenever he had the time.

Thinking of the detective brought back their awkward encounter of the other night. Part of her wished the detective had kissed her (again), and part of her was relieved he had not. She sighed and continued to make her way to the market.

Guin was a creature of habit, at least about some things. The farmers market being one of them. She always stopped at Jimmy's Java first, to get some coffee, then she made her way clockwise to the various vendors. As Ris was away, she didn't buy as much as she normally did. But she still managed to fill up her two bags, with some granola, shrimp and crab cakes, cheese, a small bag of vegetables and fruit, and a box of pastries from Jean-Luc's.

"How's it going, Jake?" Guin asked the red-headed

young man in charge of Jean-Luc's booth.

"Great, Ms. Jones. What can I get for you today?"

Guin eyed the various pastries on display. Everything looked so good. How did one choose?

"I'll have a *pain aux raisins*, a *pain au chocolat*, and…"

She paused.

"And a mocha eclair."

Jake smiled and carefully placed her selections in a box.

"How's Jo?" asked Guin.

Jake's cheeks turned a delicate shade of pink.

"She's good. She's been a big help at the bakery. Jean-Luc says she's a natural."

Jo was a close friend of Jake's, who also tended bar at the Point Ybel Brewing Company. She had always had a passion for baking and had leapt at the chance to work in a real French bakery when Jean-Luc was in desperate need of help.

"Tell her I said hi," said Guin, smiling at the young man.

"Will do," he replied.

Guin carefully placed her box of goodies in her cart, then turned to go.

"See you at the bakery!" she called.

Jake smiled back at her.

It took all Guin's willpower not to devour the pastries on her way home. But she hated getting crumbs in her car. However, as soon as she had arrived back at the condo and had put away her groceries, she immediately cut the *pain aux raisins* and the *pain au chocolat* in half, took a quick bite of each, then placed half of each on a plate and made herself some scrambled eggs. When the eggs were ready, she slid them onto the plate, then took the plate and her to-go mug of coffee to the dining table.

She took a bite, then realized she had left her phone in

her bag. She took another bite of egg, then of the *pain au chocolat*, then got up to retrieve it, so she could read the paper online.

"Huh," she said, staring down at it. "Guess I forgot to turn you back on before I left."

She pressed the power button, then entered her password. As soon as the phone had booted, her message light began to flash wildly.

She looked at the time. It was a little after 9:30. Who could be messaging her early on a Sunday?

"Oh God, I hope it's not mom," she said, bracing herself before opening her messages.

She took a deep breath and tapped the app to open it.

There were messages from Shelly and Ginny and Ris.

She opened the one from Ris first. He had messaged her just a few minutes ago and wanted to know if she could do a video chat.

"How about at 10 Sanibel time?" she wrote him back.

She waited a minute to see if he would reply before checking her other messages.

"Great!" he wrote her back. "See you soon. :-)"

Guin smiled. They had both been so busy, they had only done a video chat once since he left. It would be good to catch up.

She was about to open the message from Ginny when her phone started vibrating. It was a video chat request from Ris. She smiled and accepted.

"I thought we were going to chat at 10," she said.

"I didn't want to wait," he replied, grinning back at her.

They spent the next thirty minutes catching each other up. It sounded like Ris was having an amazing time. He had spent several days in the Philippines and had gone diving there. He showed her a few of the specimens he had found. They were gorgeous.

"You're not supposed to export a lot of the shells," he told her. But because they were going to be used for scientific purposes, he was allowed to take a few samples with him. Still, he confessed to having been a bit nervous at the airport.

He also described some of the different foods he had eaten, both in the Philippines and Cambodia. Some of it sounded quite tasty, some of it disgusting.

"I'm no Andrew Zimmern," he had chuckled, referring to the host of *Bizarre Foods* on the Travel Channel. "But when in Rome, or in Cebu…"

When he had finished telling Guin about his adventures, he had asked her what she had been up to.

"Nothing as exciting as what you've been doing," she replied, wondering for the tenth (or was it twentieth?) time if she should have gone with him. Though the idea of deep-sea diving (which terrified her) and eating strange foods in no way appealed to her. And Ris was so busy most days, they probably would not have seen much of each other, except in bed at night. Though that could have made up for it. Maybe.

"Oh, come on," he said. "There must be some new restaurant or store opening on Sanibel or Captiva that piqued your interest."

Suddenly Guin felt depressed. Was that all she was good for, writing restaurant reviews and new store announcements? True, she wrote about other things. But since she had moved to Sanibel, she had mainly written lighter fare: profiles of islanders, write-ups of charitable events, human interest stuff. And, okay, a handful of front-page pieces about missing mollusks and murders. But those were few and far between. Sanibel wasn't exactly the crime capital of Southwest Florida, for which Guin and most people who lived or vacationed there were grateful.

"Well, I am doing this kind of interesting profile. You ever hear of an ornithologist by the name of Bertram McMurtry? He wrote *The Field Guide to Birds of Southwest Florida* and a half-dozen other birding books."

"You mean Birdy? Remind me to tell you about the time Birdy and I nearly got arrested down in the Keys," Ris said, grinning.

Guin rolled her eyes. Of course Ris knew Birdy.

"Yeah, well, I'm doing a big piece on him for the paper. As a matter of fact, I need to finish it up, so I can get it to Ginny first thing tomorrow."

"Well, tell him I said hello."

"I doubt I'll be seeing him again anytime soon. He's off on some other adventure first thing tomorrow."

"That's Birdy, always off to somewhere," said Ris. "Last I heard, he was off to Patagonia."

"That was his last trip," said Guin, "He's been on Sanibel this week, giving tours and lectures over at Ding Darling."

"Did you get to go bird watching with him?" asked Ris.

"He gave me a private tour—and invited me to a party in his honor."

"Did he make a move on you?"

From his expression, Guin couldn't tell if he was concerned or joking.

"As a matter of fact, yes," she said.

Ris laughed, which annoyed Guin.

"Typical Birdy," he said, shaking his head.

"What's that supposed to mean?" asked Guin, definitely annoyed now.

"Just that Birdy likes pretty ladies, almost as much as he likes pretty birds."

"Well, I'm taken," said Guin, huffily.

Ris smiled warmly at her.

"I miss you," he said. "I wish you were here with me."

Guin touched the screen.

"I miss you, too. But I'll see you in Sydney, soon."

"Not soon enough," he said. "You got the tickets?"

"I did," said Guin. "Thank you."

Ris had insisted on buying her ticket to Australia, and she had finally acquiesced.

He smiled at her again.

Guin loved that smile. It revealed two dimples on either side of his face. And she loved when his hair was longer, like it was now. It made it wavy. She wished she could run her hands through it.

"What are you thinking?" he asked her.

"I was thinking I wanted to run my hands through your hair," she replied.

Unconsciously, Ris ran a hand through his hair.

"I should have had it cut right before I flew over here. I can practically tie it back in a ponytail," he said, frowning.

"I like it longer," said Guin. "As long as you don't put it in a man bun," she added.

Ris chuckled.

"Duly noted."

They chatted for a few more minutes, then Ris let out a yawn.

"I should probably let you go," said Guin. "It's late there, yes?"

There was a 12-hour time difference between Cambodia and Sanibel.

"Yeah, and I've been getting up very early. I'm typically dead by nine o'clock."

"Well, get some sleep," said Guin. "We can talk in a few days."

"I'd like that," said Ris, trying to suppress another yawn.

Guin smiled.

"So where are you off to next?"

"Malaysia, then Indonesia," he replied.

He let out another yawn.

"All right. Get to bed," Guin said, smiling at him.

Ris smiled back.

"Wish you were in bed with me."

Guin's cheeks felt warm.

"I'll message you this week," he said. "Goodnight."

"Sweet dreams."

Ris smiled, then they ended the call.

Guin got up and walked around the condo. The cats were still asleep on her bed. She looked down at them and smiled. Ah, to be a cat.

Though she needed to finish up her profile, and do some other work, she wasn't in the mood. She thought about going to the beach, but she didn't like going after ten, especially on a Sunday. Too many people.

She did some stretches, then glanced over at her computer.

Suddenly she remembered she hadn't checked the rest of her messages or her email.

She retrieved her phone and opened her messages again. Ris had sent her an emoji, the one blowing a kiss. She smiled and replied with the same one.

Next, she opened a series of texts from Shelly, who wanted to know all about the party.

Guin started to text her back, then deleted what she wrote.

She opened the text from Ginny instead. It was a bit unusual for Ginny to text her on a Sunday, though it wasn't unheard of.

I wonder what's up? she thought. Probably checking on me, making sure I'll have the article about Birdy to her in the morning, Guin mused.

She opened the text.

"CALL ME WHEN YOU GET THIS," Ginny had written in all caps.

Guin immediately speed-dialed Ginny's number.

"What's up?" she asked, as soon as Ginny answered.

"I need you to get over to the hospital."

"Why? Are you okay?" asked Guin, worriedly.

"I'm fine. It's Birdy. He didn't show up for breakfast this morning. And when Kathy went to check on him, he was delirious. Started screaming at her, telling her to stay away from him. Kathy said it was just awful."

"Oh my God!" said Guin. "Is he ill?"

"They called 911 and an ambulance took him to the hospital."

"Is he going to be okay? What's wrong with him?" Guin asked, not letting Ginny get a word in. "Could it be something he picked up in South America? Though he's been on Sanibel for, what, a week now? Could he have the flu? Though that doesn't usually make you delirious. And he seemed fine last night."

"Are you done now?" Ginny asked.

Guin felt her cheeks growing warm.

"Yeah, sorry. So, do they know what's wrong with him?"

"I don't know, but I want you to find out."

"Why don't you just ask the Wilsons?"

"The hospital won't tell them anything. Only family," Ginny replied.

"The Wilsons are closer to family than I am, so I doubt they'll tell me anything either," said Guin, confused.

"I told Kathy to tell the hospital you were his fiancée," said Ginny. "She and John followed the ambulance over there. Kathy called me when they told her they weren't allowed to give out any information, except to family. She thought I might know of some way to get information since I was able to get information about Joel when he had his heart attack."

"WHAT?!" said Guin.

"Mr. McMurtry did seem awfully fond of you," said Ginny, chuckling slightly. "And who's to know?"

"Well, Birdy for one," said Guin.

"He's in no state to say anything."

Guin sighed. She knew she was beat.

"Fine. So, what do you want me to do?"

"I want you to get yourself over to the hospital as soon as you can. Kathy and John are already there."

"Fine. Give me a few minutes. Then I'll head over. Which hospital?"

Ginny gave her the name and address and Kathy's cell phone number.

"Text her as soon as you've parked," said Ginny. "And let me know what you find out."

"Okay," said Guin. "And what do I do if they question me?"

"They won't," said Ginny. "Just act concerned. Kathy and John will cover for you."

Guin didn't like it one bit, but she knew better than to argue with Ginny.

"Anything else?" she asked.

"Not right now. You almost done with that profile?"

Guin rolled her eyes.

"Almost. You still planning on running it this week?"

"Absolutely!" said Ginny. "But first, find out what's up with Birdy."

"Can I go now?" asked Guin.

"Yes," said Ginny. "Just text or call me later."

"Will do," said Guin. Then she ended the call.

"Well, pussycats," she said, looking at the two now-awake felines. "I have to head out for a bit. Wish me luck."

The cats gazed up at her, then closed their eyes and went back to sleep.

CHAPTER 8

Guin arrived at the hospital less than an hour later. She had texted Kathy Wilson as soon as she had parked her car, and Kathy had met her in the lobby.

"Ginny told you the plan?" Kathy asked her.

"That I'm supposed to pose as Birdy's fiancée and find out what's wrong with him?"

"Yes," replied Kathy.

"What about you and John?"

"They'll only release information to family."

"But technically a fiancée isn't family," Guin pointed out.

"Close enough," said Kathy. "I'll take you up to his room. Then you can ask one of the nurses what's wrong with him."

Guin sighed and allowed Kathy to guide her to the elevator.

"I don't think this is going to work, but I'll give it a shot."

Kathy patted her on the arm and pressed the button for the elevator.

Kathy knocked on the door to Birdy's room. A nurse opened it.

"I have Birdy's fiancée here to see him."

The nurse eyed Guin.

Kathy had told Guin to imagine someone she loved was

in that hospital bed, dying, so she could play the part. Immediately Guin called up an image of her father on his deathbed. Tears immediately started to well up in her eyes.

"How is he?" Guin said, her voice catching.

"Not good," said the nurse, still standing in the doorway.

"May I see him?" Guin asked, a pleading look in her eye. The nurse sighed.

"Very well, but don't be surprised if he doesn't recognize you."

Guin would have been surprised if he did.

"Thank you," she said, smiling at the nurse.

"I'll just wait in the hall," said Kathy, smiling kindly at Guin and the nurse.

Guin nervously entered the room, not knowing what to expect. She immediately spied Birdy, hooked up to a bunch of equipment, an IV in his arm. His eyes were closed.

"Is he asleep?" Guin asked the nurse, quietly.

At the sound of her voice, Birdy's eyes flew open. He looked terrified, then turned to look at Guin.

Guin composed herself and went over to him. In for a penny, in for a pound, she said to herself. She stood near the bed and smiled down at him.

"How are you, darling?" she asked him. "You've given us an awful scare."

She mentally asked Ris for forgiveness. Though, knowing Ris, and knowing Ris knew Birdy, he would probably find this whole scene amusing. She bit her lip.

Birdy looked up at her. He seemed confused.

"Do I know you?" he asked Guin.

"Of course you do," said Guin, smiling down at him. "Don't you remember? We were just together last night."

It wasn't a lie.

Birdy continued to look up at her, then smiled. Guin smiled back at him.

"You remember me now?" Guin asked.

"A kiss would help," he said.

Guin looked over at the nurse, who was shaking her head.

"I'm afraid that's not allowed," Guin said. "But as soon as you're better, I'll give you all the kisses you want."

She mentally crossed her fingers.

"Come closer," he asked her.

Guin looked again at the nurse, checking to make sure it was okay.

The nurse gave her a warning look, but Guin ignored it, taking a step closer to the bed.

There was a sheen of sweat on Birdy's face and neck, and he looked awfully pale.

"Are you an angel?" he asked her. "You look like an angel."

Clearly, he was hallucinating. Though, with her fair skin and strawberry-blonde hair, which fell in ringlets around her face, Guin could, in certain circumstances, be mistaken for one of those angels you saw in Renaissance paintings.

Guin smiled down at him.

"No, I'm not an angel. I'm your fiancée."

"Now I must be in Heaven," he said, grinning up at her.

He tried to sit up but struggled.

The nurse immediately came over.

"Please, Mr. McMurtry. Just lean back against the bed."

"Could I please have a glass of water, and a moment alone with my fiancée?" he asked her.

The nurse got him a glass of water, which she placed on the tray beside him. She then glanced from Birdy to Guin.

"Just for a minute. I'll be right outside the door if you need me," she said to Guin.

"Thank you," said Guin.

Guin waited for the nurse to leave. As soon as she had,

Birdy grabbed Guin's wrist. Guin froze. His hand felt ice cold.

"I need you to help me. They're trying to kill me."

Guin stared down at her wrist.

"Who's trying to kill you?" she asked.

Birdy dropped her hand and sat back in the bed, clearly exhausted.

"I'm not sure."

"But you have an idea," Guin replied.

Birdy closed his eyes. Guin waited. A few seconds went by and she became concerned. She gently touched his shoulder and his eyelids fluttered open.

"Would you like a sip of water?" she asked him.

"Please," he croaked.

She lifted the cup of water and helped him to drink. Then she placed it back on the tray.

"Why do you think someone's out to kill you?"

"Poisoned," he said, closing his eyes once again.

"You think you were poisoned?" Guin asked.

Just then the nurse re-entered the room, followed by a doctor.

The doctor looked at Guin.

"I'm Guinivere Jones, Mr. McMurtry's fiancée," she said, extending a hand. "How is he?"

"As you can see," said the doctor, nodding towards Birdy and ignoring Guin's hand.

"Any idea what the problem is, what caused this?" Guin asked. "He seemed perfectly fine when I saw him last night."

"We're running a bunch of tests," replied the doctor, looking at his clipboard.

Guin looked over at Birdy. His eyes were still closed, and his face seemed slick with perspiration.

"Will he…?"

Guin didn't want to finish the sentence, not in front of

Birdy, in case he was conscious.

"I need to check the patient," said the doctor. "Please step outside."

Guin knew she was being dismissed.

"Okay, thank you," said Guin. She looked over at Birdy. "I'll be back," she told him.

She headed to the door, then stopped and glanced back. The doctor was examining Birdy. She paused to see if she could tell what he was doing, but it was pointless. Quietly, she opened the door and stepped outside.

"Well? Is he going to live?" asked John Wilson, the moment the door had shut behind Guin.

Guin looked around for his wife.

"Where's Kathy?"

"She had to make some calls. You find out anything?"

"Not really," said Guin.

"Did he say anything to you?"

Guin wondered if he meant Birdy or the doctor.

"Birdy thought I was an angel," Guin finally replied.

Mr. Wilson let out a laugh.

"That's Birdy for you," he said. "Did he say anything else?"

"He asked for some water."

Guin was not going to tell him that Birdy thought he had been poisoned. She didn't want to upset the Wilsons needlessly.

The two of them stood there in the hall, staring at the door to Birdy's room. Several minutes later, the doctor and the nurse emerged. Guin gave the doctor a hopeful look, the look she imagined a worried fiancée would give.

"How is he?" asked Guin. "Is he... is he going to be okay?"

"Why don't you walk down the hall with me?" said the doctor. "I need to check on a few more patients."

The doctor was a pleasant-looking man, probably in his thirties or early forties, Indian or Pakistani, or of Indian or Pakistani descent. Guin followed him as he made his way down the hall. She half expected John Wilson to follow them, but he hung back.

"So?" asked Guin.

"We're running some tests, like I said," replied the doctor, who wasn't really paying attention to her.

"Any chance he could have been poisoned?" Guin asked.

The doctor stopped.

"Why do you ask?"

"Mr. McMurtry, Birdy"—Guin wasn't sure how to refer to him—"thought someone had poisoned him."

"Hmm…" said the doctor.

"Could someone have?" Guin repeated.

"It's possible," replied the doctor. "Hopefully, the tests will tell us more. I understand that he recently traveled in South America."

"Yes," said Guin. "But he's been back in the States for over a week."

"Still, he might have caught something there. Anyway, Ms.…."

"Jones," said Guin.

"Anyway, Ms. Jones, I'm afraid I don't have any more information to give you at present. We should know more in a day or so."

"So, you're going to keep Birdy here, at the hospital?"

The doctor looked at Guin as though she were slow.

"Of course," said Guin, feeling herself blushing. "He's probably in no shape to be released."

"Hardly," said the doctor. "He's in no shape to go anywhere at present. And we need to bring that fever down."

His expression softened.

"I promise, we will let you know if anything changes."

"Thank you, doctor…"

Guin couldn't remember if the doctor had given his name. She didn't think so.

The doctor smiled at her.

"Gupta, Sanjiv Gupta."

"Thank you, Dr. Gupta," Guin said, smiling back at him.

"Just make sure the hospital has your contact information," he said, stopping outside a patient's room. He reached into a pocket and pulled out a card. "You can also text me if you have any questions. The information is there."

"Thank you," Guin said, glancing at the card, then placing it in her pocket.

The doctor opened the door and disappeared inside the room.

Guin stood in the hallway, debating what to do. Should she look for the Wilsons? Call Ginny? She thought about flipping a coin but decided to go downstairs and call Ginny first. She could always follow up with the Wilsons after she spoke with Ginny. Not that there was anything to report.

Ginny picked up after just a couple of rings.

"Well?" she asked.

"They're running some tests," Guin replied. "The doctor says they should have results in a day or two."

"Did you get a chance to talk to Birdy?" asked Ginny.

"I did," said Guin. "Briefly."

"And?"

Guin debated what to tell Ginny, then decided to tell her the truth.

"He thinks he was poisoned."

"Did he happen to say who he thinks poisoned him?"

"Ginny, the man is running a high fever and is clearly not himself."

"So, you don't think he could have been poisoned?"

Guin hesitated.

"I don't know."

"Well, let me know as soon as you hear anything. Did they buy you being his fiancée?"

"I think so," said Guin.

"Good. Well, I need to go. Get me that profile, stat. Then I want you to start work on a follow-up piece."

"Seriously?" asked Guin.

"Don't you want us to the run the story before the News-Press does?"

She had a point.

"I still need to edit the profile. Then I'll shoot it over to you. You said I could have until Monday."

Ginny sighed.

"Fine. Get it to me Monday. You going to stop by the office Tuesday?"

That was the day Guin typically stopped by the *San-Cap Sun-Times* office, which was located on Periwinkle Way. Ginny, who had lived on the island for over thirty years, knew practically everyone and everything that went on around town, and Guin enjoyed listening to her tell tales about the "good old days," as well as more recent goings-on on Sanibel and Captiva.

"If my slave-driver of a boss doesn't have me working overtime."

"Very funny," said Ginny. "By the way, I have a few more story ideas for you."

Guin thought she heard a male voice in the background.

"Gotta go," said Ginny. "Joel and I are off to Useppa for lunch."

Guin was about to say, "Have fun!" but Ginny had already ended the call.

CHAPTER 9

Guin pocketed her phone and was about to head back upstairs to find the Wilsons when she heard her name being called. She turned to find them hustling toward her.

"Glad we caught up with you," said Mr. Wilson, panting a bit.

Guin waited for him to catch his breath.

"How is he? Did the doctor say anything?"

"They're running some tests," Guin replied. "Dr. Gupta said they should have the results in a day or so."

"Any idea what's wrong with him?" he asked.

"We didn't get that far," said Guin.

"I do hope the poor boy is okay," said Mrs. Wilson. "I was frankly terrified. You should have seen him earlier this morning."

She shook her head at the memory.

"It took two EMTs to get him into the ambulance," she continued. "I've never seen anything like it. Wouldn't let us go near him."

Mr. Wilson put a comforting arm around his wife.

"There, there. He's in good hands now. He'll be right as rain before you know it."

He smiled down at her and gave her a reassuring pat. She looked up at him and smiled.

"I hope so."

"I know so," he replied. "And I'm never wrong."

Guin sighed. Another couple who seemed truly in love. Something about seeing old married couples who still clearly cared about each other made Guin wistful. She had honestly thought she and Art, her ex, would be one of them. Until he cheated on her with their hairdresser. That had ended badly. And he had tried to woo Guin back. But Guin had had enough, and she was in a new relationship with Ris.

She looked at the Wilsons.

"The doctor gave me his card. I'll follow up with him tomorrow."

Guin paused.

"I should give the hospital my information."

She took a step toward the information desk, then stopped.

"What about Birdy's family?"

"He doesn't have any immediate family, at least as far as we know," said Mr. Wilson. "His parents were killed in an automobile accident years ago."

"How awful!" said Guin.

"Yes, it was quite a shock," said Mrs. Wilson. "Birdy was on one of his birding trips when it happened. Couldn't get back for several days."

"And no siblings?" asked Guin.

"Not that we know of," said Mrs. Wilson. "Birdy doesn't like to talk about his family."

"Any chance of an actual fiancée or a wife?"

"There was someone in the past, but with his travel schedule, it's been hard for him to maintain a long-term relationship," explained Mrs. Wilson. "We were hoping, maybe, he'd eventually settle down."

"You know that Birdy is perfectly happy the way things are," Mr. Wilson said to his wife. "And he has no problem finding female companionship, if you know what I mean," he said to Guin.

Guin smiled politely. She knew exactly what he meant but didn't want to go there.

"So how did you two meet Birdy?" Guin asked, trying to change the subject.

"He was down here, on Sanibel. It was his first visit here," replied Mrs. Wilson. "He'd been invited by the Ding Darling Wildlife Society."

Mr. Wilson nodded.

"Some friends invited us to join them on one of his private tours," Mrs. Wilson continued. "And he was so charming."

"Reminded us a bit of our son, Johnny, who lives in California," said Mr. Wilson.

"We don't see Johnny very often. Always too busy," said Mrs. Wilson. "And when we heard Birdy needed a place to stay the next year, we invited him to come stay with us."

"Got plenty of room," said Mr. Wilson.

"And he's been staying with us ever since," said Mrs. Wilson. "He's like a second son to us."

Mr. Wilson nodded his head in agreement.

Guin smiled.

"I'm so glad you found each other."

She glanced over at the desk, then back at the Wilsons.

"Do you know when visiting hours are?"

"I imagine you can come whenever you like, seeing as how you're Birdy's fiancée," said Mr. Wilson, grinning at her.

Guin felt uncomfortable. She hated lying. Would she now be expected to sit by Birdy's bedside, to keep up the ruse? If it was Ris in that bed, she would.

"I'm going to go ask at the desk and give them my information."

She walked over to the desk and asked the woman there about visiting hours. She was informed that they ran from nine in the morning to nine at night, though there were quiet periods when guests were asked to wait in designated waiting areas. And patients could also request no visitors.

"And how can I get alerted if there's a change in my fiancé's condition?" Guin asked the woman.

"You'll need to leave your information with the supervising nurse or doctor."

Guin thanked the woman and walked back over to the Wilsons.

"It's pretty much as you thought," she said.

"You will come back and check on Birdy, yes?" asked Mrs. Wilson. "And keep us posted?"

"Of course," she said. She mentally cursed Ginny for getting her involved.

"Well, we need to head off to a luncheon," said Mrs. Wilson. "But we'll check in later. You okay, dear?"

"I'm fine," Guin lied. "I'll go back upstairs and check on Birdy before I go and give the nurse my information."

"Capital idea!" said Mr. Wilson.

Guin gave him a weak smile.

"Enjoy your lunch."

She would probably grab something from the hospital cafeteria.

They said their goodbyes and Guin headed toward the elevators.

Birdy was asleep when she entered the room. The nurse had explained that they were keeping him mildly sedated. Guin asked if it would be okay if she sat there and kept him company while he slept, and the nurse had told her it was fine and to press the nurse-call button if Birdy needed anything.

Guin had settled herself in a chair and was browsing the

news on her phone when she heard a voice.

"My angel."

She looked up to see Birdy smiling at her.

Guin put down her phone and got up.

"Are you the angel of mercy or the angel of death?" he said.

Guin had to admit, the man had a certain rakish charm to him, even in his weakened state.

"Neither. I'm your fiancée. Don't tell me you've forgotten already?"

Might as well play the role to the hilt, Guin told herself.

Birdy's brow furrowed.

"Fiancée? Funny, I don't remember having a fiancée," he said. He continued to look at Guin. "But you do look familiar. Come closer, so I can get a better look at you. You're a little blurry."

Guin went over to the bed, keeping a little distance between them.

"A little closer, please," he said, giving her a smile and gently patting the bed.

Guin hesitated, then told herself she was being ridiculous and stood next to the bed.

"That's better," he said, smiling at her.

Guin stood there, not sure what to do.

Birdy studied her.

"Where did we meet again?"

Guin thought about lying, but it wasn't her style.

"On one of your private birding tours."

"Did you enjoy it?" he asked.

"Very much," she replied.

He smiled.

"And when did I propose to you?"

"Shortly thereafter."

Again, it wasn't a lie. Birdy had proposed, albeit facetiously, or so she thought, after Guin had made him coffee.

"Funny, I don't remember."

"It was a bit of a whirlwind romance," Guin said.

"Have we set a wedding date?" Birdy asked.

"No," Guin quickly replied.

"Oh?" asked Birdy. "I thought that was the first thing women wanted after a man proposed, to set a date."

Guin thought quickly.

"Well, I am not most women, and you were supposed to be heading off to Australia and New Guinea."

"Oh right, New Guinea. I forgot all about New Guinea," he sighed. "I was so looking forward to that trip."

"Well, hopefully, you'll be out of the hospital in a few days, and you can go then."

Birdy stared at something across the room. Guin waited. A minute later he turned back to her.

"I'm a bit embarrassed to say this, but I can't remember your name. Must be the fever, or the drugs."

Guin smiled down at him.

"Guin."

"Guin?" asked Birdy.

"It's short for Guinivere."

Birdy smiled.

"So I'm marrying a queen."

"First you need to get better."

"I feel better already, having you here, Guinivere."

"Guin is fine."

"I rather like Guinivere."

He gave her a rakish smile.

"And I shall be your Lancelot."

"Actually, my brother's name is Lancelot, so…"

Birdy chuckled.

"Very well. Though—"

Guin cut him off.

"Don't say it."

"You have no idea what I was going to say," said Birdy.

"Whatever it was, don't say it."

"Fine. I've already forgotten what it was anyway."

His eyes started to close, and a few seconds later Guin thought she heard him gently snoring. She slowly moved away from the bed, so as not to disturb Birdy. She had nearly made it to the door when—

"Get back!" Birdy shrieked.

Guin quickly turned, thinking he was talking to her. He was sitting up in bed, his eyes wide open, but he was looking somewhere out in the distance.

"Get back, I say!" he yelled again. "I know the truth, and—"

He slumped back against the bed.

Guin rushed over to the bed and felt Birdy's forehead. He was burning up. She immediately pushed the nurse-call button.

A nurse had appeared two minutes later, and Guin had explained what had happened. She immediately began checking Birdy's vital signs and asked Guin to step out of the room.

"Is he going to be okay?" Guin had asked her. But the nurse had been too busy to respond.

Guin had now been waiting outside of Birdy's room for 15 minutes, as another nurse and a doctor had gone in. She was tempted to go in herself but thought it wiser to stay outside. Finally, one of the nurses left the room.

"Is he going to be okay?" Guin asked.

"The doctor's with him," the nurse replied.

Guin knew that.

"His fever spiked again. We're working to bring it back down."

"Thank you," said Guin, as the nurse hurried off.

How did loved ones do it? she wondered, standing there. She barely knew Birdy, and hadn't particularly liked him, and now she was terrified he wasn't going to make it. She shook her head.

A few minutes later, the doctor, not the one she had met before, came out.

"How is he?" Guin asked.

The doctor looked at her.

"And you are?"

"Guin Jones, his fiancée."

She was almost starting to believe it.

"He's stable, for now," the doctor replied.

"Can I see him?"

"He's asleep," replied the doctor. "We gave him a sedative. Best to wait until tomorrow morning to see him. By then we should hopefully have some test results."

"Okay. Thank you," said Guin, not sure what to say.

The doctor moved away, no doubt off to check on some other patient, and Guin stood staring at the door to Birdy's room. She remained there for several minutes, part of her wanting to go back in to make sure Birdy was okay. But the doctor had said he was asleep and to come back the next morning.

"Fine," said Guin, aloud. "I'll be back tomorrow, Birdy. Try to get better."

She touched the door to his room, then left.

CHAPTER 10

Guin returned to the hospital the next day. Birdy seemed a bit better, but the doctor had told her he needed to stay in the hospital at least another day, until his fever had broken.

Guin asked the doctor if they had discovered the source of Birdy's illness. He said they were still waiting for some of the lab work to come back. She had wanted to ask him more questions, but he had been in a hurry.

Birdy had been asleep when she had arrived, so she had sat quietly by his bedside, reading on her phone. But as if sensing her presence, he opened his eyes a few minutes later and smiled when he saw her.

"You came back," he said.

"Of course," said Guin.

He tried to sit up, but the effort clearly pained him, and he flopped back against the bed.

"You need some help?"

"Everything hurts," he said.

"Can I get you some water?" Guin asked, noticing his cup was empty.

"What I'd really like is some Scotch, but I'll settle for water," he replied.

Guin smiled. Clearly, he was feeling a bit better. She went to refill his water cup, then placed it on the table next to his bed. She could see him struggling to raise himself up to drink it.

"Here, let me see if I can raise you up a bit."

She looked around and found the button to raise the bed and adjusted it, so he was more upright.

"Thanks," he said.

Guin handed him the cup, and he took a sip.

"So why are you here?" he asked her.

"What do you mean?" said Guin.

"I don't have a fiancée," he said, looking right at her.

"Though you did propose to me," Guin replied, with a grin.

Birdy looked confused.

"You proposed to me in my kitchen. I made you coffee, and you asked me to marry you."

Birdy leaned back and closed his eyes. A few seconds later he opened them and turned to look at Guin. He stared at her. Then a slow smile spread across his face.

"Now I remember. As I recall, you didn't accept."

"I did not."

"A shame," said Birdy, taking Guin in.

Guin felt herself blushing.

"Have you ever been married?" Guin asked him.

"No, though I came close one time."

Guin gave him a curious look.

"It's a long story," he said.

"It must be hard being on the road all the time," Guin said, sympathetically.

"It is, but I don't mind," said Birdy. "Women on the other hand..."

"Women what?" asked Guin.

"I used to take women with me on my trips, the more adventurous ones."

Guin wasn't sure if by "adventurous" he was referring to the women or the trips.

"It never worked."

"Ah," said Guin, not knowing what to say.

He stared off into the distance for several seconds. Guin waited. Finally, he turned back to face her.

"So why are you posing as my fiancée? Not that I mind," he said, smiling.

Guin felt herself blushing again. She had to admit, he had a rather nice smile.

"It was my boss's idea. She runs the paper and is friends with the Wilsons. The hospital wouldn't tell the Wilsons anything, as they're not technically family. So they called Ginny. Ginny and Joel, he's her partner, aren't technically married, though they've been together forever. Joel had a heart attack a little while ago. And Mrs. Wilson, Kathy, wanted to know how Ginny was able to get information about him. She told them to tell the hospital that I was your fiancée."

"Very clever of her."

"Well, she was taking a big risk, if you ask me," said Guin. "You won't tell, will you?"

Birdy eyed her, like a hawk in search of his next meal, Guin thought.

"I'll make a deal with you," he said.

Guin held her breath.

"I'll go along pretending you're my devoted fiancée, and, in return, you'll help me figure out who poisoned me."

"We're not sure you were poisoned," said Guin. "It could have been food poisoning, or something you picked up in South America or on the plane."

"Are you going to help me or not?" he said, his finger hovering over the nurse-call button.

Guin hesitated.

"Fine, but I need you to tell me why you think you were poisoned."

Birdy pursed his lips.

"You're just going to have to trust me," he repeated.

They stared at each other for several seconds.

"Fine," said Guin. "But I'm going to need something to go on."

Birdy leaned back against the bed and closed his eyes.

"I'm tired," he said.

Guin was going to press him, but just then one of the nurses entered and made a beeline to Birdy. Guin watched, silently, as the nurse took his vitals and asked him a few questions. When she was done, she read him his lunch options and asked him what he preferred.

"A nice juicy steak with mushrooms and onions," he replied.

"I'm afraid that's not on the menu," said the nurse.

Birdy sighed.

"Just bring me whatever," he said, closing his eyes and leaning back against the bed.

She pressed something on her iPad, or what looked like an iPad.

"I need to check on a few more patients," the nurse said when she was done. "But if you need something, just press the nurse-call button."

"I'm good," said Birdy.

Birdy and Guin watched as the nurse left the room.

"I should probably get going too," said Guin.

"Must you?" asked Birdy.

Guin was about to reply when the door to the room flew open and a very tall woman entered. Her ash-blond hair was tied back in a ponytail and she was dressed as though she had just come from a fashion shoot.

"Darling! I came as soon as I heard!"

Guin stared as the woman brushed past her and went straight to Birdy's side and clasped his right hand.

"Hullo, Bettina," Birdy sighed. "You really didn't have to come."

"Nonsense, darling. What kind of agent would I be if I

didn't take care of my best client?"

Guin made to leave, but Birdy stopped her.

"Don't go," he called.

"I'm not going anywhere until you get out of here," said Bettina.

"Not *you*," said Birdy, clearly annoyed, "*her.*"

"Hmm?" said Bettina, turning to see what, or who, Birdy was looking at. "Oh. Who are you?" she asked, taking in Guin and making a face as though she had just eaten something that disagreed with her.

Guin opened her mouth to answer, but Birdy cut her off.

"This is Guin Jones, my fiancée."

"Your *what*?!" said Bettina, spinning back around to face Birdy.

Guin did her best to suppress a smile.

"My fiancée," repeated Birdy, calmly.

"Since when?" asked Bettina, clearly not happy about the news.

"Since he proposed to me," Guin answered.

Birdy grinned at her.

Bettina spun around to face Guin, then turned back to Birdy.

"You're marrying *her*?!" she said, gesturing at Guin. "She's not even your type!"

"And what is my type?" asked Birdy, giving Bettina a withering look.

Bettina opened her mouth to reply but thought better of it and closed her mouth.

Guin stood by the door, eager to leave.

"Well, I should let you two catch up. I'll come back later."

"Wait, don't go yet," said Birdy.

He turned to Bettina.

"Bettina, could you give us a minute… alone?"

Bettina made a face, then stomped to the door.

"I'll be just outside if you need me," she said, looking at Birdy and ignoring Guin.

Guin waited a few seconds before saying anything. Birdy patted the bed, signaling for her to come over. She hesitated, then moved closer.

"Are you going to tell her the truth?" asked Guin.

"Do you want me to?" Birdy replied.

"It's not really my call," she said.

Birdy closed his eyes, then opened them several seconds later.

"I think I like having you as my fiancée," he said, smiling up at her. "Especially if it annoys Bettina."

"I'm honored," said Guin, "but..."

"Don't worry about Bettina," Birdy replied. "She'll get over it."

"If you say so," said Guin.

"She'll probably be on the next plane back to New York."

He winced.

"Does it hurt a lot?"

"I've been better," he said. "Whatever they have dripping into my vein is definitely helping. Any idea when I'll get out of here?"

"Not until your fever has broken," said Guin.

Birdy sighed.

"Will you come see me later? Maybe we could have dinner together?"

Gone was the arrogant Birdy she had met just the other day. In his place was this entirely different Birdy. Well, not entirely different. But more vulnerable.

"It would be my pleasure," said Guin. "And maybe over dinner you can tell me why you think you were poisoned."

"Maybe," said Birdy, smiling up at her.

He closed his eyes again.

"So, see you around five?"

"I'll be here," said Guin.

Birdy reached out his hand and Guin gently squeezed it. Then she turned around and left. In the hall, Bettina was talking into her cellphone, clearly not happy. She glared at Guin as she passed by.

Guin held up her hand in a parting wave, then headed to the elevator. She pressed the down button and waited. A few seconds later, the doors to one of the elevators opened to reveal the Wilsons.

"Guin! How is he?" asked Mrs. Wilson. "Is he okay?"

They stepped into the hallway, and Guin took a couple steps back, letting the elevator doors close.

"Better," she said. "But he's still in a lot of pain."

"Can't they do anything?" Mr. Wilson asked.

"They're doing all they can," said Guin.

The Wilsons exchanged a look.

"Well, we just thought we'd stop by and check on him," said Mrs. Wilson, "seeing as he's all alone."

"Actually, his agent, Bettina, is here."

"She flew down from New York?" asked Mrs. Wilson.

"Apparently so," said Guin.

"Probably worried about losing her best client," said Mr. Wilson.

"Well, she seemed none too happy to see me," said Guin.

"I'll bet," said Mr. Wilson.

Guin wondered what he meant but didn't say anything.

"Well, I should get going. Nice to see you two. I'm sure Birdy will be happy to have you here."

"Will you come back later?" asked Mrs. Wilson.

"Yes, I told Birdy I'd have dinner with him."

Mrs. Wilson smiled.

"That's nice."

"Well, goodbye," said Guin.

She pressed the button for the elevator and the Wilsons made their way down the corridor to Birdy's room.

CHAPTER 11

Guin arrived home a little while later, but she found it difficult to work. Her mind was still on Birdy. But she knew Ginny would be after her if she didn't submit the article. Finally, around 4:30, after reading over what she had written and deciding it was good enough, she mailed the article about Birdy to Ginny. She left out the part about Birdy falling ill, closing with a call to readers to follow Birdy's adventures on his blog.

She got up and stretched. Then she headed to the kitchen and poured herself a glass of water. She took several sips, then leaned against the counter. The clock on the microwave said it was 4:40.

"Time to go see Mr. McMurtry," she said aloud.

She grabbed her purse and her keys and said goodbye to the cats. Then she headed out the door.

Upon entering the hospital, Guin didn't bother stopping at the front desk. She went straight to the elevators and up to the third floor. As she was about to enter Birdy's room, she heard raised voices. She stopped to listen. It sounded like two women arguing.

She knocked on the door, then entered.

Standing on either side of Birdy's bed were Bettina and one of the nurses whom Guin had seen earlier. Neither looked happy. Nor did Birdy, who was lying in bed with his eyes shut.

"Am I interrupting something?" Guin asked. "If so, I can come back later."

Bettina glared at her.

"Thank God you're here," said Birdy, opening his eyes and turning towards her.

"You're awake," said Bettina, looking at him.

"Hard to sleep with the racket you're making."

Bettina made a face.

Guin wondered if she had been there all afternoon.

"I was just trying to explain to Ms. Betteridge here that we cannot release patient information without the patient's approval," explained the nurse.

"But how can I help him if I don't know what's wrong with him?" Bettina whined.

The nurse gave Guin an imploring look, though Guin had no idea what she was supposed to do.

"Bettina, could you step outside for a minute?" asked Birdy, breaking the impasse. "I'm sure you have some more calls to make. And I'd like a minute alone with my fiancée."

Bettina glared at Guin.

"Fine. I'll be in the hall, making a hotel reservation."

"You're not flying back to New York?" Guin asked.

"Not tonight," she replied.

"Do you need help?" Guin asked, though she immediately regretted it.

"I'm good," she replied, giving Guin a disparaging look.

Guin, Birdy, and the nurse watched as she exited the room.

"Thank God," said Birdy, leaning back and closing his eyes again after she had gone.

"Do you want me to go, too?" asked Guin. "If you and your agent have things you need to discuss…"

Birdy opened his eyes and looked at her.

"No, stay. I can't deal with Bettina right now."

Guin smiled, despite herself.

"Would you like your dinner now, Mr. McMurtry?" asked the nurse.

"Sure, why not?" he replied. "Gotta build up my strength, right?"

The nurse smiled at him, then left.

"How are you feeling?" asked Guin.

"Better, now that you're here," he replied, smiling at her.

"So, have they figured out what's wrong with you?" Guin asked.

"Not yet. The doctor's supposed to stop by to check on me any time now."

As if on cue there was a knock on the door and Dr. Gupta entered.

"Were your ears burning?" asked Birdy.

Dr. Gupta reached up and touched his ears.

"No, why?" he asked, confused.

Birdy smiled.

"Sorry, it's just an expression. We were just talking about you."

"I was asking Mr. McMurtry if you had figured out what was wrong with him," said Guin.

"As a matter of fact," the doctor began.

He looked over at Birdy.

"It's okay, doc. Anything you can say to me, you can say to Guin here. She's my fiancée."

He grinned at Guin.

"According to the preliminary lab results, you're suffering from mandragora poisoning," said the doctor.

"Mandragora?" asked Guin, confused. "What's that?"

"You may know it better as mandrake root," replied Dr. Gupta.

"Mandrake root?" asked Guin. "Like in Harry Potter?"

The doctor, who had children and was familiar with the

Harry Potter books, smiled at her.

"People often take mandrake root to help with bowel trouble or stomach ulcers, but it can be very dangerous if not used properly—and can cause tachycardia, dizziness, blurred vision, and hallucinations."

"I know all about mandrake root, doctor," said Birdy, interrupting, "and I assure you, I've never taken the stuff."

"Well, your condition was almost certainly caused by the ingestion of mandragora, based on chromotographic identification."

Birdy made a face.

"So he *was* poisoned?" said Guin.

"As I was saying," continued the doctor.

"I knew it!" said Birdy, cutting him off.

"You also appear to have contracted some sort of virus. Have you recently traveled in South America?"

"Yes, I was recently in Chile and Argentina, studying birds."

"Ah," said the doctor. "That would explain it."

"Is he going to be okay?" asked Guin.

"He should be, in a few days," replied the doctor.

"What does that mean?" asked Birdy.

"It means we're going to keep you here in the hospital for a few more days."

Birdy made a face.

"But I feel better already."

"Good. Let's keep it that way," said the doctor. He glanced down at his wrist, which had some sort of smart watch. "I need to go see a few other patients, but I'll check back on you in the morning."

"Thank you, doctor," said Guin.

He gave her a slight nod, then left.

No sooner had he gone than Bettina returned, grinning.

"Good news?" asked Birdy.

"Darling, you remember I told you I was trying to land that *author*?"

"You mean—"

"No names," she said, cutting him off and looking at Guin.

Guin did her best not to roll her eyes.

"Well, I happened to recall he had a place in Naples. And wouldn't you know, he's there right now. We're going to have a drink later, and I'm sure I'll be able to convince him to sign with me," she said.

"Good luck," said Birdy.

"Luck has nothing to do with it," Bettina replied.

She glanced down at her watch.

"Well, I should get going if I want to get to Naples and freshen up. If you need anything, darling, give me a call or shoot me a text."

"I'll be fine," replied Birdy.

Bettina glanced over at Guin, then back at Birdy.

"Very well. I'll see you tomorrow."

"Thanks for checking on me," said Birdy.

"Of course!" she said. "Well, gotta run. Nice meeting you, Gwen."

"It's *Guin*," Guin said, more to herself, as Bettina was already halfway out the door.

"Thank God," said Birdy, as soon as Bettina had gone.

"She is a bit of a handful," said Guin.

"She means well, though," said Birdy. "And I don't know what I'd do without her."

Guin was about to make a suggestion when the door opened again. It was the nurse, with Birdy's dinner.

"Here you go, Mr. McMurtry," she said.

She put the tray of food down, then raised Birdy's bed, so he was fully upright.

"I'll be back in a little while to check on you."

"Thanks," he said.

Guin watched the nurse as she left.

"Alone at last," said Birdy.

Guin turned to look at him.

"You should eat."

Birdy looked down at the tray. There was what looked like a piece of roast chicken, with some sort of mixed vegetable and a whole grain roll. He made a face.

"You want it?" he said, looking at Guin.

"Eat," said Guin. "I'll get something later. Besides, you need to build up your strength. The sooner you're better, the sooner you can get out of here."

"Good point," he replied.

He looked at the roll.

"They could have at least given me some butter."

"You want me to see if I can go find some?" Guin asked.

Birdy looked down at the tray and sighed.

"I'll live."

"I hope so," said Guin. "Now eat up. You need me to cut up that chicken?"

He made a face.

"I'm not an invalid."

He picked up the knife and fork began cutting up the chicken.

"See? Perfectly fine," he said, waving a bite of chicken at her, then putting it into his mouth.

Guin smiled.

"Go on, eat the rest."

Birdy grimaced but ate the rest of the chicken.

"You feel a little better?" Guin asked when he was done.

"A bit."

"Good. Now tell me," she said, pulling the chair she had been sitting on closer to the bed, "who might want to poison you?"

CHAPTER 12

Guin had left the hospital feeling frustrated, and she was still frustrated. Birdy had refused to tell her who he thought might have poisoned him, insisting it was too dangerous to tell her. Indeed, he worried he might have already placed her in danger by allowing her to pose as his fiancée. Though Guin thought that was ridiculous as most people, at least outside of the hospital, knew it wasn't true. Still, Birdy had argued, the risk was too high.

Guin had rolled her eyes and tried to reason with him.

"How can I help you if you won't tell me who might want to poison you?" she had asked him.

But he wouldn't budge. And Guin wound up leaving in a huff, telling Birdy that if he wouldn't let her help him, she would just go.

She had phoned Ginny upon leaving the hospital, but Ginny hadn't answered. So Guin had left her a voicemail. It was now after nine, and Ginny still hadn't returned her call. Guin was tempted to call her again when her phone started buzzing.

She grabbed her phone in the hope that it was Ginny, but it was a text from her brother Lance, wanting to know how she was doing. Instead of texting him back, she called him.

"Isn't it a bit late for you to be calling?" Lance asked. "I thought you were usually in bed by 9:30."

"Ha, ha," said Guin, not amused. "If you thought I was asleep, why did you text me?"

There was a slight pause on the other end of the line.

"Well, since you wanted to know what was up, maybe you can help me," said Guin.

"Shoot. What can big brother help you with?"

"So remember I was telling you I was working on this big profile, of the ornithologist Birdy McMurtry?"

"Vaguely," said Lance. "Is he cute?"

"Some would say so. Though he's not my type."

"Your type being…?"

"Can you please not interrupt?"

"Fine," said Lance, a bit huffily. "Pray, continue."

"So I went to this party for Birdy Saturday, and he seemed totally fine. The next morning, however, he was apparently raving like a lunatic, threatening the hosts, and had to be taken to the hospital."

"Must have been some party," said Lance.

Guin ignored him.

"Anyway, the people he's staying with called 911, and an ambulance took him to the hospital over in Fort Myers. But since they're not family, and Birdy apparently doesn't have any family, Ginny came up with the brilliant idea of telling the hospital that I was his fiancée."

"Wait, how did Ginny get involved?"

"She's friends with the Wilsons, the couple who are hosting Birdy. She and her partner aren't legally married, and he was recently in the hospital, and—"

Lance cut her off.

"I get the idea. So, does Harry Heartthrob know you're engaged to be married to another man?"

Guin glared at the phone.

"You know I hate when you call him that, *Lancelot.*"

"Fine. Does Dr. Hartwick know about your little scheme?"

"It's Ginny's scheme, and no, not yet. Besides, there's nothing to tell. It was just a means to find out what was up with Birdy."

"You mean it was a way for the paper to get the scoop," said Lance.

Guin sighed.

"Yes, but if the guy really has no one.... Though there's that horrible agent of his."

"Agent?" asked Lance.

"This woman who handles all of Birdy's bookings. Looks like a Ralph Lauren model and has a major attitude. *Anyway*," she continued, "the hospital bought me being Birdy's fiancée, and I've been over there checking on him. He's convinced he was poisoned."

"Like food poisoning or poison poisoned?"

"Poison poisoned."

Lance whistled, then paused.

"You sure he didn't OD on something?"

"The doctor said he had mandrake root poisoning, but Birdy swore he never took the stuff."

"Mandrake root poisoning?" asked Lance.

"It's an herbal supplement. Apparently very big in Europe. Cures lots of things. But you take too much and it can make you really sick and hallucinate."

"Sounds great," said Lance.

Guin ignored his sarcastic tone.

"*Anyway*, I asked him to tell me who might have wanted to poison him, but he refused to say."

"Did he tell you why?"

"He said it would be too dangerous."

"I feel like I've seen this movie before. Let me guess, you're going to investigate anyway."

"You don't think I should?" Guin asked.

"Would it make any difference?" Lance replied.

There was silence on the other end of the line.

"You like this guy, the bird watcher?"

"I don't want him to die," Guin replied.

"That's not what I asked, but whatever. Look, I know you. And it's no good telling you not to do something. You're just going to do it anyway. Just be careful. I only have one little sis, and I'd like to keep it that way."

"Thanks, Lance. I love you, too. But how do I get Birdy to confide in me?"

"You could always sleep with him."

"Lance!"

"Fine, be a prude. It always works for me whenever I want Owen to tell me something."

"Yes, but Owen is your husband," Guin retorted.

"And you don't have a husband," Lance replied.

Guin was about to say something snarky, but she stopped herself.

"Can we change the subject, please?"

"Hey, you're the one who brought up the poisoned bird guy," said Lance. "But I'm more than happy to talk about myself."

Guin smiled.

"So, tell me, what have you been up to?"

And he did.

By the time Guin got off the phone with her brother, she was feeling much better. Lance had a way of doing that, which is probably why she had called him. Instead of checking her messages, she turned off her phone and got ready for bed. She would figure out what to do about Birdy in the morning, after a good night's sleep.

And, indeed, the following morning Guin felt much better and was determined to get the truth out of Birdy. She made herself some coffee and took care of the cats, then she took a shower and put on a pretty sundress and a little makeup. She wouldn't be taking Lance up on his suggestion of sleeping with Birdy, but she knew from experience a little strategic flirting could go a long way.

She looked herself over in the full-length mirror and smiled at her reflection. Life on Sanibel definitely agreed with her. Except for acquiring a few more freckles, and the tendency for her hair to frizz, she looked good: healthy and happy.

She turned on her phone and waited for her messages to load. There was a voicemail from Ginny. She quickly listened, then called her back, even though it was early.

Ginny picked up after a few rings.

"And what can I do for you this bright morning?"

"I'm heading over to the hospital to see Birdy," Guin replied.

"You've been spending a lot of time over there," said Ginny. "Is there something I should know?"

"Hey, you were the one who set up this cover, so I could keep tabs on him."

"Easy there, Red."

"Sorry," said Guin. "Anyway, the reason I called you is that the tests came back. And it appears Birdy was poisoned."

"I knew it!" said Ginny. "What was it?"

"Mandrake root," Guin replied.

"Mandrake root?" said Ginny.

"They sell it in health food stores. People take it for ulcers and constipation and all sorts of stuff. The doctor thought Birdy had ingested some, you know, taken a supplement or something, but Birdy swears he's never touched the stuff."

"It's possible he could be lying," said Ginny.

"True, but I don't think he is."

"Go on," said Ginny.

"So that leaves poisoning. Birdy even said as much, but he clammed up when I asked him why anyone would want to poison him."

"Did he give a reason for not telling you?"

"He said he didn't want to endanger me."

Ginny snorted.

"Men."

"I know, right? Anyway, I tried my best to wheedle it out of him, but he wouldn't budge. So I left. But now I have a plan."

"You do? Care to share it with your boss?"

"No, but I was hoping you would give me permission to get Craig involved. He has more experience with this kind of thing than I do."

Craig was Craig Jeffers, the paper's fishing reporter. He had been a crime reporter in Chicago before retiring to Sanibel and had won a bunch of awards for his work. He had been content to fish and spend time with his wife, Betty, but Ginny had lured him out of retirement to cover fishing for the paper. Then she had gotten him to return to covering crime after the murder of noted Captiva real estate developer Gregor Matenopoulos. Since then, he and Guin had worked together on a number of stories.

"Go ahead and give Craig a shout. I'm sure he'd be more than happy to help you."

"You sure it's okay?" asked Guin.

"As long as he gets me his fishing column."

"Great. Thanks Ginny."

"No problem," Ginny replied. "Keep me posted. I know Kathy and John have been worried sick about Birdy and blame themselves."

"I don't see how it could be their fault," said Guin, who had seen the couple at the hospital and knew how they felt about Birdy.

"Well, he did get sick at their house."

"That's just a coincidence," said Guin.

She glanced up at the clock on the microwave.

"Hey, Ginny, I need to go. I'll check in with you later."

"You going to stop by the office?"

"On the way back from the hospital."

"Okay, see you then."

They ended the call and Guin immediately called Craig.

"Hello?" came a cheery female voice.

"Betty? It's Guin Jones."

"Oh, hello dear. I imagine you want to speak with Craig, yes?"

"If he's available," said Guin.

"Just a minute. He was trying to fix the faucet in the kitchen."

Guin waited while Betty went to get Craig.

"He'll just be a minute, Guin. Do you want to wait, or should I have him call you back?"

Guin debated. She really wanted to get to the hospital, and she didn't like talking on the phone in the car.

"Do you think he'll be long?" Guin asked.

"Hello, Guin?"

It was Craig.

"Hi," said Guin. "I hope I'm not disturbing you."

"Nope. Just trying to fix a leaky faucet."

"Any luck?"

"I'll let you know. What can I do for you?"

Guin explained the situation with Birdy.

"So how can I help?" he asked.

"I was hoping you could look into Birdy's background, see if he's had any run-ins with any unsavory characters."

Craig chuckled.

"Been watching old movies again?"

"You know what I mean."

"I do," said Craig. "And what are you up to this fine day?"

"I'm going back to the hospital to see Birdy. Hopefully, he's feeling better and will talk to me."

"Good luck with that," said Craig.

He didn't sound confident.

"Thanks. I'll check in with you later."

"Okay," said Craig.

They hung up, and Guin shoved her phone into her bag and grabbed her car keys.

CHAPTER 13

Guin could tell Birdy was feeling better by the smile on the nurse's face. Birdy had no doubt been flirting with her.

Guin cleared her throat.

"Darling!" Birdy called from the bed. "Come over here and give us a kiss."

Guin gave him a look.

"It's fine," said the nurse, misreading Guin's expression. "He's doing much better."

Birdy patted the bed.

Guin could feel her cheeks burning. Why had she agreed to this ruse?

She forced herself to walk to the bed and leaned over and gave Birdy a peck on the cheek.

"How are you feeling?" Guin asked.

"Much better," he replied. And, indeed, he looked much better today. "I'm just waiting to see the doctor. Hopefully, they'll let me out of here soon."

"The doctor should be in shortly," said the nurse. "Do you need anything before I go?"

"Now that Guin's here, I have everything I need," said Birdy, smiling at Guin.

Guin felt embarrassed but forced herself to smile back at him.

The nurse looked at the two of them and sighed.

"Nice to see folks so in love," she said. "Well, call if you need anything."

Guin watched as nurse left. As soon as she was gone, she turned to Birdy.

"Laying it on a bit thick there," said Guin, giving him a mildly chastising look.

Birdy grinned.

"Well, we are supposed to be engaged. And I have to say, I'm warming to the idea."

"Well, cool it," Guin replied. "I'm already spoken for— and it wasn't my idea to pose as your fiancée."

"Touchy, aren't we?" said Birdy, still grinning. "Come on, be a good sport. I was only having some fun. God knows I could use a little fun."

Guin felt bad. Here was Birdy, in a hospital bed, his trip cancelled or at least postponed, and she was picking a fight with him.

"Sorry," said Guin. "I get a little sensitive around flirtatious, good-looking men."

"Oh, so you think I'm good looking, eh?" said Birdy, sitting up a little taller and giving her that rakish smile.

Guin felt herself coloring.

"You know you're good looking," said Guin.

"And you, Ms. Jones, are a very attractive woman. So what's the harm with a little flirting?"

Guin sighed.

"My husband—make that my *ex*-husband—was also a good-looking man who liked to flirt. In fact, he was so good at flirting that he flirted his way into the bed of our hairdresser," said Guin.

"Ouch," said Birdy, no longer smiling.

"Yeah," said Guin. "But I've moved on, and now I'm seeing someone."

"Someone who is hideous and would never dream of

flirting with anyone, no doubt," said Birdy, a smile playing on his lips.

Guin laughed.

"As a matter of fact, he's also very good looking and women find him irresistible. I have no idea what he's doing with me."

Birdy gave her a look.

"What?" asked Guin.

"Nothing," he replied.

Time to get this conversation back on track, thought Guin.

"So, about who might have poisoned you…" Guin began.

"All that matters is I'm doing better, and I want to get out of here," he stated.

"Yes, but if someone poisoned you, what makes you think they won't try again?"

Birdy looked thoughtful.

"Look, I'm a reporter, a good one, too," said Guin. "I've helped solve several tricky cases on Sanibel. Let me help you. Even if you don't want my help. I'll just go investigate anyway."

Birdy closed his eyes and leaned back in his bed.

Guin waited.

"Fine," he said, a minute later.

He opened his eyes and looked at her.

"So, you'll tell me?" Guin said.

Birdy nodded.

"For a while now, I've had an arrangement with this company, Natura Natraceuticals," Birdy began. "They sell homeopathic remedies and natural supplements."

"Do they by any chance sell mandrake root?" Guin asked.

"Yes," said Birdy.

"So what's your involvement with them?" asked Guin.

"If you would let me finish," said Birdy.

"Sorry," Guin said.

"Bettina arranged it. One of their executives attended one of my talks and was very impressed. Thought we could do some business. So he reached out to her with an offer."

"What kind of offer?" asked Guin.

"Over the years, I've learned a lot about the local flora in the rain forests and jungles I regularly visit, medicinal plants and herbs and things, which I talk about in my lectures. I've become pretty knowledgeable. Natura was looking for someone who could identify potential herbal supplements for them. And in return for tracking down potential supplements and serving as a spokesperson, they would pay me a lot of money."

"Sounds like a good deal all around."

"It was, or so it seemed, until around a month or so ago," said Birdy.

"What happened?" asked Guin.

"They asked me to bring them samples of certain plants, plants that are considered unsafe if not processed or used properly."

Guin raised her eyebrows.

"Did you agree?"

"Not at first," said Birdy. "But they assured me that the plants were only for research and could potentially help thousands of people."

"Go on," she said.

"I agreed, but regretted my decision after getting stopped by Customs," he explained.

"Were you detained?"

"Briefly. Fortunately, I managed to talk my way out of it, but they kept the samples. Then came some other stuff."

"Other stuff?" said Guin.

"There were some stories."

"Stories?" asked Guin.

"Lawsuits, actually, against Natura, claiming their natural supplements were making people sick. In some cases, very sick. Some of the people were just kids. They were ingesting supplements I helped source."

Guin gave him a sympathetic look.

"So I told Natura I wanted out."

"And did they let you out of your contract?"

"No," said Birdy. "They threatened to sue me if I tried to break it."

"What did you do?"

"I threatened to go public with what I knew."

"So you think someone at Natura is trying to send you a message?"

"I do," said Birdy. "Mandrake root is one of Natura's biggest sellers, though it's mostly sold in Europe. Still…"

"That's the drug you were poisoned with," said Guin.

"Exactly," said Birdy.

"And you didn't take the stuff yourself?"

"No," said Birdy. "I know some people swear by mandrake root, and I'll admit, I've tried more than a few herbal supplements over the years, but…"

"So the question is, who slipped it to you and when?"

"It must have been at the party," Birdy replied.

Guin had thought the same thing.

"But who could have done it?" asked Guin. "There must have been a hundred people, maybe more, plus the caterer and the musicians."

"I don't know," said Birdy, leaning back against the bed.

"Was there anyone from Natura there?" asked Guin.

"Not that I know of," said Birdy. "Though it's possible."

"Well, we should figure that out," Guin stated. "I'll check out the guest list for the party, see if anyone there worked for or was affiliated with Natura." She paused. "And I'll check out the caterer and the musicians. It will take some doing, but I have just the guy to help me out."

"You trust him?" asked Birdy.

"With my life," said Guin. "He's a retired crime reporter from Chicago. Well, semi-retired, I guess. He mostly covers fishing now."

Birdy didn't look confident.

"So is there anyone else who would want to poison you, maybe another ornithologist or wildlife photographer, or an angry ex?"

"Ornithologists are not exactly known for being a bloodthirsty lot," said Birdy, "though I know a few who are jealous of my success."

"Jealous enough to want you sidelined?" asked Guin.

"Unlikely, but possible," said Birdy. "I think someone from Natura is far more likely."

"And what about an ex?" asked Guin. "Any former girlfriends with an axe to grind?"

Birdy thought for several minutes.

"Not that I can think of. I always tell the women I date that I'm not interested in a long-term relationship, and I make sure to send them something nice when the relationship ends."

"Seriously?" she said. Birdy was very naive if he really believed telling women he wasn't interested in a long-term relationship and sending them a gift would make everything okay when he broke up with them.

"Let's assume not everyone you dated understood the ground rules and was satisfied with a parting gift," Guin continued. "Was there anyone who took the breakup a bit harder than most, maybe someone you had dated for a while?"

Birdy thought for a minute.

"There was Georgina..."

Guin waited.

"She was rather upset when I broke things off."

"What happened to her?" Guin asked.

"She wound up marrying a duke or something," said Birdy. He looked up at Guin and grinned. "She's practically royalty now. Lives just outside of London and has two adorable toddlers, a boy and a girl."

Guin wanted to hit him.

"Anyone else? Anyone who didn't rebound with a member of the British royal family?"

Birdy looked thoughtful again.

"No, not that I can think of. Like I said, I treated all my paramours very chivalrously."

"I'm sure," said Guin, sarcastically. "Well, I'll start checking out the guest list. If you think of anything, or anyone else who might want to poison you, let me know."

She made to leave, but Birdy stopped her.

"You're going, so soon?"

"I have a lot of work to do."

"Can't you stay a few minutes more? Please?" he said.

He looked so earnest, Guin felt her heart melt just a little.

"Oh, all right," she said. "But just for a few more minutes."

Birdy smiled.

"Thank you."

They spent the next little while pleasantly chatting. Birdy told Guin all about his upcoming trip, which he would be delaying, and Guin told him a bit about her family. They were so deep in conversation that they didn't hear the doctor enter.

"Ah, Mr. McMurtry, I see you are doing better."

"Much better, doctor," he replied. "Any chance you'll spring me soon?"

"Let me take a look," the doctor replied.

He examined Birdy (Guin retreated to the other side of

the curtain), then reviewed Birdy's chart.

"Your fever is down, and it would seem the poison is out of your system," the doctor informed him. "However, we want to monitor you for another day. If you don't have a setback, I don't see why you shouldn't be released tomorrow or the day after."

"I'm ready to go now!" Birdy said, swinging his legs around and preparing to stand up. "See?" he said, taking a few steps, then collapsing.

Guin and the doctor rushed to help him up and get him back in bed. The doctor made a face.

"You are still quite weak, Mr. McMurtry. We don't want to discharge you until you are strong enough to walk on your own."

"Yes, doctor," Birdy sighed, leaning back in his bed.

Guin could tell he was frustrated. She didn't blame him. She would feel the same way in his position.

The doctor finished making some notes.

"Do you have any questions for me?" he asked Birdy.

"No," said Birdy, who was clearly angry at having to stay in the hospital another day.

"One of my colleagues will check on you later," said the doctor. "But if you need anything…"

"I just need to get out of here and get back to work," said Birdy, a bit petulantly.

"I understand, Mr. McMurtry," said the doctor. "Now, if you will excuse me…"

He nodded to Guin, and she watched as he left the room.

"I need to go, too," she said.

"Fine," said Birdy. "Leave. I'll just be lying here, all by myself."

Guin rolled her eyes.

"I'm sure the Wilsons plan on stopping by. What about your family?"

"I have no family," said Birdy, clearly in a mood. "And my fiancée clearly doesn't love me enough to stay."

Guin was about to say something when the door flew open.

In rushed a six-foot-tall blonde Amazon.

"Darling, how are you? I had the most dreadful evening." Bettina.

Birdy looked over at Bettina, then at Guin, which caused Bettina to look in Guin's direction.

"Oh, you," Bettina said, looking down at her, clearly not pleased to see Guin.

"Nice to see you, too, Bettina. I was just leaving."

"Well, don't let me keep you," she replied.

Guin stopped.

"Aren't you flying back to New York?"

"I've decided to stay a few days," Bettina replied. "I want to make sure Birdy is back to his old self before I fly back up north." She turned to look down at him. "I've managed to reschedule most of your Australia and New Guinea trip. You think you'll be able to get out of here by this weekend?"

"If not, shoot me."

Bettina gave him a big smile.

"That's my Birdy."

"Well, I should get going," Guin said.

"Yes, run along," Bettina replied, not looking at her.

"Will you come back later?" asked Birdy.

"Of course," said Guin, detecting the plea in his voice.

Ignoring Guin, Bettina began to regale Birdy with details from her evening with the author, which had seemingly not gone well.

Guin shook her head and made her way out of the room.

CHAPTER 14

Guin stopped at the *San-Cap Sun-Times* office on her way home from the hospital. Ginny was on a call but had indicated that Guin should wait for her to get off. Everyone was busy, so Guin waited by the front desk, checking her messages on her phone. Both Shelly and Ris had texted her.

"When are we getting together?" Shelly had asked her. "I feel like it's been forever."

"You want to go shelling tomorrow morning?" Guin texted her back.

"It's a date!" Shelly replied seconds later. "Name the beach and the time."

"Beach Access #4 at 7:15?"

"C u there!" Shelly typed back.

One down, one to go, thought Guin.

What time was it in Cambodia? Guin wondered. Or had he moved on? She started to type "time in Cambodia," then stopped.

"Miss you, too," she texted him back. "You want to do a video chat this week? Let me know what works for you."

She had just hit "send" when Ginny came rushing up to the front desk.

"Sorry about that," she said to Guin. "Important advertiser."

"No worries," Guin replied. "Everything okay?"

"Everything's fine now," said Ginny. "He was just upset that his ad didn't appear closer to the front. But as I explained to him, that cost more, and the man is a notorious cheapskate."

Guin smiled.

"Let's go back to my office," said Ginny, taking Guin by the arm. "Then you can tell me all about you-know-who."

Guin followed her back and took a seat.

"So?" said Ginny, after taking a seat behind her desk.

Guin then told her everything she knew about Birdy, with Ginny only occasionally interrupting her.

"Good work," said Ginny, when Guin had finished. "Let me know what you and Craig find out."

"Will do," said Guin.

"And I have a couple of other pieces I want you to work on."

"The ones you mentioned in your email?"

"Yes," said Ginny. "As you know, Valentine's Day is in just a few weeks."

"And I'm going to be meeting up with Ris in Sydney, as I told you."

"Yes, yes," said Ginny, dismissively. "But before you go, I want you to do a roundup of romantic things to do on and around Sanibel for Valentine's Day."

Guin groaned.

"Really? Couldn't you assign that to one of your other writers?"

"No, I want you to do it. After all, you met Dr. Heartthrob on Valentine's Day, and look what happened."

"Fine," Guin said, realizing that resistance was futile. "Is there anything in particular you have in mind?"

Ginny smiled.

"Actually, I quite like the idea of including some non-traditional ways to spend the holiday, though I know a number of stores and restaurants have special events planned."

She rooted around in her desk, opening and closing folders, until she found the folder she was looking for.

"Here you go," she said, sliding it across the desk to Guin. "Here are a bunch of press releases I've received, along with some notes and contacts. That should give you a good head start."

"Thanks," said Guin.

"I also want you to review this new place that's opening over in Tahitian Gardens. It's called the Paper Fig Kitchen."

She slid over a piece of paper, which Guin took a look at.

"Is it a take-out place?"

"Yes, and they do catering," said Ginny. "Anyway, it sounds intriguing. And I know how you love good food."

Guin did love good food. Though since Ris had left, she wasn't cooking as much, and she missed his cooking.

"Sure," Guin said. "No problem. Happy to do it."

"Excellent," said Ginny.

"Anything else?" asked Guin.

"You want more? Because you know I have several stories…"

"No, no, I'm good," said Guin, getting up. "I'm assuming you want these two as soon as possible."

"If not sooner," said Ginny, smiling at Guin.

Just then Ginny's phone rang.

"I'll see myself out," Guin said, as Ginny picked up the handset.

Ginny waved goodbye as Guin let herself out.

Guin made her way to the front of the office, waving to Jasmine, the head designer, and a few other people she knew. Then she took her leave.

She paused by the Mini to check her messages again. There was one from Birdy, asking her to bring him some "real food." She smiled.

She got in the car and headed to Bailey's General Store. Birdy wasn't the only one who could use some real food. By the time she had finished, she had enough food to survive a hurricane, or it felt that way. In reality, she had only bought enough food to tide her over for a few days. She also bought ingredients to make chocolate chip cookies. That should cheer Birdy up, she thought, assuming he was allowed to eat them.

She paid for her groceries, then packed them into the tiny trunk of the Mini.

"Oh my God," said Birdy, later, eating one of the chocolate chip cookies Guin had brought for him. "This may be the best chocolate chip cookie I've ever had."

"I just hope it doesn't make you sick," said Guin.

"I don't care," said Birdy, taking another bite. "At least I'll die happy now."

He took another bite and moaned.

"You wouldn't also happen to have a thermos of your world-famous coffee?" he asked her.

"No, sorry," said Guin.

"I'll just have to console myself with another cookie then," he said, grabbing another one out of the container. "Seriously, you could make a fortune with these cookies," he told her, waving the cookie around.

"When was the last time you had a chocolate chip cookie?" Guin asked.

Birdy thought for several seconds.

"I don't recall. But if I had had one this good, I would definitely have remembered it."

Guin looked skeptical.

"Well, I'm glad you're enjoying it. Just try not to OD."

She watched as Birdy began eating the second cookie.

He finished it and reached for another, but Guin stopped him.

"Wait a few minutes. I don't want you to get sick."

"I feel fine," he said, a bit petulantly.

Guin gave him a look.

"Fine," he said. "I'll wait a few minutes. Would you mind getting me a glass of water? I'm still a bit shaky on my feet."

Guin went over to the sink.

"Did the Wilsons come by to see you?" she asked, placing the glass next to him.

"They did," said Birdy. "Kathy brought me this."

He held up a bird-watchers coloring book. Guin laughed. Birdy smiled.

"I love it," said Guin. "Do you need some crayons or magic markers?"

"She brought me both," he said, smiling at her.

"Well, I should probably get going…" said Guin.

She had been there for over half an hour.

"Please stay a little longer," said Birdy, looking up at her.

"All right," said Guin. "But just a little while longer. I need to get to work on figuring out who might have poisoned you."

She had hoped to start when she had gotten home from the grocery store, but the cookies had taken longer than she thought.

"Thank you," said Birdy. "So, did I tell you about the time I was nearly killed by a bunch of Chinese poachers in Indonesia?"

"Poachers?" said Guin.

"They were in search of the rare helmeted hornbill, which I was there to photograph," Birdy explained. "The helmeted hornbill has a solid red beak, which is known as 'red ivory' on the black market and sells for several times the price of elephant ivory. It's illegal, but that's only made it more valuable. Their tail feathers are also highly prized."

Birdy paused.

"I saw the poachers sneaking around, so I made a fair bit of racket, in hopes of scaring the bird away."

"Did it work?" asked Guin.

"It did, but the poachers were none too pleased. Next thing I knew, they were aiming their guns at me."

"How did you escape?"

"I fired back at them, then hightailed it out of there."

"You had a gun?" Guin asked, her eyebrows going up.

"You think I could defend myself in the jungle with a pair of binoculars and a camera?"

Guin felt a bit stupid, but what did she know? She couldn't imagine a bird watcher carrying a gun, but then the only bird watching she had ever done was over at Ding Darling.

"Could the poachers have followed you to Sanibel?" she asked him.

"Possible, but highly unlikely. I'm not sure they even knew who I was, just some interfering Caucasian trying to deprive them of their trade."

He probably had a point, Guin thought.

Just as she was about to ask him a question, there was a knock at the door and one of the nurses she had seen before entered, along with yet another doctor.

Guin glanced over at the container of chocolate chip cookies, feeling a bit nervous. The doctor followed her eyes and smiled.

"Chocolate chip?" he asked.

"Yes," said Birdy. "And I'm willing to share, but only if you promise to let me out of here."

The doctor chuckled.

"I'm afraid I'm immune to bribery."

"Please, have one," said Guin, holding out the container.

"Thank you," said the doctor, "but I'll pass."

Guin looked at him. He was very lean. Probably a runner and didn't eat sugar.

"You don't know what you are missing," said Birdy.

"I'm sure," said the doctor.

He reviewed Birdy's chart, then looked over at him.

"Dr. Gupta will be back to check on you in the morning. If he gives the okay, you can go home tomorrow."

"Thank God," Birdy said. "No offense, doctor," he quickly added.

"No offense taken," replied the doctor. "We just want to make sure you're stable. Are you able to walk around at all?"

"Take a look," said Birdy.

He swung his legs over the side of the bed and took a few steps. Guin watched nervously, holding her breath.

"You see?" he said, still standing, but resting an arm on the stand near the bed.

The doctor didn't look entirely convinced.

"Let me just examine you, then I'll be out of your way."

The nurse closed the curtain around the bed. Guin waited on the other side.

A few minutes later, the nurse drew the curtain aside.

Guin looked over at the doctor.

"Will he be okay?" she asked.

"This is my fiancée, Guinivere Jones," said Birdy.

"He's recovering nicely," said the doctor. "Like I said, a good night's rest and he should be able to be discharged."

Guin smiled.

"Well, I should get going," said the doctor. "Need to check on a few more patients. Nurse Hatchett can reach me if you need anything."

The nurse nodded.

"Thank you, doctor," Guin and Birdy said simultaneously.

"And what would you like for dinner this evening?" asked Nurse Hatchett, after the doctor had left.

"What are my choices?" Birdy asked.

She recited them for Birdy. None of them sounded

particularly appetizing. Guin had planned on making him some chicken soup, but had quickly realized she didn't have the time, so she had made him cookies instead.

"I'll have the chicken. Thank you," he said, smiling at the nurse.

She smiled back at him and left.

"I'd rather just eat your cookies, but I know what you'd say."

"You need protein," said Guin.

She was about to say something else when she felt something vibrating against her lower back. Her phone. Which was in her back pocket. She tried to ignore it, but her phone continued to vibrate.

She grabbed it to see who was calling. The word "Mom" was prominently displayed on her screen. Great. Just what she needed.

"Everything okay?" asked Birdy.

"I don't know," said Guin. "It's my mother. She's called twice now."

"Then you'd better answer it," he said.

"I'll be right back," said Guin.

She walked quickly out of the room and called her mother back, not bothering to check her voicemail.

"What?" she asked, when her mother had picked up.

"That's a fine how do you do," said her mother, indignantly.

"Sorry. Hi Mom. What's up? Is that better?"

"Barely," her mother sniffed.

"Look, Mom. I'm at the hospital…"

"The hospital?! Is everything okay?"

"I'm fine, Mom. Just visiting a friend."

"Well, in that case…"

Guin waited for her mother to continue. When she did not immediately, Guin spoke up.

"I'm kind of busy, Mom. Is there something you need?"

"I was just making some plans for when we're down there at the end of the month, and I wanted to run a couple of things by you."

"Can it wait?" asked Guin, glancing at the door to Birdy's room.

"I suppose," said her mother. "But you know how booked up things get down there this time of year."

"I promise, I'll call you later, or tomorrow. How late will you be up?"

"Philip and I are going to the theater tonight, and I have my Mandarin class tomorrow morning."

"Mandarin? You're studying Mandarin?" Guin asked. This was the first she'd heard of it.

"Didn't I tell you? Philip and I just booked a trip to China this spring, and I thought it would be useful if I spoke a bit of the language."

"Good for you," said Guin.

"You should try it," said her mother. "Could come in very handy."

"I'll consider it, but Mom, right now I need to get back to my friend."

"Anyone I know?"

Guin was torn. She didn't like lying to her mother, but she didn't want to tell her about Birdy.

"I'll tell you about it when I talk to you tomorrow. What time's good for you?"

Her mother proceeded to rattle off her schedule, which sounded far busier than Guin's.

"But I'm free between four and five," she finally said.

"Fine," said Guin. "I'll phone you tomorrow between four and five. Gotta go."

"*Dzai jee-en*," said her mother.

"What's that?" asked Guin.

"It's *goodbye* in Mandarin."

"Ah," said Guin. "Well, goodbye to you, too. Hope you and Philip enjoy your show."

She ended the call and placed her phone back in her back pocket. Then she went back into Birdy's room.

CHAPTER 15

The next morning Guin met Shelly over on West Gulf Drive. However, her mind was on Birdy.

"Penny for your thoughts," said Shelly.

"Sorry," said Guin. "Just have a lot on my mind. This whole Birdy thing has been taking up almost all of my time."

"I can think of worse ways to pass the time than with Birdy McMurtry," said Shelly, grinning at her.

"It's not like that, Shell."

"Uh-huh."

Guin made a face.

"And my mother wants to discuss her upcoming trip to Naples, which I am *not* looking forward to. And Ris is MIA, again."

"I'm sure he's just busy," said Shelly.

"Probably," said Guin.

It was funny. Things hadn't been so great with Ris before his trip. However, since he had been gone, Guin had found herself missing him and second-guessing her decision not to go with him.

Guin sighed.

"Try him again later," suggested Shelly. "Maybe he doesn't have coverage wherever he is."

"Good point," said Guin. "I just hope he's okay."

"I'm sure he's fine."

"You're probably right," said Guin. "Anyway, enough about me. Tell me how you're doing."

Shelly then told Guin about her idea to add some decorative pieces to her Etsy store.

"I have all these extra shells, so I thought I could make some picture frames and tchotchkes."

"That sounds great, Shell!" Guin replied. "And how are the kids?"

An hour or so later, after Shelly had told her about her daughter Lizzy's new boyfriend, whom she hadn't actually met, and her son Justin finally getting to start on the lacrosse team this season, and only finding a handful of halfway decent shells, mostly orange and pink scallops and some lettered olives and lightning whelks, they said their goodbyes.

As soon as she got home, Guin showered and changed and headed to the hospital. She had just missed the doctor, who, Birdy told her, had told him he could be discharged later that day, as long as he had someplace nearby to recuperate and someone looking after him. Birdy had asked the doctor about travel, but the doctor had advised against it, at least until Birdy was fully recovered. Birdy had promised to take it easy, to appease the doctor. But he fully intended to leave for Australia and New Guinea that weekend.

Guin stayed at the hospital for an hour, watching as Birdy demonstrated that he was perfectly okay by walking around the room. He certainly put on a good show.

"So where do you plan on recuperating?" she had asked him.

"At the Wilsons'," he had replied. "Speaking of whom, could you give me a ride over there?"

"They can't pick you up?" she had asked him, surprised.

"They had a thing," said Birdy. "They were very apologetic.

But they said their housekeeper and gardener would be there to look after me until they got back."

"What about Bettina?" Guin had asked.

"What about her?" Birdy had replied.

"Can't she take you over there?"

"She's busy."

"So she's not too busy to fly down from New York to Florida to see if you were okay, but she's too busy to drive you from the hospital to Sanibel?"

Guin looked skeptical, but Birdy just shrugged.

"Fine," Guin had finally said. "What time should I pick you up?"

She agreed to come get him at five, so she could get some work done in the meantime. Then she left. As soon as she got home, she went to her computer. But she found it difficult to concentrate.

"May as well work on something easy," she said, opening the folder Ginny had given her with Valentine's Day ideas.

Before she knew it, it was time to head back to the hospital to get Birdy.

She went to his room and found him arguing with an attendant.

"You make me prove I can walk on my own only to stick me in a wheelchair?" Birdy groused.

"Hospital rules," said the attendant.

Birdy grunted and sat down. The attendant picked up his bag.

"Is that all you have?" asked Guin.

"Not like I needed a suit and tie at the hospital," said Birdy.

He had a point.

Guin accompanied them to the lobby. When they got near the doors leading outside, the attendant insisted Birdy stay in the chair, though Birdy told him he was perfectly fine.

"You sure you can manage, miss?" the attendant asked Guin.

Birdy was around six feet tall and had to weigh at least 180 pounds, while Guin was just over five foot four and weighed at least fifty pounds less.

"Well…" she said.

"I'm perfectly fine," Birdy insisted.

"Why don't I bring my car around? I'll just be a minute." She looked over at the attendant.

"I can wait," he replied.

Birdy opened his mouth to object but quickly shut it at the look he received from Guin.

"Fine," he growled.

A few minutes later, Guin pulled up in the Mini. She got out to help Birdy, at the same time as the attendant moved to help him, but he held up a hand. He then proceeded to lift himself out of the wheelchair and walk to the car.

"Allow me," said the attendant, placing Birdy's bag in the trunk, then shutting it.

"Thanks," said Guin. "You good?" she asked Birdy.

"Let's get out of here," he said.

She waved goodbye to the attendant, then put the Mini into gear.

Birdy was unusually silent on the drive to Sanibel.

"Everything okay?" Guin asked him.

"Just have a lot on my mind."

"Okay if I put on some music?"

"Go ahead," he replied, staring out the window.

Guin put on her favorite jazz station.

As they crossed over the Causeway, she smiled. The sun was setting, and the sky was alight with reds and oranges, yellows and pink. There was a reason people referred to this stretch of road as "the happy lane."

She glanced over at Birdy. He had nodded off and was snoring quietly.

Around twenty minutes later, she pulled into the Wilsons' driveway. The outdoor lights were on, as were some lights inside the house. Guin wondered if the Wilsons had cut their trip short after inviting Birdy to recuperate at their place.

She turned off the engine and nudged Birdy.

"Hmm?" he asked, sleepily.

"We're here," Guin replied.

She got out of the car, went around to the passenger side, and opened the door.

"You need a hand?" she asked.

"I think I can manage," he replied.

He got out of the car and nearly tripped. But Guin was there to catch him.

"You okay?" she asked him.

"I am now," he said, moving his body closer to hers and leaning on her.

"Let's get you up to the house then."

They took a couple steps, then Guin stopped.

"Oh, I almost forgot your bag," Guin said. "Stay here. I'll just go get it."

She turned and walked back to the Mini.

As she opened the trunk of the car, she heard a faint sound, like wind rushing by, and then a gasp and a loud thump.

She turned to see Birdy lying in the driveway, face down, blood streaming around him.

"Oh my God! Somebody, help!" she screamed up at the house.

She knelt beside Birdy's body and felt for a pulse.

"Thank God," she said.

He was alive.

She moved her face close to his ear.

"Birdy, can you hear me?"

He didn't respond.

"I'm calling an ambulance. Just stay with me. Please."

She whipped out her phone and pressed 9-1-1.

"This is an emergency," she said to the operator. "Someone's been shot at…" she gave the 911 operator the Wilsons' address and told them to hurry.

"Stay with me, Birdy," she said again, holding his hand.

She looked up at the house. She thought she detected a figure by the window, but it quickly disappeared. Should she go ring the doorbell? She looked back down at Birdy. Better to stay with him.

She continued to hold his hand and tell him everything would be okay. Then she realized the shooter could still be lurking nearby and could very well take a shot at her. But she held her ground. The ambulance would be there soon.

A couple more minutes passed, though it felt like an eternity, and she thought she heard a sound. She immediately reached for her phone and called Detective O'Loughlin's mobile number.

"Ms. Jones, to what do I owe the honor?" said the detective, in his usual snarky tone.

"No time, detective. Someone just took a potshot at Birdy McMurtry in the Wilsons' driveway while I was getting his bag. I called 911, but I'm—"

"I'll be right there," said the detective, cutting her off. "Get to someplace safe."

Guin looked around.

"He's unconscious and bleeding in the driveway. I can't move him, and I can't just leave him here."

"Sit tight, I'll be right there," said the detective.

"I'm not going anywhere," said Guin.

She looked up at the house again, thinking surely someone must have heard the commotion and would check to see if everything was all right. But there was no movement, at least none she could detect from where she was crouched.

She looked down at Birdy and gently laid a hand on his face.

"Stay with me, Birdy," she ordered him.

"You still there?" asked the detective.

Guin had put the phone down, forgetting to end the call with the detective.

"Yeah, I'm still here," she replied.

"I'm almost there," said the detective.

The one nice thing about being part of the Sanibel Police Department was that you could drive as fast as you needed to. Something Guin wish she could do, the speed limit on Sanibel being 35 mph.

Guin heard the rustling sound again. It was coming from some palms. She froze. Could it be the shooter? If so, she was a sitting duck. But she refused to leave Birdy lying there. She lay on the ground next to Birdy, whispering in his ear.

She felt a breeze and held her breath, thinking it was another bullet. But it was just the wind. Seconds later, she heard a siren. She was too scared to look up. She just prayed it was coming there.

The siren became louder, until it was practically on top of her.

She looked up to see an ambulance and a police car—and two EMTs rushing towards her, along with Detective O'Loughlin and Officer Pettit.

"Thank God you're here," she said, getting up.

"You okay?" asked the detective, helping her to stand. "You hurt?"

Guin looked down. She had blood on her shirt and pants.

"I'm fine. It's Birdy's," she said, noticing the blood.

Guin turned to watch the EMTs as they examined Birdy.

"Will he live?" Guin asked.

"We need to get him to the hospital," the male tech replied.

He and the female tech wheeled over a stretcher and gently lifted Birdy onto it.

"Can I go with him?" Guin asked, as they wheeled Birdy to the ambulance.

"You his wife?" the male tech asked.

"Fiancée," Guin replied.

The detective shot Guin a look, but she ignored him.

The female tech was about to say something when the detective cut her off.

"I'll take you," he said to Guin, taking her arm.

"I'm fine," she replied. "Really."

"We'll meet you at the hospital," the detective said to the EMTs.

They closed the rear door of the ambulance and got in.

Guin went to get into the Mini when the detective stopped her.

"Where do you think you're going?"

"The hospital," said Guin, shaking his arm off.

"Not until you tell me what happened here," said the detective.

"Please, let me go to the hospital," Guin begged, feeling like she was about to cry. This was all her fault.

"You know, I could order you to come to the police department, Ms. Jones," he said, looking at her.

Guin pulled herself together.

"I promise to tell you everything I know, detective. But right now, I need to find out if Birdy is going to be okay."

Suddenly, Guin pictured Bettina. She would need to tell her what happened, the Wilsons, too.

"You're coming with me," said the detective, taking Guin's arm.

"I told you, detective, I need to go to the hospital!"

She tried jerking loose, but the detective held firm.

"I'm taking you to the hospital. You can tell me everything you know on the way there."

"What about Officer Pettit?" asked Guin, looking over at the handsome young officer who had accompanied the detective. She had known Officer Pettit since she had worked with him to solve the case of the missing Golden Junonia the year before.

"He can drive your car over to the police department. You can pick it up later."

Guin looked over at Officer Pettit, who had been waiting patiently by the detective's car. He nodded to them.

"Okay, fine," she said.

She followed the detective to his vehicle. He instructed Officer Pettit to take Guin's Mini over to the police department, and Guin handed him the keys.

"Thanks," she said.

"No problem," Officer Pettit replied, smiling at her.

That taken care of, the detective walked around to the passenger side of the car and opened the door for Guin. She climbed in. A few minutes later they were en route to the hospital.

CHAPTER 16

"Fiancée?" the detective asked her, as they drove to the hospital. "What about the marine biologist?"

Guin sighed.

"It was Ginny's idea. Birdy fell ill right after the Wilsons' party. He was staying with them, and when they went to check on him the next morning, he was ranting and raving. The Wilsons called an ambulance, and the EMTs took him to the hospital. But when the Wilsons tried to find out what was the matter with him, the hospital said they could only share that information with family. So they called Ginny, because, you know, Joel, and she told them to tell the hospital that I was Birdy's fiancée."

The detective looked at her, shook his head, then focused on the road. For the next several minutes, neither of them said a word.

"Did you see the shooter?" the detective asked Guin.

"No," she replied. "It all happened so fast. And it was pretty dark. We were heading to the house, and I had gone back to get his bag out of the trunk when I heard this sound, almost like a whistle. Then, next thing I knew, Birdy was on the ground and there was blood everywhere. I thought he was dead, but I checked, and he had a pulse and was breathing, though barely."

The detective asked Guin a few more questions, which

Guin answered to the best of her ability. But as she had not seen the shooter, and had been absorbed with looking after Birdy, she wasn't able to give him much help.

"I did see someone inside the house. At least I thought I did," she said. "Both the housekeeper and the gardener were supposed to have been there. But no one came out."

"And you say the Wilsons are away..."

"That's what Birdy told me. I thought his agent would pick him up from the hospital, but she had something, too. So I agreed to take him to the Wilsons'."

"Agent?" asked the detective.

"She handles all of his bookings," Guin explained.

Guin looked over at the detective, but his expression was as Sphinx-like as ever. Seriously, the man should take up professional poker. He'd kill at Texas Hold'em.

Finally, they arrived at the hospital. The detective parked by the Emergency Department, then escorted Guin inside.

"Let me do the talking," he told her.

They walked up to the admitting area.

"We're here to check on a patient," the detective told the woman behind the glass. "He was just brought in from Sanibel. The name's Bertram McMurtry. Gunshot wound."

The detective showed the woman his badge.

"He hasn't been admitted yet," replied the woman, after pressing a few keys on her computer. "You say he was just brought in?"

"Yes," said the detective.

"Give me a minute," she said, still looking at her screen.

The attendant got up and started to head toward one of her coworkers when Guin piped up.

"He was just a patient here," she called. "He was discharged earlier this evening. I'm his fiancée."

The detective shot her a look, which she ignored.

The attendant turned around and went back to her computer.

"Ah, got it," she said. "You say he was brought back in just a few minutes ago?"

"Yes, he was shot," Guin replied. "We followed the ambulance here."

"Hey, Mick, we get any gunshots the last few minutes?" she called to a man a few feet away.

"I'll go see," replied the male attendant.

Guin and the detective waited. A few minutes later, Mick returned and went over to the woman at the desk.

"Did you locate him?" Guin asked, looking from one attendant to the other.

The detective presented his ID to the male attendant.

"Detective O'Loughlin, Sanibel PD."

"He's here, unless there's another guy with a gunshot wound who was brought in from Sanibel."

"Is he going to be okay?" asked Guin.

"They're taking him into the OR now," said Mick.

Guin looked over at the detective.

"Let us know as soon as you hear anything," he told Mick. "We'll be in the waiting area."

"It could be a while," Mick informed them.

"Here's my information," said the detective, handing him a card. "Make sure someone contacts me as he's out of surgery."

The attendant took the card and shoved it into a pocket, then turned to help someone else.

"Come on," said the detective, leading Guin over to the waiting area.

She followed him over but was too on edge to take a seat.

"Do you think he'll be okay?" she asked the detective.

Even though she knew it wasn't her fault, she felt guilty about Birdy getting shot. Not that she could have prevented it.

"I don't know," replied the detective. "It didn't look

good, but I'm not a doctor."

Guin began to pace.

"Why would someone take a shot at him? I don't understand."

She suddenly stopped.

"Birdy said he thought someone poisoned him. Could it be the same person?"

The detective looked at her.

"Poisoned?"

"The doctor said Birdy had ingested mandrake root. That's what caused him to fall ill. But Birdy swore he never touched the stuff—and said someone must have poisoned him."

The detective looked skeptical.

"Why would he lie?"

The detective raised an eyebrow.

"Come now, Ms. Jones. Don't tell me you never did something you shouldn't have, then lied about it afterward."

Several images immediately popped into Guin's brain, and she felt her cheeks getting warm.

"Point taken. But in this case, I think Birdy was telling the truth."

"And you know this because...?"

Guin couldn't explain. She barely knew Birdy, but she felt in her gut that he was telling the truth.

"You're going to have to trust me, detective."

The detective ran a hand over his face. He looked weary.

"You don't have to stay here," Guin told him. "I'm fine waiting on my own."

He was about to say something when his phone rang.

"I need to take this," he said, looking at the screen.

Guin gestured for him to go ahead.

He moved to a more secluded spot, where no one could hear him. A few minutes later, he came back over.

"I need to go. Let me take you back to the police department. Chances are Mr. McMurtry is going to be in surgery for a while and won't be able to see visitors until the morning.

Guin hesitated. Then she went over to the window.

"Excuse me," she said to the woman she had spoken with earlier.

The woman looked up at her.

"I'm Guin Jones, Mr. McMurtry's fiancée."

Guin had said it so many times now, it almost felt real.

"Will someone let me know when he's out of surgery?"

"Here, fill out this form," said the attendant.

Guin looked at the form and realized she knew nothing about Birdy, not his middle name, or birthday, or where he lived—and began to panic.

The detective saw her distress and came over to the window.

"I'm sorry, Ms. Jones here is in shock," the detective explained to the attendant. "As Mr. McMurtry was just a patient here, I'm sure his information is still in the system."

"Yes, but..." began the attendant.

Guin did her best to look like someone suffering from shock.

"I'm sure the information hasn't changed in the last six hours," continued the detective. "Ms. Jones here will give you her information, as she is his next of kin. If someone could contact her when Mr. McMurtry is out of surgery..."

The attendant sighed.

"Go ahead," she said.

Guin wrote down her cell phone number as well as her email address.

"Here," she said. "And thank you."

"Come," said the detective, gently taking her arm and leading her away.

They walked to the exit, Guin looking back one last time as they reached the double doors.

"I feel funny leaving," she said.

The detective stopped.

"No one knows he's been shot," she continued. "Except for me."

"And the person who shot him," replied the detective, his face grave.

Guin involuntarily shivered.

"You sure you're okay?" he asked her. "Maybe we should have you checked out."

"I'm fine," Guin replied, wrapping her arms around herself.

They reached the detective's car. Guin stopped and turned toward the detective.

"So how did the shooter know where to find Birdy? He had only just been released from the hospital, and only a handful of people knew where he'd be."

The detective looked at her.

"You don't think..." she began.

Just then her phone started to buzz. She grabbed it, thinking it was Ginny, replying to her message. But it was Ris.

"Ris!" she said, gaily, trying to mask her anxiety.

The detective raised an eyebrow. Guin turned away from him.

"How are you?"

"I'm fine," Ris replied. "Sorry if I've been a bit incommunicado. Been a pretty busy few days, and the cell service here is horrible. Are you okay?"

Guin glanced over at the detective. She was definitely not okay, but she didn't want to worry Ris.

"Everything's fine," she lied. "Hey, can I call you back in a bit? I'm kind of in the middle of something."

"You sure you're okay?" he asked. "You sound a bit funny."

"Must be the connection," said Guin. "Can I ring you back in a couple of hours?"

"I'm heading out at eight local time here. I'm twelve hours ahead of you. If you can't talk later, I can always try you tonight, my time, that is, your tomorrow morning."

Guin felt torn. She desperately wanted to speak with Ris, but the hospital parking lot was not the place.

"Fine. If you don't hear back from me in an hour, try me tomorrow morning. That is tomorrow morning Sanibel time."

"Okay," said Ris. "I miss you."

"I miss you, too," said Guin. "Bye."

She ended the call and looked over at the detective.

"You tell him about your new fiancée?" he asked her.

Guin made a face.

"No. Besides, there's nothing to tell," she retorted.

She opened the passenger-side door and got in, slamming it shut after her. The detective got in the driver's side and turned to Guin.

"You want to grab something to eat?" he asked her.

"I'm not hungry," she said.

"Suit yourself," said the detective. "But I know a little place a few blocks away where you can get a killer burger, fries, and a milkshake."

"I'm good," said Guin, crossing her arms in front of her and looking out the window.

Just then, though, her stomach let out a loud gurgle. It had been hours since she had eaten anything, and she suddenly realized she was hungry.

She turned and looked at the detective.

"Fine, let's go."

The detective gave her a self-satisfied smile and started the car.

CHAPTER 17

"Five Guys? Your 'little place' is Five Guys?" Guin said, as the detective parked in front of the fast food restaurant.

"You got a problem with Five Guys?" asked the detective.

"No, but..." Guin began.

The detective got out of the car.

"Fine," said Guin, opening the passenger-side door.

She followed the detective into the restaurant. He ordered a bacon cheeseburger, fries, and a Coke.

"Ms. Jones?"

Guin stared at the menu.

"I'll have a little burger with lettuce and tomato and a black-and-white milkshake," she told the young man behind the counter.

"Would you like some fries with that?" asked the young man.

"I'll just have some of his," Guin said, looking at the detective and smiling.

The cashier announced the amount and the detective gave him cash.

"I would have been happy to have paid," Guin said, as they made their way to the soda machine.

"I think I can handle it," said the detective, as he filled up a large cup with Coca-Cola.

Guin helped herself to some water.

They found an empty table and sat.

Guin took out her phone and placed it on the table, looking down at it.

"I doubt that he's out of surgery," said the detective.

"I know," said Guin. "I just feel so…"

She trailed off.

"Nothing you can do," said the detective, stoically.

Guin stared out the window.

"You planning on going to Spring Training?" asked the detective, breaking the silence a couple minutes later.

"I hadn't really thought about it," said Guin, turning back to face him.

The detective was a diehard Boston Red Sox fan, having grown up and lived in the Boston area most of his life. And his office was full of Red Sox paraphernalia. Guin was also a baseball fan, a New York Mets baseball fan, having grown up in New York City and gone to games with her father when she was a little girl, her brother having no interest in baseball. She and the detective had attended a couple of games together the previous summer and had enjoyed themselves. Then he had disappeared, and they hadn't gone to a game since.

"I've never been to First Data Field," he continued.

"Are the Red Sox playing the Mets there?" asked Guin.

"Not this season," replied the detective. "But I'd be happy to watch the Mets beat the Yankees. The next best thing."

He grinned, and Guin laughed.

"It's a date, assuming we can get tickets," she said.

"I'll take care of it," said the detective.

They lapsed into silence again, though it was quickly broken by their number being called.

"I'll get it," said the detective, getting up.

He returned a minute later with their food and some ketchup. Guin devoured her little burger and sighed contentedly as she sipped her milkshake. The detective grinned.

"What?" she said, noticing him smiling at her, a sight that always disconcerted her.

"I like a woman who enjoys her food," he replied.

They finished their meal, then got up to go.

The detective drove them back to the Sanibel Police Department and escorted Guin to her car.

"Please thank Officer Pettit for me."

"Will do," said the detective, opening the driver's side door for her.

Guin hesitated before climbing in.

"You'll let me know if you hear anything from the hospital?" she said, looking up at him.

"You may hear first," he replied.

"Thanks for dinner," she said, getting in.

"My pleasure."

The detective closed the door after her, then turned to go.

"Detective!" called Guin out her window.

"Yes, Ms. Jones?"

"You know I'm going to be covering this for the paper."

The lights around the police department illuminated the detective's face. He did not look happy. Instead of replying, he turned and made his way up the stairs to the police department.

Guin started the Mini and slowly backed out.

As soon as she got home, Guin called Ginny, but she didn't pick up. So Guin left her a message, telling her to call her back ASAP. Then she phoned Craig. Fortunately, he was home, Craig rarely being out after nine on a weeknight, unless it was Friday, Poker Night.

Guin filled him in on all that had happened. He whistled.

"We need to start running down those leads," she announced. "I'm betting whoever tried to poison Birdy may have taken that shot or hired whoever did."

"Sounds plausible," said Craig. "I did some preliminary checking. My money's on Natura. I read some articles about them. It seems a number of people have tried to sue them. Also, any company with a name like 'Natura Natraceuticals' doesn't sound on the level."

Guin smiled. Despite his wife being a bit of a health nut, Craig was deeply suspicious of anything that sounded too good to be true.

"Fine. Keep investigating Natura. I'm going to look into one Bettina Betteridge," said Guin.

"The agent?" said Craig. "You got a bad feeling about her?"

"Something about her rubbed me the wrong way."

"You sure it's not jealousy?" asked Craig.

"Phht," said Guin, immediately dismissing the idea. "I have zero personal interest in Birdy or who he sees. Not that he's seeing Bettina. I just find it a little odd that she showed up here so soon after Birdy fell ill and then was nowhere to be found when Birdy was discharged from the hospital."

"Fine, you research the agent. Anyone else you want me to check out?"

Guin thought for a minute.

"We should probably look into Birdy's other business dealings and competitors."

"You think some bird watcher wanted to knock him off?"

Guin suddenly formed a cartoon image of an elderly

birdwatcher, à la Mr. Magoo, with a pair of binoculars and a gun, and had to stop herself from laughing out loud.

"I admit, it doesn't sound likely, but you never know."

"And we need to run down the guest list for the party." Guin paused. "I'll take care of that."

"Sounds like a plan," said Craig. "I'll run a background check on Mr. McMurtry, do a little digging into his business dealings, and see what else I can find out about Natura. Though since you were the business reporter, maybe you want to do a little poking around into the company."

"Good point," Guin replied. "I'll look into Natura. Maybe one of my former colleagues knows something about them."

She paused.

"I just hope Birdy's going to be okay."

"It's not your fault, Guin," Craig told her.

"That's what the detective said," she answered. "But I still feel guilty."

"Well, don't," said Craig. "Now go get a good night's sleep."

"I'll try," said Guin. "But it won't be easy. Say hi to Betty for me."

"Will do," he said.

She ended the call, then got ready for bed as she suddenly felt very tired.

Guin got up early the next morning, despite not having slept well. It was still dark outside, but the sun would be coming up soon.

The cats were still asleep, curled up on either side of her. Not for the first time, she wished she was a cat.

She sighed and got out of bed. May as well go to the beach, she thought.

She went into the bathroom and splashed some cold

water on her face. Then she tied her hair in a ponytail, threw on a pair of capris and a long-sleeved top, and headed to the kitchen.

The cats, now wide awake, beat her there, and Fauna immediately started to cry. Guin stared down at her.

"Let me guess, you're hungry," she said.

Fauna meowed louder.

Guin opened the door to the pantry and pulled out a can of cat food. The meowing got louder and more insistent.

"Geez. Give me a sec, will ya?" she said, looking down at the black cat.

She pulled back the lid and grabbed a fork. Immediately, Fauna and Flora raced to their bowls. Guin knelt and scooped the contents of the can evenly between the two bowls. Both cats lunged, head first, into the food.

Guin shook her head, then grabbed their water bowl and refilled it. Then she got herself some water from the fridge. She took a few sips, then put the glass down.

"Phone," she said aloud, realizing it was not in her back pocket.

She walked back into the bedroom and retrieved it from the nightstand. She turned it on and headed back toward the kitchen. There was a voicemail from Ginny. Guin would call her back later.

She quickly checked her email. Nothing urgent. Then she put the phone in her back pocket, grabbed her fanny pack and her keys, and left.

It was still pretty dark when she arrived on West Gulf Drive. She had just stepped onto the beach when she felt her phone vibrating. She took it out. It was Ris.

"Am I catching you at a good time?" he asked her.

"I'm on the beach," she replied, walking down to the shoreline.

"Which one?"

"West Gulf, Beach Access #4."

"Are there a lot of people there?" he asked.

Guin looked around. There were a few shell seekers, but no one in her immediate vicinity.

"Just a few hardy souls. It's a little chilly this morning, and still a bit dark. What's it like over there?"

"Beautiful. The beaches here are amazing. I heard they filmed a season of *Survivor* right around here."

"Huh," said Guin, who was not a fan of reality TV shows.

They chatted for a few minutes, Guin staring out at the water as they talked.

"Who's there with you?" asked Guin, hearing what sounded like a woman giggling in the background.

"Just the daughter of our host," Ris replied.

Guin raised an eyebrow.

"She's nine, Guin. One of the guys was doing a magic trick for her."

Guin felt embarrassed. It was as if Ris could read her mind.

"Well, I should probably let you go," she said.

"Yeah, we're about to head out to dinner. But I'm glad we got to speak."

"Me, too," said Guin.

Guin could hear someone calling Ris's name.

"Gotta go," he said. "I'll message you tomorrow."

"Sounds good," said Guin. "Goodnight."

"And Guin," said Ris.

"Yes?"

"I love you, and I can't wait until we're together again."

Guin felt her cheeks growing warm.

"I love you, too," she said. "Bye."

They ended the call and Guin put her phone away.

She looked out at the sea.

"Hey Neptune!" she called. "How about tossing me a junonia? Though I'd settle for a Scotch bonnet."

She stood there for several seconds, looking down, as the waves gently lapped against the shoreline. Nothing. Guin sighed, then began to slowly walk west.

CHAPTER 18

It had not been a good morning for finding shells, and Guin was feeling restless. She made herself a pot of coffee when she had gotten back to the condo and had gone to take a shower while it was brewing, ignoring the cats' cries for more food.

"I just fed you!" she had snapped at them.

The warm shower relaxed her a bit, but she had too much on her mind. She kept replaying the scene in the Wilsons' driveway. Clearly someone wanted Birdy dead. But who?

She toweled off, applied some body lotion, and combed her hair, which was in desperate need of a trim. Then she threw on a pair of capris and a t-shirt and went to get some coffee.

She was staring out at the golf course, her mug warm in her hands, when she felt something brush against her leg. Fauna.

"I'm not feeding you again until noon," she told the black cat.

The cat continued to rub against her and purr.

"Fine," said Guin, bending down and stroking the cat, which elicited a louder purr.

Guin smiled and continued to pet the cat for several seconds. As if sensing petting was to be had, Flora trotted over and sat down in front of Guin.

"You want some petting, too?" Guin asked her.

As if in response, the multicolored cat began rubbing herself against Guin.

"Okay, okay," said Guin.

She sat down and proceeded to pet each cat.

Several minutes later, feeling more relaxed, she stood up, much to both cats' annoyance.

"Sorry, team. I've got work to do."

She took a sip of her coffee, which was now lukewarm, then placed it in the microwave. When it was done, she took the mug into her office/bedroom.

She had left her phone on her desk and saw she had a missed call. Ginny. She immediately called her back.

"Are you okay?"

"I'm fine, Ginny," Guin replied.

"Of all the times to not have cell service," she muttered.

"Really, it's okay," Guin repeated.

"It's not okay," said Ginny. "You could have been killed, Guinivere."

"But I wasn't," said Guin.

"And poor Birdy. What that man has been through."

"Have you heard something?" asked Guin.

In her haste to call Ginny back, she hadn't checked her other messages.

"I just got off the phone with Kathy. He's in ICU. Thankfully the bullet missed any major organs. But in his weakened state…"

Guin let out a sigh of relief. Though how had the Wilsons found out about Birdy before she had? She shook her head. The important thing was that he was alive.

"So he's going to be okay?"

"It's too early to say," Ginny replied, "but according to Kathy he appears to be out of any immediate danger."

"I should go see him," Guin said.

"They're not allowing any visitors."

"Not even his fiancée?" Guin asked.

Ginny chuckled.

"No. No one except your friend the detective."

How did Ginny know so much? Then again, she had spies everywhere. Though to call them "spies" might have been a bit uncharitable.

"But," began Guin.

"But nothing. You can see him later. The best way you can help Birdy is to help figure out who would want to harm him. I've already chatted with Craig. He said you two were on top of it."

Guin wondered if Ginny ever slept. She always seemed to know what was going on the island, no matter the hour.

"When did you speak with him?" Guin asked, curious.

"Earlier this morning."

"Ah," said Guin. "So where were you last night?"

"Out on my friend Digby's new yacht. He's got it moored up on Captiva and took a few of us out for a late-night spin."

"Nice," said Guin. "So, do I know this Digby? I don't think you've mentioned him before."

"That's probably because he doesn't come to Sanibel and Captiva very much anymore. Made a killing on Wall Street and now invests in startups and travels the world."

"So what was he doing back here?" asked Guin, curious.

"He has some business here," said Ginny. "Anyway, he's only here for a short time. And it's been ages since Joel and I saw him. So…"

"Well, I'm glad you had a good time," said Guin.

"Yes, well, and while I was out drinking Champagne on some yacht, my star reporter nearly got herself killed."

Guin rolled her eyes.

"I told you, I'm fine, Ginny, except for being worried about Birdy. I can't believe the shooting was random."

"No," Ginny agreed. "But I can't imagine who would want to harm him. Everyone loves Birdy."

"Clearly, not everyone," said Guin. "Anyway, Craig and I are working on some leads."

"Good, good. Keep me updated. I'm assuming you've spoken with the police."

"Yes. Detective O'Loughlin accompanied me to the hospital."

She paused.

"Though, speaking of the detective, I need to give him a call."

"Okay," said Ginny. "I need to run, but call or text me with any news."

"Will do," said Guin.

She paused.

"You said before you spoke with Kathy Wilson."

"Yes."

"When?" asked Guin.

"Early this morning. Why?"

"I thought they were away," Guin said.

"They were," Ginny replied, "but they heard about Birdy being shot in their driveway and rushed back."

"Had the police informed them?"

"I assume so," said Ginny. "Listen, I really have to go, Guinivere, but keep me posted. The other papers are going to be all over this, but we have the inside track. And I'd like to keep it that way. This is a big story."

"I'll do my best," said Guin.

"Good," said Ginny. "Well, ta-ta for now."

They ended the call and Guin stared at her computer. Where to begin?

She opened a new document and began to type, laying

out everything she knew so far, from Birdy falling ill after the party and being rushed to the hospital to his being shot at shortly after they arrived at the Wilsons'. Then she ran a search on him.

She had placed her phone, ringer off, in a drawer and now took it out. The text message, voicemail, and email notifications were all lit. Guin groaned.

She called her voicemail first. The first message was from Kathy Wilson, letting her know she had heard the news, had felt just awful she and John had not been at home, and that Guin should call her as soon as she got the message. Guin deleted the message then played the next one. It was from her mother, who had an urgent question and wanted Guin to call her. Guin sighed and deleted the message. Why couldn't she have just texted her the question? She made a mental note to phone her mother back later.

Next she checked her text messages. Shelly had some big news she wanted to share and had asked Guin to call her ASAP. There was also a message from Craig, saying he had found something interesting.

Guin was torn. Her first inclination was to call Craig, but she knew that if she didn't reply to Shelly, Shelly would just keep texting her. So she picked up the phone and called her.

"Oh my God!" Shelly practically shrieked when she picked up. "You'll never guess what happened!"

Before Guin could reply, Shelly continued.

"I got a booth at the big downtown Naples art show! I was on the waitlist, and apparently someone backed out, and now I'm in!"

"That's wonderful, Shelly!" Guin said, truly happy for her friend.

"I know, right? This could be huge. You know I've applied several years in a row. I still can't believe it!"

"You'll do great, Shell."

"You'll come, of course."

"Of course!" said Guin. "I'll even help you out, if you need someone, providing I'm free. When is the show?"

"Near the end of March. Oh my God! I'm so excited!"

Guin smiled.

"Will you be able to finish your project for the Artistic division and do the Naples show?"

"I'm nearly done with my piece for the Artistic division. I just need to make more jewelry for Naples. But I've got time. Oh, I'm so excited!"

"Congratulations," said Guin. "I'm very happy for you."

"Thanks. I knew you'd be excited," said Shelly. "So when are we getting together to celebrate?"

"Soon," said Guin. "Right now, however, I need to get back to work. There's a big story Ginny needs me on."

"Ooh," said Shelly. "Anything good?"

"I can't say," said Guin.

"Not even a hint?" asked Shelly.

"Sorry, Shell."

"Well, I guess I can wait and read it in the paper," Shelly said. Though, by her tone, Guin could tell she wasn't happy about it.

"Thanks, Shell. I promise I'll text you about getting together later."

"Okay," she said. "I should probably go make some jewelry."

"You do that," said Guin.

They said their goodbyes, then Guin immediately called Craig. He picked up after three rings.

"What's up?" asked Guin.

"I came across something interesting."

"Yes?" said Guin.

"I did a little more research on Natura Natraceuticals."

"And?" said Guin. She had thought Craig was going to leave that to her, but no matter.

"It's registered in the Cayman Islands."

"So?" said Guin.

"The Caymans are an infamous tax haven. A lot of shady companies incorporate there."

"And some not so shady ones, too," said Guin. "Just because a company incorporates there doesn't mean it's got something to hide."

Craig made a harrumphing sound.

"Yeah, well…"

"Anything else?" asked Guin.

"I'm still digging."

Neither said anything for several seconds.

"You speak with the detective?" he finally asked her. "I heard McMurtry's in ICU."

Guin made a face. Did everyone know about Birdy, except for her?

"I haven't spoken to him this morning. Why, did you speak with him?"

Craig said that he hadn't.

They spoke for a few more minutes, until Craig said he had to go.

CHAPTER 19

Next, Guin called Kathy Wilson, though she was unsure what to say.

"It's too dreadful," Mrs. Wilson had exclaimed, shortly after picking up. "Who would want to do such a thing, to Birdy of all people?"

"I know," said Guin. "It's awful."

"And to think it happened on our property!" Mrs. Wilson continued. "What is the world coming to?"

"Do you have any idea who would want to harm Birdy?" Guin asked. "Has he had a run-in with anyone on the island?"

"Everyone on Sanibel loved Birdy," Mrs. Wilson said.

"What about other people?" Guin asked. "Does Birdy have any rivals, maybe someone with a professional or personal grudge?"

There was no response for several seconds.

"Mrs. Wilson?" Guin asked. "Are you still there?"

"I was just trying to think of anyone who might have resented Birdy's success."

"And?" Guin asked.

"Well, there's James Hornsby," she replied. "He's always been jealous of Birdy. He was Birdy's mentor. A classic case of the student eclipsing the teacher."

Guin wrote down the name.

"Do you know where he lives?"

"Sorry, no. I know he was teaching at Cornell, but that was a while back."

Guin made a mental note to do a Google search for him. "Anyone else?"

"There's poor Briony," said Mrs. Wilson, a bit wistfully.

"Briony?" asked Guin.

"Briony Betteridge," replied Mrs. Wilson.

"Briony Betteridge?" asked Guin. "Any relation to Bettina Betteridge?"

Mrs. Wilson sighed again.

"I'm afraid so."

Guin waited.

"They're sisters."

"Ah," said Guin. "And what is, or was, Briony's beef with Birdy?"

"How much time do you have?" asked Mrs. Wilson.

Guin waited for Mrs. Wilson to continue.

"Briony and Bettina have been rivals practically since birth," she began.

Guin had never really experienced that kind of sibling rivalry. She and Lance had never fought over anything. Or if they had, it was minor.

"Whatever one of the sisters got, the other one wanted," Mrs. Wilson continued.

"So where does Birdy fit in?" asked Guin.

"Briony dated Birdy. Though I'm not sure 'dated' is the right term. Briony was totally obsessed with the man."

"Briony dated Birdy?" asked Guin.

"It was years ago," Mrs. Wilson explained. "That's how Bettina met him. Briony was an up-and-coming photographer. Did society portraits. Rather successful. She was also a bit of a nature buff and had signed up to go on one of those nature photography trips, which Birdy happened to be leading. By the end of the trip, the two of them were an item. But it didn't last. It never does with Birdy. Briony was devastated. Next thing you know, she was trying to beat Birdy at his own game. But of course, she couldn't compete. Not that her work is bad, mind you. But she's no Birdy."

"How do you know all of this?" asked Guin.

"I've known Clarissa Betteridge, Briony and Bettina's mother, forever. We were sorority sisters. She was the one who suggested we go hear Birdy."

"Do you know where Briony is now?" asked Guin.

"No," replied Mrs. Wilson. "I haven't seen her in ages."

"Do you think Bettina would know where she was?"

"It's possible," said Mrs. Wilson. "Though, as I said before, the two aren't exactly close."

"Do you know how I can get in touch with Bettina?"

Mrs. Wilson gave Guin Bettina's mobile number.

"Oh, I almost forgot," said Guin. "Could I get a list of everyone who worked the party, as well as those who attended?"

"Why?" asked Mrs. Wilson.

"There may have been someone there who shouldn't have been, who had something against Birdy."

"I already gave the list to that detective."

"O'Loughlin?" asked Guin.

"Yes, I believe that was his name."

"Could you send it to me, too?"

"Why do you need it?" Mrs. Wilson asked.

"I'm covering the story for the paper."

"That's right," she replied. "Of course Ginny would want to cover this. I'll send it over to you as soon as we get off the phone."

"Thank you," said Guin.

"So, do you know of anyone else, anyone at all on Sanibel

or nearby, who might want to harm Birdy?" Guin asked again.

Mrs. Wilson thought for several seconds.

"No, not off the top of my head," she finally replied. "Like I said, everyone here adores Birdy."

Clearly, not everyone, thought Guin, but she kept that thought to herself.

"Well, I should get going," said Guin. "Thank you for your help, Mrs. Wilson."

"Please, it's Kathy. And if you do go to the hospital later, let me know how our Birdy is faring. John said we should wait until he's out of intensive care."

"Will do," said Guin.

She paused.

"Speaking of Birdy, how were you able to find out he was in the ICU?"

"John knew someone who knew someone."

"Ah," said Guin, not pursuing the matter.

They said their goodbyes, then ended the call.

Guin looked down at her notes. The number of suspects had just increased, and she had a lot of work to do.

CHAPTER 20

"Detective O'Loughlin, please."

Guin had decided to give the detective a call shortly after speaking with Mrs. Wilson.

"Who's calling, please?" asked the police department operator.

"Guin Jones."

"One moment," said the operator.

Many seconds later, she came back on the line.

"I'm sorry, he's unavailable right now. Would you like to leave a message?"

"Just put me through to his voicemail."

"Okay," said the operator. "Have a nice day."

"You, too," said Guin.

Guin waited for the telltale beep, then left the detective a message, asking him to call her back as soon as possible.

When she was finished, she turned over her phone and woke up her computer.

Guin had been staring at her monitor (and out the window), trying to decide where to start. Finally, she typed "Briony Betteridge" into her search engine, which seconds later displayed hundreds of results. She clicked on Images first.

There were photos of and by Briony from various

fashionable magazines, parties, and gossip sheets. Guin clicked on one of Briony smiling, holding a camera. Superficially, she resembled her sister: tall—the word *willowy* sprang to mind—with long, straight, ash blonde hair. She could have been a model.

Guin scrolled through the Images gallery and found a few photos of Briony with Birdy. They made a handsome couple, Guin thought. She clicked on one to get a closer look. In the photo, no doubt taken a while ago, Briony was beaming. Birdy was smiling, but it seemed a bit forced. Or perhaps that was Guin's imagination.

She wondered what the age difference was between the two and, in a new tab with a couple of clicks, discovered that Birdy was 10 years older than Briony.

Next, she went to Briony's website. Briony was clearly a talented photographer. Or good at photographing people. There were dozens of portraits and party shots.

Guin next did a search for "Birdy McMurtry and Bettina Betteridge." As expected, there were dozens of results. She clicked on Images and found photos of the two of them. In nearly all of them, they were in the same pose, standing next to each other, with Birdy's arm around Bettina, both smiling for the camera. Guin wondered if the two of them had also dated. It wouldn't surprise her. The resemblance between the two sisters was striking. So was Briony jealous of Bettina's relationship with Birdy?

Guin spent the next hour or so finding out what she could about each woman, typing notes as she went. Both were attractive, seemingly successful, and had relationships with Birdy. But could one of them have tried to kill him? It didn't seem likely, but, as Guin well knew, love did funny things to people, as did rejection.

Guin went back to Briony's website. There was a link on the website to gallery shows. She clicked on it.

"Well, well, well," she said aloud.

It turned out Ms. Briony Betteridge had a gallery show in Naples at that very moment, and the opening reception had been the Friday before the Wilsons' party for Birdy. Could Briony have snuck into the party and poisoned Birdy? Though how would she have even known about the party? And realizing the poison hadn't worked, would she really have come back and taken a shot at Birdy a few days later? Guin made a face. It did seem a bit preposterous. Okay, more than a bit, but....

"I need to speak with Briony—and Bettina," Guin said aloud.

She grabbed the piece of paper where she had written Bettina's number down and sent her a text, asking when the two of them could talk. Not that Guin really wanted to spend time with Bettina, but Bettina would be able to tell her who might have borne a grudge against Birdy, and she wanted to know more about the sisters' relationship with him.

"You bet we're going to talk!" Bettina replied. "And you're going to explain to me how you let my star client get shot!"

Guin froze. Of course someone had told Bettina about Birdy. Stupid of her to not have anticipated she would be angry.

She immediately called the hospital to check on Birdy. After being transferred several times, she was put in touch with a doctor.

"I'm Guin Jones, Mr. McMurtry's fiancée," Guin explained, when the doctor came on the line. "How is he?"

"He's in serious condition," the doctor replied.

"Is he conscious?"

"Not as yet."

"Can I see him? I was told he wasn't allowed visitors."

"They've moved him into a semi-private room. So you can visit him during normal visiting hours."

"So I could come see him this evening?" she asked.

"Up until nine," replied the doctor.

"Is he going to be okay?" Guin asked.

"I can't give you an answer at this point."

"At what point can you give me an answer?" Guin asked, becoming frustrated.

"That depends on Mr. McMurtry," said the doctor.

Guin sighed. This was like talking to the detective.

"Thank you, doctor," Guin said, as politely as she could.

"You're welcome," he said. "Hopefully, we will have more to tell you in the next day or so."

Guin ended the call and paced around her bedroom. Part of her wanted to rush over to the hospital, just to make sure Birdy was actually alive. But she wasn't sure how that would help or what was to be gained.

Suddenly, Guin realized her phone was buzzing. It was Bettina. She debated answering it but finally did.

"Hi Bettina."

"So, is he going to live? That stupid hospital won't tell me a thing."

She was clearly upset.

"I was just on the phone with the doctor," Guin replied.

"And?"

"He's in serious condition," Guin replied. "I'm heading to the hospital now."

"I'll meet you there," said Bettina.

Guin was about to say something, but Bettina had already ended the call.

Guin stood staring at her phone. Should she call Bettina back and tell her to wait? Though if anything, Bettina had more of a right to see Birdy than she did. Unless she was the killer. Though Bettina had supposedly not shown up in

Florida until after the party. Guin would need to double check that. But for now, she would need to get to the hospital. She grabbed her bag and her keys and headed out the door.

Guin parked the Mini and went into the hospital. She looked around but didn't see Bettina. She realized they hadn't discussed where they would meet. Bettina had hung up before Guin could ask her. But if Bettina was staying in Naples, it would take her a bit longer to get to the hospital.

Guin took another look around the lobby but didn't see her. It was possible she had gone upstairs to Birdy's room. She went to the front desk and asked where she could find Bertram McMurtry and said she was Birdy's fiancée. The woman asked to see a photo ID and Guin handed over her driver's license.

The woman examined Guin's license, then typed something into her computer.

"Okay, you can go up," she told Guin.

"You didn't say what room," Guin told her.

"My bad," said the woman. She looked tired, as if she had been answering questions all day, which she probably had. She gave Guin Birdy's room number and told her how to get there.

"Thank you," said Guin. "By any chance has a tall, willowy blonde also asked to see Mr. McMurtry, just before I got here?"

"A tall, willowy blonde?" said the woman. "No, I don't think so. I think I would have remembered her."

"Okay. Thank you," said Guin. "If someone fitting that description comes in in the next few minutes, would you tell her Guin already went up? Her name is Bettina Betteridge."

"Will do," said the woman. "Though I'm about to leave for

the day. But I can leave a note for Doris. She's on after me."

"Thanks," said Guin.

She then headed toward the elevator.

Guin knocked softly, then entered Birdy's room. She hadn't ever visited someone in intensive care before, and she was a bit overwhelmed by all the machines. There were two beds in the room, divided by a curtain. Birdy was in the first bed. He looked asleep.

Guin went over and stood next to him. There were various tubes coming out of, or rather going into, him. Guin reached out a hand and gently placed it on his arm.

"Oh Birdy. I'm so sorry. This is all my fault."

Even though she knew there was probably nothing she could have done to have prevented Birdy from getting shot, she still felt responsible.

Suddenly he stirred. Guin nearly shrieked in surprise.

Birdy's eyes fluttered open, and he turned to look at her.

Guin smiled down at him.

"Welcome back."

He opened his mouth, then winced.

"Should I get a nurse?" she asked, concerned. It looked like he was in pain.

Before he could answer, a nurse came into the room. She looked from Guin to Birdy.

"He's conscious," said Guin.

"So I see," said the nurse.

She went over to Birdy.

"How are you feeling, Mr. McMurtry?" she asked him.

He again opened his mouth, but he seemed unable to speak.

"Here, have a little water," the nurse said, refilling his cup.

He drank some, then immediately started coughing, then wincing.

"Drink slowly," advised the nurse.

She held the cup up to his lips and had him take another sip. This time he didn't cough.

"You had us worried there," said the nurse, putting the cup down.

"Sorry," he rasped.

"I forgive you," said the nurse, smiling at him. "The doctor will be here shortly."

"Food," rasped Birdy.

"I'll have to check with the doctor," said the nurse. "We'll probably have to start you off with broth and some toast."

Birdy made a face.

"Trying to kill me," he rasped.

"We're trying to heal you," said the nurse. "If I wanted to kill you, I'd make you go eat in the cafeteria," she said and laughed at her little joke.

Birdy did not look amused, but Guin smiled.

"I'm just going to go find the doctor, tell him you're awake," said the nurse. "You going to behave?"

Birdy closed his eyes.

"I'll make sure he behaves," said Guin.

"And you are?" asked the nurse, turning to look at Guin.

"Sorry," said Guin. "I'm Guin, his fiancée."

"Okay, but no nookie," said the nurse, looking over at Birdy.

"I promise," said Guin.

The nurse left the room.

Less than a minute later the door flew open.

"Oh my God!"

Bettina.

"You had me scared to death, Birdy!" she said, rushing over to his bedside and ignoring Guin.

She stopped just short of the bed, taking in all the various machines and monitors.

"I'll have to cancel the Australia and New Guinea tour," she said and began rummaging in her bag for her phone.

Guin stared at her.

Bettina looked up and glared at Guin.

"What?"

"Nothing," said Guin.

"I know what you're thinking," said Bettina. Though Guin doubted it. "You're thinking, what kind of cold bitch is she, thinking about business when poor Birdy is lying in a hospital bed, practically at death's door?"

Apparently Bettina did know what Guin was thinking. She continued.

"Well, Birdy *is* my business. And if he wants to stay in business, he needs to keep his fans and partners happy. And the sooner I let the people in Australia and New Guinea know what's up, the better it will be. Of course, they won't be happy. They'll have to refund everyone. But, hopefully, we'll be able to reschedule. The important thing is for Birdy to get well."

She said this last bit while furiously typing on her phone.

Guin looked at Birdy. He was leaning back against his pillow, his eyes still closed.

"Birdy?" she asked. "Are you okay?"

He didn't respond.

Guin felt herself begin to panic. Then she checked his monitor. It seemed fine, but what did she know? All she knew about such things was what she had seen on those hospital procedurals on TV. But surely if he had gone into cardiac arrest, something would start beeping or that bouncing light would flatline. That's what happened on all those shows.

She leaned over, putting her face very close to Birdy's.

"Whatever are you doing?" asked Bettina.

"Checking to see if he's still breathing," replied Guin.

"And?" said Bettina, momentarily stopping what she was doing.

"He appears to be okay," said Guin.

"If you consider this"—Bettina waved her hand around—"okay."

"Let's step outside for a minute," suggested Guin.

"Why?" asked Bettina, looking at Guin suspiciously. "Is there something you're not telling me?"

"No," said Guin, trying to control her annoyance. "I'd just like to ask you a few questions, and Birdy could probably use some peace and quiet," she said, lowering her voice.

Bettina still eyed her suspiciously.

"Don't you want to find out who shot Birdy?" Guin asked her.

"Fine," said Bettina, putting her phone back in her bag. "But just for a few minutes."

Guin walked to the door and held it open for Bettina.

CHAPTER 21

Guin looked for a quiet place for the two of them to chat, but there didn't appear to be a sitting area nearby. So she settled for a quiet looking spot down the hall from Birdy's room, at the end of the corridor.

"Yes?" said Bettina, crossing her arms.

Guin took a deep breath and exhaled.

"So, you probably know Birdy better than anyone," she began, hoping to soothe the other woman. "Do you know of anyone, anyone at all, who might want to harm him? Anyone who might have been jealous of him, of his success, or who he had butted heads with?"

"*Of course* people were jealous of Birdy," said Bettina, as if Guin's question was the stupidest one she had ever heard. "That's the lot of famous people like Birdy. But want to kill him?" She looked down at Guin, as though such an idea was ludicrous. "Everyone loves Birdy."

"Including your sister, apparently," Guin said, not allowing herself to be intimidated, even though Bettina towered above her.

Bettina did not look pleased.

"Who told you that?" she snapped.

"It doesn't matter," said Guin. "What matters is, would Briony ever do anything to harm Birdy?"

Bettina looked like she was about to say something,

something not particularly nice. Then her expression changed, and she sighed.

"I know Bri was very upset when Birdy broke up with her and nursed a grudge against him for a while. But she's moved on."

"Did you know that she currently has a show in Naples?"

For a minute, Guin thought Bettina was going to feign ignorance.

"I did, but Naples isn't exactly close to Sanibel," she replied. "I should know. It must have taken me nearly two hours the other day. I don't know how you people can stand the traffic. It's worse than the Hamptons."

Guin sympathized with her about the traffic. During high season, it did get pretty bad on Sanibel. But it wasn't as though Naples was at the other end of the country.

"Anyway, what's your point?" asked Bettina.

"Is it possible Briony found out about Birdy being on Sanibel and came here?"

"I told you, the two of them were over years ago."

"Yes, but isn't it possible she still had feelings for him? And when she found out he would be on Sanibel, she decided to pay him a visit?"

"Look, I may not get along with my sister, but no way would she take a shot at Birdy."

"What about poisoning him?" asked Guin.

"Poisoning him?" asked Bettina.

"When Birdy was in here before, the doctor said he had been poisoned."

"I thought it was some bug he had picked up in Argentina, or a bad shrimp."

"Well, according to the tests the hospital ran, it was mandragora poisoning."

"Mandragora poisoning?" asked Bettina, looking confused.

"It's a root. Better known as mandrake. Some people

take it to help with ulcers or constipation or joint pain. But take too much, and it can make you very ill."

Bettina continued to look at Guin.

"The doctor thought Birdy might have taken some the day of the party, but Birdy swore he never touched the stuff. When they first brought him in, Birdy swore he had been poisoned. Though no one believed him because he was out of his mind," Guin explained.

"And you honestly think my sister could have driven over here and snuck some mandrake root into his, what? His drink? His food?" said Bettina, looking skeptical.

Guin ignored her tone.

"Is it possible," Guin said slowly and clearly, "that Briony could have found out about the Wilsons' party, wangled her way in, and then poisoned Birdy?"

"It's possible Briony knew about the party," Bettina said, begrudgingly. "But poison Birdy? I don't think she's that stupid. And as much as I love Birdy, he did love those homeopathic cures. Every time he goes on one of his trips, he chats up the locals to find out what they use to cure headaches and bug bites and stuff. That's why I knew he'd be perfect as a spokesman for Natura. They're a huge maker and distributor of natural supplements."

"Well, Birdy swore to me and the doctor that he hadn't ingested any mandrake root, at least knowingly," said Guin.

Bettina gave her another skeptical look.

"Speaking of Natura, though," said Guin, "did you know Birdy was planning on severing his contract with them?"

"*What?*" Bettina practically squawked.

"He apparently has some issues with the company."

"Well, that's news to me," said Bettina. "Did he speak with Dick or Digby? He hasn't said anything to me."

"Digby?" asked Guin. Why did that name sound so familiar? "Who are Dick and Digby?"

"Dick Grayson is the head of Marketing at Natura and Digby, otherwise known as J. Douglas Blyleven, is the CEO. And no, I don't know why people call him Digby. Probably some college or baseball nickname. He briefly played in the big leagues."

"Blyleven..." said Guin, immediately recognizing the last name. "Any relation to Bert Blyleven, the pitcher?" Guin asked.

"A cousin," replied Bettina. "Though Digby was never as good as Bert. Blew his arm out his first season in the majors and got a job on Wall Street instead. Made a killing, then began investing in companies."

"And how did he become involved with Natura?" Guin asked.

"He was an early investor," Bettina replied. "Then when the company exploded and needed to bring in a professional to run it, Digby stepped in. Though he rarely goes to the office these days. Spends most of his time on his yacht."

"And I understand you were the one who hooked Birdy up with Natura."

"Yes," said Bettina. "It was one of my better deals, if I do say so myself."

She smiled at the thought.

"And Birdy didn't say anything to you about getting out of it?" Guin asked her again.

"No."

Guin was about to ask Bettina another question when a phone started ringing.

Bettina reached into her bag and pulled out her mobile. She looked at the screen.

"I need to get this," she said to Guin.

She turned her back to Guin and took a few steps away from her.

"Darling!" said Bettina. "I was just about to call you back.

No, really!'"

Guin shook her head as Bettina walked down the hall. She waited a minute, then decided to go back and check on Birdy.

The doctor was with him when she entered the room, and Birdy's eyes were open again. He smiled weakly at her as she entered.

"Hi, I'm Guin, Birdy's fiancée," Guin said, extending her hand to the doctor, a woman.

The doctor, who was holding a tablet, did not shake it.

"I'm Dr. Sanger," she said.

"How is he?" Guin asked.

"As I was just saying to Mr. McMurtry, he's a very lucky man. He literally dodged a bullet."

"Though not nearly lucky enough," said Birdy, with a pained smile.

"It could have been much worse," said the doctor. "The bullet just missed your major organs."

"Lucky me," said Birdy, clearly not feeling very lucky.

"So, what's the prognosis?" Guin asked.

"Good," said the doctor. "We're going to keep him here for a couple days, make sure there's no infection or internal bleeding. Then, if all looks good, he could be out of here this weekend."

Birdy made a face.

"That is, as long as he obeys his doctor and the nurses and takes it easy," said the doctor, giving him a stern look.

"I'll make sure he takes it easy," said Guin. Though, from what little she knew about Birdy, that wouldn't be easy. But maybe Bettina would help.

As if summoning her with a thought, Bettina flounced into the room.

"Ciao, darling!" she said into her phone, then placed it in her bag.

"That was Giancarlo," she said, looking at Birdy. "He sends his best."

"That's very sporting of him," Birdy replied.

"Who's Giancarlo?" asked Guin.

"One of Bettina's many admirers," said Birdy.

Bettina made a face.

"He's a client," she said, looking at Guin. "Italian racecar driver turned author."

"Bettina got him his first book deal. Now he's in love with her," Birdy piped up from the bed.

Bettina made a sound, like "pshaw," and waved the comment away.

"Well, if you all will excuse me," said the doctor, who had been writing something on the tablet.

"Of course," said Guin. "So if he continues to improve, no setbacks, he should be able to leave here this Saturday?"

"Or Sunday," said the doctor.

"Not sooner?" asked Bettina.

The doctor and Guin looked at her.

"What?" said Bettina.

"Good day," said the doctor. "The nurses know how to find me, if you need anything," she said to Birdy as she left the room.

"So what's new with Giancarlo?" asked Birdy.

"They're talking about turning his book into a movie."

"Nice," said Birdy.

Guin cleared her throat.

"Bettina, if you could spare me a few more minutes?" she said, indicating that she wanted to talk to her in private.

"Is something up?" asked Birdy.

"Your *fiancée* here wants to know who might have wanted to take a shot at you."

"And I would appreciate you helping her, as I am in no position to," he said, looking at Bettina.

"Fine," said Bettina. She turned to Guin. "You want to talk some more? Let's talk."

"Outside, please," said Birdy, closing his eyes. "I need my beauty rest."

Guin could have sworn she saw him smile.

"Shall we?" said Guin, gesturing toward the door.

"Fine," said Bettina, clutching her bag, which Guin thought had probably cost several thousand dollars.

Guin held the door open, and Bettina strode out.

CHAPTER 22

"So there's no one else you can think of who might wish to harm Birdy?" Guin asked Bettina again.

Bettina looked annoyed.

"Look, Ms. Jones, I have no doubt that there is some ornithologist or bird photographer out there who wishes she or he was as successful as Birdy is. But take a shot at him? No way."

Guin was frustrated. If Bettina didn't suspect anyone....

"So, have you seen your sister since you've been here?" Guin asked.

"No," said Bettina.

"Even though she has a show in the area…"

"As I told you before, Ms. Jones, my sister and I are not particularly close."

"But you knew about her show."

Bettina pursed her lips.

"What about the Wilsons?" Guin asked.

"What about them?" asked Bettina.

"Might they be in contact with her? I know your mother and Mrs. Wilson are close. Could they have told her about Birdy being on the island?"

Bettina sighed.

"It's possible. But shouldn't you be asking them? And it's not as though Birdy's lectures are a secret."

She had a point.

Suddenly a phone started buzzing. Bettina's again.

Bettina reached into her bag and pulled out her mobile, looking down at the screen.

"I need to get this," she said. "If you're done?"

"For now," Guin replied. But Bettina was already moving away from her.

Guin sighed, then walked back into Birdy's room. He was watching something on TV.

"Hope I'm not interrupting," she said.

"No, not at all. So, you and Bettina have a nice chat?"

"Not really," said Guin.

Birdy chuckled, then winced.

"What?" Guin asked.

"Bettina's not the easiest person to get along with."

"Tell me about it," said Guin.

"But she means well," Birdy replied. "I would be lost without her."

"What about her sister?"

"Briony?" asked Birdy.

"Unless she has another one," said Guin.

"Nope, just the one. What about her?"

"I understand the two of you dated, back in the day."

"I think I know where this is going," said Birdy, with a sigh. "Yes, we dated. Probably longer than we should have. She didn't take the breakup well and went a little psycho on me. But I haven't heard from her in ages."

"Did you know she has a show over in Naples? The opening reception was the night before the Wilsons' party for you."

From the look on Birdy's face, it seemed as though he hadn't known, or was a very good actor.

"She has a show in Naples? Is it any good? Did Bettina know? She didn't say anything to me."

"She knew, but she claims she hasn't seen Briony."

"It's possible," said Birdy. "The two of them aren't particularly close."

"By any chance do you recall seeing Briony at your party?"

Birdy closed his eyes and leaned his head back.

"Everything from that night is a bit of a blur," he said. He opened his eyes and looked at Guin. "But I can't believe Kathy and John would have invited her."

"It's possible she snuck in. There were a lot of people there."

"I guess it's possible," said Birdy.

Guin made a note to ask Ginny for photos from the party. There was a good chance the *San-Cap Sun-Times* had had a photographer there.

"Also, did you know the CEO of Natura was on Captiva?"

"Yeah, I had heard his yacht was here."

"Does he know about you wanting to get out of your contract?"

"It's possible," said Birdy.

"And does he know you threatened to go public with what you knew?"

Birdy closed his eyes again, then opened them a minute later and looked at Guin.

"You think Digby hired someone to shoot me?"

"You tell me," said Guin.

Birdy leaned back. Guin waited.

"Do you think they'd really try to kill me?" he asked her.

"Maybe they were just trying to send a warning," Guin said.

"Maybe," he said.

"So who at Natura did you speak to?" Guin asked.

"Dick Grayson, the VP in charge of Marketing."

"Dick Grayson, like in Batman and Robin?" asked Guin. Birdy smiled.

"They even refer to him as the Boy Wonder."

"Ouch," said Guin.

"He's fine with it," said Birdy. "Thinks it's a hoot."

"So Dick Grayson is the person you told, about wanting to get out of your contract?"

"Yes."

"Why didn't you just tell Bettina?" Guin asked. Birdy sighed.

"I should have. I was trying to keep her out of it."

"But surely she'd find out, eventually," said Guin.

"I know," said Birdy. "I wasn't thinking."

He closed his eyes again. He was clearly uncomfortable.

Guin felt slightly guilty for asking him all these questions, but she needed answers if she was to find out who was trying to kill him.

"So is it possible that Digby being on Captiva at the same time as you isn't a coincidence?"

"I don't know," said Birdy.

Guin looked at him. He looked very pale and tired.

"I should let you get some rest."

She turned to leave when a nurse came in.

"I'm sorry, Miss, visiting hours are ending in a few minutes."

"That's fine," said Guin. "I was just leaving."

Birdy reached out a hand towards Guin. She took it and gently squeezed it.

"It's going to be all right," she said. "I'll come see you again tomorrow."

The nurse began checking Birdy's vitals. Guin excused herself. She was eager to get back to her computer and type up everything she had learned, even though it was late. She stopped in the lobby to check her phone, which, unlike

Bettina's, had been silenced. No word from the detective. Typical.

"Screw it," she said.

She entered his mobile number and was surprised when he picked up.

"Were you ever going to call me back?" she asked him.

"I've been busy," he replied.

"Well, I've been busy, too," she said. "We need to talk."

"About?" asked the detective.

"Who's trying to kill Birdy McMurtry."

The detective sighed.

"Can't you leave the detective work to the police, Ms. Jones?"

"No, I cannot, not when the man was shot right in front of me. Besides, I have some information you might be interested in."

"You want to tell me what it is?" said the detective.

"Not right now. I'm at the hospital."

"Fine, meet me at the police department at eight tomorrow."

"Fine. I'll even bring breakfast."

"Can I go now?" asked the detective.

"Yes," said Guin. "Unless there's something you want to tell me."

"I'm good. See you tomorrow."

Guin was about to say goodnight, but the detective had already hung up.

CHAPTER 23

Guin arrived at the Sanibel Police Department promptly at eight, carrying a box of breakfast pastries from Jean-Luc's Bakery and two cappuccinos. She checked in at the front desk, telling the young officer that Detective O'Loughlin was expecting her. After a brief call to the detective, she was buzzed back.

"Breakfast is served," Guin said, placing the box of pastries and the tray of cappuccinos on the desk in front of the detective, the only spot that wasn't covered with paperwork or Red Sox paraphernalia.

The detective grabbed a cappuccino and took a sip.

Guin took the other cappuccino and sat in the chair opposite the detective's desk.

They sat there, drinking their cappuccinos in silence, for several seconds.

"Well?" said Guin, finally, looking at the detective.

"Well what?" asked the detective.

"Aren't you going to see what's in the box?" Guin asked, a smile curling around her lips. "Or would you rather trade it for what's behind the curtain?"

The detective glanced at Guin, then opened the box. Inside were two croissants, two *pains aux raisins*, and two *pains au chocolat*.

"Take something," said Guin. "Personally, I recommend the *pain aux raisins*."

The detective looked thoughtful.

"Don't tell me you're on a diet, detective."

"Fine," he said, grabbing the raisin danish and taking a bite. "You happy now?"

Guin smiled.

"Very. But you know what would really make me happy?"

The detective gave her a look.

"If you'd share with me what you knew about the McMurtry case."

The detective took another bite of the danish.

"Not bad, for a French guy."

Guin waited. But the detective seemed in no hurry to share. Finally, after he had taken another sip of his cappuccino and another bite of the pastry, she couldn't take it anymore.

"So, any idea who's out to get him?"

"Ms. Jones, how many times have I told you…"

"Oh, come on, detective!" Guin said. "I already know about Briony and Natura."

"Then why do you need my help?" he replied. "Sounds like you've got everything covered, Nancy Drew."

Guin made a face.

"Why do you have to be so difficult? It's not like I'm asking you to give away state secrets. Just remember, that could have easily been me lying in the Wilsons' driveway."

The detective's face looked grim.

"Which is why I don't want you sticking your nose into this case. You could have been killed. The person who shot McMurtry is still out there. Next time, it could be you."

Guin shivered involuntarily.

"But don't you see? That's why I need your help," she said. "If someone is gunning for me, don't I have the right to know who it is?"

The detective grunted.

"Fine. It appears to have been a professional hit, or else someone who was very skilled at long range. We're tracking some leads, but it's going to take a while."

"So you think it was a hired gun?"

"Looks that way, but I'm not willing to commit to that theory just yet."

"Do you think whoever it was will try again?" Guin asked.

"I don't know," replied the detective. "If the goal was to kill McMurtry, then, quite possibly, yes. If it was just to scare him…."

He shrugged.

"Great," said Guin, clearly not happy. "So, do you think the shooter is the same person who poisoned him, or are we talking about two different people?"

The detective took another bite of the danish and drank his cappuccino. Guin felt her frustration increasing.

"What about Briony Betteridge, his ex? You speak with her? She has a photography show in Naples. And there's Digby Blyleven, the head of Natura. His yacht is currently anchored off Captiva. Did you know that Birdy was trying to get out of his contract with them and had threatened to go public with some confidential information?"

The detective looked over at her.

"Seriously, you should take up poker," said Guin, squeezing the arms of the chair. "You'd kill."

The detective finished off his cappuccino.

"I need to get to work," he said, getting up and moving toward the door. "So, if you'll excuse me, Ms. Jones…"

"But!" said Guin, standing and facing the detective.

The detective raised an eyebrow.

"Fine. But the least you could do is throw me a bone," said Guin, more huffily than she would have liked.

"First you need to learn how to heel," said the detective.

"Ha," said Guin, not in the least bit amused. "At least tell me you're looking into Briony and Digby."

"If I told you, would you leave?"

"Yes," said Guin.

"We're looking into Ms. Betteridge and Mr. Blyleven's possible involvement."

"Aha!" said Guin, brightening.

"But that is all I am going to tell you."

He walked the rest of the way to the door and held it open.

"Fine," said Guin. "I'll go. But I'll be back."

"I have no doubt," said the detective.

Guin was about to head out when the detective called out to her.

"Aren't you forgetting something?"

Guin turned around, confused. The detective held up the box of pastries.

"Keep them," said Guin. "I'm sure there's some hungry officer who would be grateful to receive a pastry from Jean-Luc's."

She turned and walked briskly out of the police department and down the stairs.

"Why does he have to be so difficult? Would it kill him to share what he knows?" she grumbled as she went.

She got to her car, reached into her bag, and yanked out her phone. Hopefully, Craig had some information to share with her.

She entered his number and waited. His wife Betty picked up.

"Hello?" she said.

"Betty?"

"Yes?"

"Betty, it's Guin. Is Craig there?"

"I'm afraid he's out fishing this morning."

"Ah," said Guin.

"You can try him on his cell phone. Though you know how he gets when he's out on the water."

"I do," said Guin. "Wouldn't want to disturb the fish."

Betty chuckled.

"Shall I tell him you called?"

"Please," said Guin. "And I'll send him a text, just in case he's checking his phone."

"Probably a good idea," said Betty. "I heard about that young man who got shot. Just awful. Sanibel used to be such a peaceful place."

Guin could hear her sigh.

"It still is, Betty." She paused. "Well, I need to go. Tell Craig I called."

"I will. Take care of yourself, Guinivere."

Guin ended the call and stood in the parking lot. She wasn't ready to go back home and sit in front of her computer. She needed answers.

"What I need is to talk to Briony—and Digby," she said aloud.

But she didn't want to approach Digby until she had done some more research.

"Briony it is," she said.

She looked down at her phone and realized she didn't know how to contact her. Bettina had claimed the two were not in touch and had no idea how to reach her sister, which Guin suspected was a lie. Suddenly she had an idea. She entered the number on her phone and waited as it rang.

"Hello?" came a pleasant female voice.

"Mrs. Wilson?"

"Yes, speaking."

"It's Guinivere Jones."

"Ah, Guinivere. How's our Birdy doing? I've been

meaning to get over there, but...."

"He's doing better. The doctor even said he may be discharged this weekend."

"That's wonderful!"

"Anyway, I'm calling because I need your help," said Guin.

"Of course," Mrs. Wilson replied.

"I'm trying to get in touch with Briony Betteridge."

"Did you ask Bettina for her number?"

"I did, but Bettina claims they're not in touch."

Mrs. Wilson chuckled.

"Do you know how I can get in touch with her?"

"I could reach out to her mother. I owe her a call."

"Would you?" asked Guin. "That would be great."

"I'll do it as soon as we get off the phone," said Mrs. Wilson, "and I'll call you back."

"Or you can text or email me the information," said Guin. "If that's easier."

"Call me old fashioned, but I still prefer to talk on the phone," said the older woman.

"That's fine, then. Give me a call after you speak with Mrs. Betteridge."

"Will do. And please send our apologies to Birdy. John's been bogged down with some business thing, and it's been difficult to get to the hospital. Though I know that's not a good excuse."

"You're welcome to go to the hospital with me," said Guin. "I was planning on going over there at lunchtime."

"Unfortunately, I have a luncheon I must attend. Otherwise I'd go with you. I'll just make sure John carves out some time to go with me later, or else tomorrow."

"Okay then," said Guin. "I'll let you go. Let me know if you're able to get Briony's information."

They said goodbye, then Guin ended the call.

She was still in the parking lot by the police department and wasn't sure what to do next. It was possible Mrs. Wilson would call her right back, in which case she didn't want to be behind the wheel, driving back to the condo. On the other hand, Mrs. Betteridge might not even be at home, or she could be asleep. (It wasn't yet nine o'clock.)

Guin sighed. She could always go to the library. It would be opening in a few minutes, and it was close by. And if Mrs. Wilson called her back, she could easily excuse herself.

Her plan made, she got in her car and drove over to the library, even though it was within walking distance.

A few minutes later, she was seated in front of a computer, doing research on Natura.

"Whoa," she said.

When she had typed "Natura Natraceuticals" into the search engine, it produced thousands of results.

She was so lost in reading about the company that she jumped when her phone started buzzing.

"Hello?" she said, in a loud whisper. She had completely lost track of the time.

"Guinivere, it's Kathy Wilson. Sorry I took so long getting back to you. I have Briony's cell phone number. Her mother said that's the best way to reach her."

"Hold on a sec," Guin said, reaching for her pen and a piece of paper.

She took down the number.

"Thanks, Mrs. Wilson."

"Please, call me Kathy, dear."

"Thanks Kathy," said Guin, with a smile. "I really appreciate it."

"I just hope she wasn't involved."

"You didn't say anything to her mother, did you?"

"Goodness no," said Mrs. Wilson. "I told her you were writing an article about Briony's show for the local paper here and needed to get in touch with her."

Guin smiled.

"Good thinking."

"I need to go but do let me know if I can help with anything else," said Mrs. Wilson. "You received the guest list I sent you, yes?"

Guin had almost forgotten.

"I did! Thank you for that."

She would need to review it when she got home.

They ended the call and Guin immediately phoned Briony. Briony didn't pick up, so Guin left a message, explaining that she was a reporter with the *Sanibel-Captiva Sun-Times*, looking to do a story about Briony's new show. Then she turned back to the computer.

CHAPTER 24

The rest of the morning went by in a blur. Guin forwarded herself several articles about Natura and Digby Blyleven. She definitely wanted to have a chat with the elusive CEO. Maybe Ginny could introduce them. The man sounded fascinating. It was hard to think, from what she had read about him, that he was a killer. But as she had learned, killers came in all shapes and colors and didn't announce themselves with nametags.

Guin glanced down at the clock on the monitor. It was nearly noon, and she had told Birdy she'd visit him at the hospital. She glanced at her phone. Neither Briony nor Craig had gotten back to her. If she hadn't heard back from Craig by three, she'd phone him again. And she could always send Briony a text.

She put a note in her calendar to go over the guest list for the Wilsons' party later. Had anyone else fallen ill after the party? If so, then maybe Birdy's poisoning was accidental.

She retrieved her phone and called Kathy Wilson.

"Sorry to trouble you again, Mrs.—Kathy," Guin began, after Mrs. Wilson picked up. "But do you happen to know if anyone else who attended your party fell ill right after?"

"I don't," Mrs. Wilson replied. "Or if they did, they didn't tell me. Why?"

"I was just wondering," said Guin.

There was a slight pause.

"Is there something else I can help you with?" Mrs. Wilson asked her.

"Not right now," said Guin.

"Well, let me know. I still feel sick about Birdy."

"It's not your fault," said Guin, who had done her fair share of blaming herself for Birdy's current condition.

Mrs. Wilson sighed.

"Maybe not, but I still feel responsible. So does John. Who would do such a thing?"

"I don't know," said Guin. "But I'm going to find out."

"Good luck," said Mrs. Wilson.

Guin said goodbye and ended the call. Then she closed the windows on her computer and signed off.

Guin arrived at the hospital a little while later, bearing a bag of goodies she purchased at Jean-Luc's Bakery: two brie, Granny Smith apple, and roast turkey sandwiches, along with several pastries.

When she showed Birdy what she had brought, his eyes lit up.

"You *are* an angel!" he said, looking from the sandwiches and pastries to Guin. "Is this all for me?"

"Well, I thought we might share. But you can have first dibs."

He immediately reached for one of the sandwiches, then hesitated.

"Take whichever one you want," Guin said. "I don't care. One's on multigrain bread, the other's on a demi baguette."

Birdy grabbed the baguette and took a healthy bite. Then another. And a third.

"Slow down!" Guin admonished. "I don't want you to choke!"

But he ignored her.

"At least have some water," she said, refilling his water glass.

He took a couple sips, then resumed wolfing down his sandwich.

Guin chuckled. He was like a teenage boy who hadn't been fed in a week. Though, having spent almost the entire week in the hospital, Birdy probably was starved for good food.

When he had finished the sandwich, he leaned back.

"Oh my God," he said, closing his eyes.

He opened them a few seconds later and turned to Guin.

"Marry me," he said. "I mean it."

"You know I didn't make those sandwiches," she replied.

"I don't care. Anyone who brings me something that good—and can make a decent cup of coffee—is a keeper in my book."

Guin laughed.

"I think the hospital has messed with your brain. And besides, Ris is already not happy with me pretending to be your fiancée. He'd be furious if I actually accepted your proposal."

Birdy looked up at her.

"Ris?"

"My beau, for lack of a better term. Harrison Hartwick. I believe you two know each other."

Birdy grinned.

"So you're dating old *Hard*wick," he said, emphasizing the first syllable. "Well, well, well. I must say, you're an improvement over the last one I met."

Guin raised her eyebrows.

"She was all right to look at," continued Birdy, oblivious to Guin's expression. "Ris has a thing for blondes. But I never thought she was right for him. I think she was an interior decorator, or something like that," he said. "So, how long have you and Hardwick been at it?"

"It's *Hart*wick," Guin said, feeling annoyed. "And it's been almost a year now."

Birdy grinned at Guin again.

"Oh, I know his last name," he said. "That's just my little nickname for him. You should hear what he calls me."

Part of Guin wanted to ask him, but she refrained.

"So, you two are a thing, eh?" continued Birdy. "Where is he? I'm surprised he hasn't visited me. Or does he not want to blow your cover? You told him all about me, of course."

Even with a gunshot wound, the man was supremely confident.

"He's on sabbatical this semester, traveling around the South Pacific in search of shells and adventure."

It came out a little sharper than Guin had intended.

"And left you here all alone?" asked Birdy.

Guin could feel her cheeks start to warm.

"I'm meeting him in Sydney next month, for Valentine's Day," she replied.

Birdy smiled, then eyed the pastries Guin had brought.

"I think I'm ready for some dessert. Which one do you recommend?"

"Well, it depends what you like," Guin said. "I personally adore their opera cake. That's that one there," she said, pointing, though he probably knew what opera cake was. "And their fruit tart is also excellent. And I got you an eclair, because…"

Birdy smiled up at her. Guin had to admit, he had a very nice smile. She could just imagine him and Ris palling around. Suddenly she envisioned the two of them with two gorgeous blondes, not unlike Bettina and Briony, and frowned.

"Is something wrong?" asked Birdy.

"Oh, sorry," said Guin, hastily. "Was just lost in thought."

Birdy glanced down at the pastry box and grabbed the eclair, which he devoured in just a few bites.

"Don't they feed you here?" Guin asked.

"Nothing like this," he replied, licking his fingers.

Guin held up the glass of water.

"Drink," she ordered.

"Yes, ma'am."

He downed the glass of water and placed the empty cup in front of her.

Guin was about to say something when the door opened and a nurse came in.

"Well, I should get going," said Guin.

"Must you?" asked Birdy.

"I must," said Guin. "Besides, I'm sure your fan club will arrive any minute."

Birdy looked confused.

"The Wilsons and Bettina."

"Ah," said Birdy.

The nurse was waiting patiently to check on Birdy.

"Go ahead," he sighed to the nurse.

He leaned back against the bed, closing his eyes, and extended an arm.

Guin smiled.

"I'll try to stop by later."

"Bring more food!" he called. "And coffee!"

Guin checked her phone when she got to the lobby. There was a message from Craig. She thought about calling him back but decided to wait. Instead she phoned Ginny.

"What's up, Buttercup?"

"Can you introduce me to Digby?" Guin asked.

"How come?"

"I'd like to ask him some questions," Guin responded.

"Oh?" said Ginny.

"About Natura and Birdy. Birdy was doing some work for Natura, but something happened, and he told them he wanted out."

"Surely, you don't think Digby is involved?"

"That's what I'd like to find out."

Ginny didn't reply.

"Please, Ginny. I know you and Joel are friends of his. But if he's got nothing to hide, what's the problem?"

"Fine. I'll ask him if it's okay. Just be prepared for him to say no. He's a bit of a recluse. And I don't know how long he's in town for."

"The Ginny I know would never take no for an answer."

Ginny made a noise that sounded like "mmph."

"Come on, Ginny."

She sighed.

"I'll see what I can do."

"That's all I ask," said Guin.

They ended the call and Guin stared at her phone.

May as well call Craig back. She called his home phone, and he answered after a few rings.

"Hey, Craig," she said.

"Hey yourself. So, you have something to share?"

"I do. I did some digging around this morning, and I wanted to compare notes."

"Where are you?" he asked.

"At the hospital. I just visited Birdy. I'm about to head back to Sanibel."

"You want to stop here on your way back?"

"That okay with Betty?" Guin asked.

"She's playing mahjong at one of her friend's."

"All righty then. I'll be there in around twenty minutes."

"See you then," said Craig.

Guin placed her phone in her bag and headed to the parking lot.

CHAPTER 25

Guin told Craig everything she had learned, about Briony (and Bettina) and Natura, and Craig told her what he had found out.

"I don't have a good feeling about Natura," Guin said.

"I told you they were up to no good," said Craig.

"But would they really send someone to poison and then shoot Birdy?" Guin asked.

Craig gave her a look.

"I've seen people taken out for less. Though that was back in Chicago."

Guin glanced over at the dining table. There was a copy of the *San-Cap Sun-Times* on it. She went over to take a look.

"May I?" she asked, lifting it up.

"Be my guest," said Craig.

Guin started flipping through the paper, stopping at the party pages.

Craig walked over and stood next to her.

"Something in particular you're looking for?"

Guin squinted down at the photos on the page. There were a handful from the party at the Wilsons' the Saturday before.

"There!" she said.

Craig looked down at the photo Guin was pointing at.

"What are we looking at?"

"There," Guin said again, stabbing her finger at one of the photos. "That blonde woman in the background. I would lay money on that being Briony Betteridge."

Craig squinted.

"How can you tell?"

"I spent the morning looking at photos of her. There are quite a lot online. The woman gets around."

"You think she could have poisoned Birdy?"

Guin looked pensive.

"I don't know, but it seems suspicious. Though why didn't Kathy Wilson mention that Briony was at the party?"

"Maybe she didn't know Briony was there. Didn't you say the place was packed?"

"True," said Guin, "but if the Wilsons had invited her, why didn't Mrs. Wilson say something?"

"Maybe they didn't invite her," said Craig.

Guin thought about that. While it was possible Briony had somehow snuck into the party, it seemed unlikely that neither the Wilsons nor Birdy had seen her. Though….

"I can see those wheels turning," said Craig.

"Briony is a society photographer. Maybe that's how she got in. Wouldn't be hard for her to claim she was photographing the event for one of the local papers. They often use freelancers."

"Hmm…" said Craig.

"I need to speak with her."

"How do you want me to proceed?" asked Craig.

Guin knew Craig was used to calling the shots and was touched that he deferred to her.

"Well," said Guin, thinking, "what would your next steps be?"

"Well, you've already spoken with McMurtry and the Wilsons, and that agent of his," said Craig. "Seems to me someone should speak to Birdy's contact at Natura."

"Could you do that?" asked Guin. "I'm trying to get a meeting with the CEO. Turns out he's a friend of Ginny and Joel's, and his yacht is anchored over on Captiva."

"You want me to go with you?" asked Craig.

Guin considered it.

"Thanks for the offer, but first I have to see if I can even get a meeting. Actually, what you could really help me with is finding out what the police know about who took that potshot at Birdy. I know you have all sorts of contacts there. And, as usual, the detective refuses to share anything with me."

Craig chuckled.

"I think Detective O'Loughlin's just not used to dealing with someone like you, *Ms. Jones.*"

"Surely, he must have dealt with reporters before," said Guin.

Craig gave her a look.

"Reporters, yes, but *you*, no."

Guin felt herself start to blush.

"I don't see why I'm any different."

Craig raised an eyebrow.

"I'll speak to my contacts at the police department, see what I can find out. And I'll see what I can find out about this contact of McMurtry's at Natura. What did you say his name was again?"

"Dick Grayson."

The side of Craig's mouth quirked up.

"I know," said Guin. "I thought the same thing. They even call him the Boy Wonder."

They stood there for a minute, neither one knowing what to say.

"Well, I should get going," Guin finally said. "I want to go over the guest list to the party, see if any names stick out."

"Sounds like a pretty big task," said Craig.

"Yeah, I'm not looking forward to it," Guin said. "But I need to see if there was someone there who had a personal connection to Birdy."

"Well, keep me posted," said Craig, walking her to the door. "Let me know if you need any help."

"You do the same," said Guin.

Guin opened the door to the condo and was immediately greeted by two yowling felines.

"I left you food!" Guin told them.

Fauna continued to meow.

"Fine," said Guin.

She marched over to the cat bowls, both of which were empty.

"If I give you a little more food, will you be quiet?" she asked the black cat.

The cat meowed back at her.

Guin looked down at Fauna, let out a puff of air, then got the bag of dry food.

"Here," she said, shaking some into each bowl.

Fauna sniffed, but she did not seem happy.

"Too bad," said Guin. "That's what there is."

She put the bag of cat food away, poured herself a glass of water, then headed to her office/bedroom.

She rebooted her computer and retrieved the guest list Kathy Wilson had sent her. There were over sixty people on the list, and, as Mrs. Wilson had told her, some of the people who attended weren't on the list. Suddenly she had an idea.

She picked up her phone and texted Bettina.

"Can you help me with something?" she wrote.

Guin waited for a response. In the meantime, she printed out a copy of the list. She would bring it with her to the hospital later. Maybe Birdy would recognize some of the names.

She went through her email, then pulled up the file containing her notes on Birdy. She added everything she had learned. There were a lot of question marks.

As she was typing, her phone pinged. She picked it up and saw that she had two text messages. One of them was from Bettina.

"What?" she had replied.

Guin rolled her eyes.

"Can I send you the list of people who attended the party for Birdy at the Wilsons'? And can you let me know if any of them might have a grudge against Birdy? Maybe some woman who was a bit obsessed with him or a jealous husband?"

"Fine," came the reply.

"What's your email?" asked Guin.

Bettina texted it.

"Thanks," Guin wrote. "I'll forward it to you now."

Guin was about to forward the email when she had another thought and pulled up the *San-Cap Sun-Times* in a new tab. She searched the site until she found what she was after, the photo from the Wilsons' party with the woman who resembled Briony. She copied and pasted it into her email to Bettina, asking if the woman was indeed Briony. Then she hit "send."

Her phone pinged again. It was another text message. Shelly.

"You want to come over for BBQ Monday?"

"Monday?" wrote Guin. Shelly and Steve usually had their barbecues on Sunday, or Saturday.

"Steve's new boss is coming to town Monday. He's never been to Sanibel. Thought we'd have a few friends over."

"Ah," said Guin. "Will the detective be there?"

"I don't know," Shelly replied. "Would you like him to be?"

Guin thought about it. A barbecue might be the perfect

place to get him relaxed and talking.

"Go ahead and invite him," Guin wrote back. "I'm sure Steve's boss would be interested in meeting the island's top detective."

"Uh-huh," replied Shelly.

"What time?" Guin texted her.

"The usual, 6."

"OK," Guin wrote. "Let me know if you need me to bring anything."

"Will do!" Shelly replied.

"Gotta go," Guin wrote. "C u Monday."

"Bye," Shelly texted.

Guin looked down at her phone. Wonder of wonders, miracle of miracles, there was a text from Briony Betteridge. Guin hadn't told her the real reason she wanted to interview her. Instead she had written that she wanted to review Briony's show. Most people leapt at the chance to have an article written about them. And Guin had said she had heard good things about Briony's work.

"When would be a good time to chat?" Guin wrote her back. "I was hoping to go see your show tomorrow morning."

It was a lie, but Briony didn't need to know that.

"Perfect," Briony texted her. "I'm still in Naples. Do you want to meet me at the gallery at 11? I can give you a personal tour."

So Briony was still around. Interesting. I wonder if Bettina knows? Guin thought.

"Sure," Guin wrote back. "That would be great."

"Excellent. See you tomorrow!" Briony responded. "Ciao"

Guin was tempted to type *ciao* back, but she stopped herself.

"All right," she said, entering the name of the gallery in her web browser, "let's check out your show."

Even though Guin would not, in fact, be doing a piece

on Briony's show, she didn't want to sound ignorant.

"Not bad," she said aloud, looking at some of Briony's photographs. She was clearly a talented photographer.

A short while later, after doing more research, she put her computer to sleep. It was late afternoon, and she felt the need to go for a beach walk. It always helped her think more clearly. And she hadn't watched a sunset from the beach in ages.

She put on a pair of capris, a t-shirt, and a light sweatshirt, grabbed her fanny pack and keys, and headed out the door.

Bowman's Beach was rather crowded. Not that much of a surprise. Sanibel's beaches were often filled with visitors and locals out to watch the sunset, which was often spectacular. People even threw sunset parties.

Guin headed west, away from the throngs. She wasn't really looking for shells, but, just in case, she kept her head down, glancing from the sand up at the horizon, so as not to miss the sun setting. As the sun began its final descent into the ocean, Guin stopped and watched. The sky was turning shades of orange, pink, and red. Then the sun disappeared below the horizon, and Guin could have sworn she saw a green flash. She sighed. No matter how many Sanibel sunsets she saw, she would never get over them.

There was still plenty of light, but Guin needed to get back to her car if she didn't want to be walking in the dark. She headed back east and spotted two dolphins making their way west. She stopped to watch them, wishing she had her camera with her.

CHAPTER 26

Guin got back to the condo and quickly changed. Birdy had probably already eaten, hospitals tending to serve dinner on the early side, but in case he hadn't, she would pick up some fried chicken over at the Pecking Order.

She arrived at the hospital a little before seven, and she could swear she saw Birdy drool a little when she presented him with the box of fried chicken, biscuits, and coleslaw.

"Did you eat already?" she asked him.

"If you call that eating," he replied, staring at the food.

Guin looked around.

"I should have brought plates."

"I'm fine eating out of the box," he said, hungrily.

"Be my guest," said Guin.

He grabbed a chicken leg and bit into it.

"Oh my God," he said, closing his eyes.

Guin smiled.

"I hope it's not cold. I kept it in one of those insulated bags, so it would stay warm."

Birdy took another bite.

"This may be the best fried chicken I've ever had," he said, his mouth full.

"Wait until you try the biscuit and coleslaw."

As if commanded, he took a bite of the biscuit.

"It's good," he said.

Guin looked in the bag for a fork. Fortunately, there were two sets of plastic utensils. She broke open a pack and handed Birdy the fork.

"Dig in," she said.

He didn't need to be asked twice.

He stuck the fork into the container of coleslaw and shoved a forkful into his mouth.

"Mmm… very good," he mumbled.

He then picked up the chicken leg and polished it off.

"When I was a kid, my folks had a woman who would take care of me occasionally. She made the best fried chicken," he said. "This reminds me of hers."

Guin smiled.

Suddenly Birdy frowned.

"Have you had dinner?" he asked Guin.

"Not yet. I was thinking we would share," she replied.

Birdy looked a bit guilty.

"Don't worry, there's a whole other box."

He immediately perked up.

Guin was reaching into the insulated bag to pull it out when her phone rang. Normally, she wouldn't have answered it, but she saw Ris's number on the screen and quickly swiped to answer it.

"Hey!"

"Finally!" said Ris. "Sorry for the delay. I've been kind of busy."

Guin saw Birdy looking at her and mouthed, "It's Ris."

"I know," he mouthed back.

Guin smiled.

"You still there?" asked Ris. "I don't have a great connection."

"I'm at the hospital," said Guin.

"Are you okay?" Ris asked.

She could hear the worry in his voice.

"I'm fine. I'm visiting Birdy."

"Let me speak to him," said Ris.

Guin put a hand over her phone.

"He wants to speak with you."

Birdy grinned and indicated for her to hand him the phone.

Guin hesitated, then handed it over.

"Just give it back to me when you're done. I want to speak with him."

Birdy ignored her.

"Hardwick!" he said, clasping the phone to his right ear. "You don't mind if I marry your girlfriend, do you?"

Guin opened her mouth to protest, then quickly closed it.

A few seconds later, Birdy was chuckling. Guin watched, trying to figure out what the two men were saying. Whatever it was, Birdy, at least, was enjoying himself.

"She's been a real lifesaver," he said into the phone. "Been at the hospital every day. Even brought me fried chicken. I'm telling you, she's a keeper."

Ris was clearly saying something back to him. Guin was dying to know what it was.

"Well, I hope to be out of here this weekend. Already had to cancel my upcoming tour."

They prattled on for several minutes. Guin had ceased paying attention, eating some of her fried chicken instead.

"Take care of yourself man," said Birdy. "Next time."

"Hey, Guin," he called. "You want to speak to your boyfriend?"

Guin quickly swallowed the piece of chicken she was eating and took the phone back from Birdy, who was grinning at her.

"Hello?"

"Just watch out for him," said Ris, a bit sternly. "Birdy

has quite a reputation with the ladies."

"Well, I'm taken, thank you," said Guin, primly.

She cast a quick glance at Birdy, who pretended to ignore her. She took a few steps away from him, hoping for a little privacy.

"How are you?" she asked.

"Good. Tired. I actually have to head out in a few minutes. We're going diving again this morning, then this evening I have a lecture at the local university here."

"Okay," said Guin, feeling a bit frustrated.

"How are you?" he asked her.

"Okay," she said. "I miss you."

"Ginny keeping you busy?"

"Always," said Guin.

"I have to go," said Ris.

Guin sighed.

"So soon?"

"Sorry," he replied. "Can I call you Sunday morning your time? I have nothing scheduled Sunday night."

"What time?" asked Guin.

She almost always went to the Sanibel farmers market Sunday mornings.

"Nine o'clock?"

"That should be fine."

"It's a date then."

"It's a date," said Guin.

"Sweet dreams," said Ris.

"Same to you. Or should I say g'day?"

"I'm not in Australia yet."

"Well, whatever the equivalent of 'have a good day' is wherever you are."

"Thanks," said Ris. "And Guin?"

"Yes?" she said.

"I love you."

Guin glanced back over at Birdy, who had turned on the television and was seemingly not paying attention to her.

"I love you, too," she said, covering the phone with her hand.

She ended the call and placed her phone in her back pocket.

"You have a nice chat?" Birdy asked her as soon as she had put the phone away.

"Very nice," said Guin.

She noticed that Birdy had eaten the rest of his fried chicken and fixings.

"I guess you were hungry," she said, smiling.

"Starving. Hospital food," he said, making a face. "So, you bring me any dessert?"

Guin stared at him.

"What about the pastries I brought you?"

"I wound up giving them to one of the nurses."

"Sorry, I've got nothing."

"Oh well," said Birdy.

"So, the doctor say when you're getting out of here?"

"With luck, tomorrow," he replied.

"That's good news, right?"

"Definitely," he said.

"Will you be going back to the Wilsons'?" Guin asked.

"No," he said. "Bettina's arranged for me to stay at the Ritz in Naples for a few days. Figured a swanky hotel would be the best place to recuperate. Lots of people to wait on me."

And probably safer, too, Guin thought.

"Do the Wilsons know?" asked Guin.

"No. Detective O'Loughlin said not to tell anyone, except for you, you being my fiancée and all," he added with a grin.

"We both know I am *not* your fiancée," Guin retorted.

"A man can dream," he replied, still smiling.

"So the detective was here, at the hospital?" asked Guin.

"Yes. Why?"

"No reason," said Guin. Though she was dying to ask what the two had talked about.

"He's actually been to visit me a couple of times. Asked me about my work with Natura, and if I had pissed off anyone recently."

Guin smiled at that. She doubted that was actually what the detective had said.

"Speaking of which," said Guin, reaching into her bag. "Do you recognize any of the names on this list?"

She handed him the printout of the guest list. He took it and looked it over. Guin waited.

A minute or so later, Birdy looked up at her.

"I know a handful of these people. Mostly friends of John and Kathy's on Sanibel and Captiva. So many people attend my tours and lectures, it's hard to remember all their names."

"Understandable," said Guin. "But do any of those names stand out? Maybe someone you, uh…" Guin didn't know how to phrase the question. "Someone you might have known a bit better than the others?

Comprehension immediately dawned on Birdy.

"You asking if I slept with anyone on the list?" he said with a grin.

Guin nodded. She was not a prude, but she felt a bit funny asking him.

Birdy looked at the list again.

"Just the caterer."

"The caterer?" asked Guin.

"You know what they say, the way to a man's heart is through his stomach."

Guin stopped herself from rolling her eyes.

"Were the two of you on good terms?" Guin asked.

"We had an understanding," said Birdy.

"And did her husband understand?" asked Guin.

"She's divorced, or she was the last time I saw her."

"So you didn't, uh, see her at the party?"

"Oh, I saw her, but we didn't have a chance to connect, if you know what I mean."

Guin knew exactly what he meant.

The caterer. The perfect person to slip poison into Birdy's food. Though she would probably be the first person the police would suspect. She made a mental note to ask the detective.

"So, um, did you see her often when you were on Sanibel?" Guin asked.

"Like I said, we had an understanding."

Guin did not understand.

Birdy sighed.

"She was busy and lonely. I was busy and lonely. One thing led to another and…"

"How did you two meet?" Guin asked.

"At the Wilsons'. Kathy and John were throwing a party for me—they usually do when I'm here on tour—and Rebecca was catering it."

"Ah," said Guin. "But you and Rebecca were on good terms?"

"Very good," he replied. "As I told the detective, Rebecca had no reason to poison me."

"That you know of."

Birdy sighed again.

"That I know of."

"And there was no one else on that list who might have had a beef with you?" Guin asked.

Birdy looked over the list again.

"Not that I know of," he said, handing the list back to her.

Guin put it back in her bag. A few seconds later, a nurse walked in.

"I'm sorry, Miss. Visiting hours are ending, and Mr. McMurtry needs his rest."

"I was just leaving," said Guin.

"Will I see you tomorrow?" asked Birdy.

"What time are you checking out?" Guin asked.

"I'm not sure," Birdy replied.

"Well, send me a text or give me a call in the morning. I have an appointment in Naples tomorrow morning, but I could swing by here or see you at the Ritz in the afternoon, if you're out of here by then."

"Okay, will do," he said.

The nurse was busy attending to him, so Guin excused herself.

She pulled out her phone when she got to the lobby and sent the detective a text.

"We need to talk," she wrote him.

She glanced at her phone. Still no reply from Bettina. She had a bunch of emails, but she ignored them. She'd deal with them later. There was also a text from Ginny, asking her if there was any way Guin could get her review of the Paper Fig Kitchen to her by Tuesday morning. Apparently the restaurant review that was supposed to have run in next week's paper had fallen through, and Ginny had a hole to fill.

Guin pursed her lips. She always ate at a place three times before writing a review. There simply wasn't time.

"I'll get it to you the following Monday," Guin typed. "Best I can do." Then she added, "Sorry."

She hit "send," then waited for Ginny to lay a guilt trip on her.

"Fine," Ginny wrote back a minute later.

Guin could tell Ginny wasn't pleased, but there was

nothing she could do about it. She put her phone back in her bag and headed to her car. Tomorrow would be another busy day.

CHAPTER 27

As Guin was driving home from the hospital, her phone rang. She thought about answering, then thought better of it. If it was important, the person would leave a message. Besides, she was nearly at the condo.

She parked the Mini in her garage and checked her phone. There was a voicemail message from Ginny. She had managed to reach Digby, and Digby had invited her (Guin) to have a drink with him on his yacht the following evening.

Guin immediately called Ginny back.

"You're a miracle worker," Guin exclaimed. "How did you get Digby to invite me on his yacht? What did you tell him about me?"

Ginny chuckled.

"I told him the truth."

"The truth?"

"I told him you were one of our star reporters and could use his help on a piece you were working on."

Guin made a face.

"Ginny…"

"Well, it's the truth," Ginny replied.

"Did you tell him what the piece was about?" Guin asked.

"I may have left that part out."

Guin sighed.

"What if he's the killer?"

"I seriously doubt that, Guinivere. Joel and I have known Digby for years. The man wouldn't harm a fly."

"It's not flies I'm worried about," said Guin.

"If it makes you feel better, you can ask Craig to come along."

"That won't be necessary," said Guin. "I can handle it."

She paused. Maybe it would be smart to bring Craig. She shook her head. No. She could do this on her own. Besides, Ginny would know where she was.

"What time am I expected?"

"Five o'clock. And wear something smart."

"Smart?" Guin asked.

"Digby's a bit old-fashioned. Likes to dress for cocktails."

Suddenly Guin formed an image of Digby decked out in yachting regalia, with one of those white captain's hats.

"Got it," said Guin. "Anything else?"

"Let me know how it goes," said Ginny.

"Will do," said Guin.

They said goodbye and Guin ended the call.

Saturday morning Guin drove to Naples, to 5th Avenue South, where Briony's gallery was located. She found a place to park near the gallery and got out.

"Cute car!" said a woman with spiky, bright orange-red hair, dressed in purple.

Guin smiled. She often got reactions like that to her little purple Mini Cooper.

"Thanks," she said.

"I've never seen a purple one before," the woman continued.

"It was a limited edition," Guin replied.

"Purple is my favorite color."

"I would have never guessed!" said Guin, eyeing the woman's head-to-toe purple ensemble.

The woman smiled back at Guin.

"Any interest in selling it?" the woman asked.

"I'm afraid not," Guin replied.

"Well, if you change your mind," said the woman.

She reached into her purple bag and pulled out a card. She handed it to Guin.

"My contact information is on the back."

Guin looked at the card.

"You're an artist?"

"Guilty," said the woman. "I was just in the gallery discussing my upcoming show."

"Ah," said Guin.

"You should come!" said the woman. "There will be wine and nibblies."

"Thanks," said Guin. "When is it?"

"At the end of the month. You can get a card from the gallery."

Guin's wheels began to turn. A gallery opening would be the perfect thing to do with her mother and stepdad.

"I'm Guin, by the way," said Guin, extending her hand.

"Dorothea Melville," said the woman. "Well, I must be running. Do come to the opening. It will be a hoot."

"I'll try," said Guin.

Dorothea waved goodbye, then walked briskly down 5th Avenue South, her long purple skirt flowing out behind her.

Guin shook her head, then entered the gallery.

She looked around but did not spy Briony. Though it wasn't quite eleven yet. She decided to have a look around while she waited. There were three different artists on exhibit, but Briony was the only photographer.

"May I help you?" asked a man dressed in a button-down shirt and slacks.

"I'm just looking," said Guin. Though she could imagine several of the pieces in the gallery in her condo. "I'm supposed to be meeting Briony Betteridge here."

"Ah, Briony," said the man, smiling. "We've sold almost all of her work."

"She's very popular?" asked Guin.

"Oh, yes," said the man. "We're fortunate to have her here. This is her first show in Naples."

"Ah," said Guin, not sure what to say.

"You should have been here for the opening," said the man.

"I'm sorry I missed it," Guin said. "Are you the owner?"

"The manager," he replied.

"It's a lovely gallery," said Guin, looking around.

"Isn't it?" said the man. "Mr. Redgrave and I personally select all the artists."

"I just met one outside. Dorothea Melville."

"Ah yes, Ms. Melville. She's part of our next show. It's coming up in just a couple of weeks."

"I'd love to attend," said Guin. "My parents will be in town, and they love art."

The man beamed.

"Of course! Here, let me get you a card."

As he walked back to his desk, the front door opened and a tall, casually but elegantly dressed blonde entered.

Guin walked over to greet her.

"Briony?"

For a moment, the woman looked confused. Then she looked down at Guin and smiled.

"I'm Guin, Guinivere Jones," said Guin, extending a hand. "With the *Sanibel-Captiva Sun-Times*."

"Of course," said Briony. "Very nice to meet you." She shook Guin's proffered hand. "Have you had a chance to look around?"

"A bit," said Guin.

"Briony!" called the manager, walking quickly toward them. "We just sold another one of your photographs."

"Which one?" she asked.

"The one of the model with the cockatoo."

"I do love that one," said Briony. "I hope it's going to a good home."

"Of course!" said the manager.

"I'd love to see it," said Guin.

"Right this way," said the manager.

He led them a little way away, to the part of the gallery where Briony's photographs were displayed.

"Here it is!"

They stopped in front of a large black-and-white photo of a beautiful black woman, dressed in a sheer white dress, with a white cockatoo perched on her shoulder. The woman was looking straight out, while the cockatoo was facing her. It was a striking image.

"It's beautiful," said Guin.

"Thank you," said Briony. "It's one of my favorites."

"I can see why," said Guin.

She looked around.

"Here, let me give you the guided tour," said Briony.

She walked Guin around the exhibit, telling her a little about each photo. Many of them featured exotic birds.

"I see you like birds," Guin said.

Briony smiled.

"What gave it away?"

Guin smiled back at her.

"I understand you studied with Birdy McMurtry."

Briony frowned.

"Who told you that?"

"I read it online, while I was doing research," said Guin.

Clearly, it was a touchy subject.

"That was a long time ago," said Briony, a bit testily. "As you can see, our styles are quite different."

"Did you know that Birdy was in the area?"

"No, and why should I care if he was?" asked Briony, clearly not happy with the direction of the conversation.

"Did you know that someone tried to kill him, while he was on Sanibel?"

"Birdy was shot? I had no idea!"

Guin eyed the other woman. She had said nothing about Birdy being shot. And there was something about the way she had replied that made Guin suspicious.

"Is he okay?" asked Briony.

Guin regarded her.

"He's alive," Guin replied. "But it was touch-and-go for a while there."

"Who would want to shoot Birdy?" said Briony, suddenly all concern.

"You tell me," said Guin, looking up at Briony, who was a full head taller.

"You don't think I had anything to do with it?" said Briony.

"Where were you Wednesday evening?"

Briony smiled. It was not a friendly smile.

"Nowhere near Sanibel."

Guin raised an eyebrow.

"I was having dinner right here, in Naples."

"Can you prove it?" asked Guin.

"My, aren't you the suspicious type? Yes, I can prove it." She looked down at Guin.

"Why are you so interested in Birdy anyway? Oh wait, don't tell me you've fallen for him! You poor thing. Don't you know? He eats up and spits out little birds like you."

Guin did not like the way Briony was looking at her.

"I haven't fallen for Birdy."

"Uh-hmm," said Briony. "You probably don't even really work for the paper. You're just here because you heard about me and Birdy and were jealous."

Guin had to suppress the urge to laugh.

"Oh, I work for the *Sanibel-Captiva Sun-Times* all right," said Guin. "But my only interest in Birdy is professional."

"You keep telling yourself that, dear," Briony said, in a patronizing tone.

"So where were you the evening Birdy was shot?"

"I was having a cozy dinner for two at Bha! Bha! here in Naples. It's an adorable little Persian bistro. You and Birdy should try it sometime."

Guin was becoming annoyed.

"I told you, I'm not seeing Mr. McMurtry."

"Then why are your cheeks turning such an adorable shade of pink?"

"Thank you for your help, Ms. Betteridge," Guin bit out.

"Aren't you going to ask me some questions about my work?"

"Why the birds?" asked Guin.

"Ah yes," said Briony, looking around. "My bread and butter is society photos. You know, party pictures and portraits. But it got to be so boring. So I thought, why not combine my two loves, nature and portraiture? *Et voila!*"

She extended her arms.

Guin had to admit, her portraits, if that's what you'd call them, were pretty unique. There was a black-and-white photo of a parrot that almost looked like a society portrait, and a portrait of a grand dame in a Chanel suit with a pigeon perched upon each shoulder.

"I understand from the manager that the exhibit is nearly sold out."

"Usually, they sell out in a few days," said Briony. "But I'm new to Naples."

"Speaking of which, why Naples?"

"Why not?" asked Briony.

"It just seems a curious place for you to have a show," said Guin.

Briony sighed.

"Well, if you must now, I'm thinking of getting a place here."

Guin eyed her.

"But why Naples?"

"Inquisitive little thing, aren't you? Well, if you must know, I'm seeing someone here."

"The person you were having dinner with on Wednesday."

"Yes."

"Name?"

"I'd rather not say."

Guin suddenly had a funny feeling.

"Let me guess, he's married."

"Separated."

"Ah," said Guin, not sure whether she believed it. "So have the police contacted you?"

Briony looked momentarily confused.

"Oh, you mean that detective fellow? Detective…"

"O'Loughlin?" asked Guin.

"Something like that," said Briony. "Medium height. Built like a boxer. Closely cropped reddish-brown hair?"

"That's him," said Guin. "So you spoke with him."

"I did, but I don't think I was very helpful."

So she had spoken to the detective. Maybe that's how she knew Birdy had been shot. But why had she played dumb before if she knew?

"Can I tell you anything more about my work?" asked Briony.

"I think I'm good," said Guin.

Maybe she would ask Ginny if she could do a little write-up of the show. It was quite good, and she knew Ginny had a hole to fill.

"What's the best way to reach you, in case I have any more questions?"

Briony produced a card.

"Thanks," said Guin, pocketing it. "Well, I should be going."

"When will the story run?" asked Briony.

"I'll let you know," Guin replied.

She made to leave when the gallery manager came hurrying toward her.

"Here's the card for Dorothea's show."

"Thank you," said Guin.

"Did I hear that you are doing a piece on Briony's photos?"

"Yes," said Guin.

"It's only on for a couple more weeks," said the manager.

"I know," said Guin. "Thanks for your time."

He escorted her out.

Guin looked at her phone. It was already after noon. She called over to the hospital to check on Birdy, but when she asked to be connected to his room, she was told he had been discharged.

That's odd, thought Guin. Why didn't he call me to let me know?

"What time was that?" Guin asked.

"I'm afraid I can't release that information," said the woman.

Guin was about to say, "But I'm his fiancée," but she thought better of it.

"Okay. Well, thank you," she said.

Birdy had said Bettina had reserved a suite at the Ritz. So she called over there.

"The Ritz-Carlton Naples!" came a cheery female voice. "How may I help you?"

"Yes, I'm looking for a guest, a Mr. Bertram McMurtry. I'm not sure if he's checked in yet. He has a reservation."

"One moment, please," said the woman.

Guin waited.

"I'm sorry, but we don't have a reservation for a Bertram McMurtry."

Guin stopped dead.

"What about for a Bettina Betteridge?"

"I'll check," said the woman.

Guin again waited.

"I'm sorry. There's no reservation listed for her either."

"Are you sure?" asked Guin. "Can you double check?"

"I'm sorry, ma'am. Maybe they're staying at a different hotel?"

Guin was sure Birdy had said Bettina was taking him to the Ritz in Naples, but maybe she had misheard?

"Thanks for your help," said Guin.

She hung up and stared ahead of her. Then she tried Birdy's cell phone. The call immediately went to voicemail.

"This is Birdy. Leave a message."

"Birdy, this is Guin. It's around 12:30 on Saturday. Where are you? Please call me back or send me a text when you get this."

She left her number, said she hoped he was okay, then hung up.

"Where did you fly off to, Birdy?" she said aloud.

CHAPTER 28

Guin called the detective on his cell phone, praying he'd pick up. Of course, it went to voicemail.

"Detective, it's Guin. Ms. Jones. I can't find Birdy. He left the hospital and didn't check into his hotel. I'm worried. Please call me back when you get this."

She hung up and looked around. She hadn't realized she had walked so far. She turned and headed back towards her car. Where was Birdy?

She sent the detective a text, nearly colliding with a couple as she was typing.

"Sorry!" she said.

The couple gave her a look and continued on.

Guin put her phone in her bag and was soon back at her car.

She unlocked the Mini and paused. Who else might know where Birdy had gone? The Wilsons!

She called over to their house. A woman picked up.

"Wilson residence."

"Is Mrs. Wilson there?" asked Guin.

"She's not home right now," said the woman.

"May I speak with Mr. Wilson?" Guin asked.

"He's not here," said the woman.

"Well, when they get home, or if they call in, could you please tell them that Guin Jones called and to call me back? It's urgent."

"Okay," said the woman.

"Here's my number," added Guin.

There was silence on the other end of the line.

"Do you need me to repeat it?" Guin asked.

"I got it," said the woman.

"Okay, thank you," said Guin.

The phone went dead.

Well, she wasn't very helpful, thought Guin. Then she remembered she had Mrs. Wilson's cell phone number. She retrieved it and sent her a quick text, hoping she actually checked her text messages.

Who else would know where Birdy might be?

"Bettina!" she said aloud. "She would definitely know."

Just then her stomach decided to remind her she hadn't eaten anything in hours.

"I'll feed you in a minute," she said, looking down.

She found Bettina's number and pressed "call." The phone rang several times, then went to voicemail. Guin sighed.

"Hey, Bettina, it's Guin. Is Birdy with you? I called the hospital, and they said he'd been discharged. And I called the Ritz, but there's no reservation for him, or for you. Is everything okay? Call or text me when you get this."

She ended the call and put her phone back in her bag. Her stomach rumbled again.

"Fine," she said aloud. "Let's go get some lunch."

Guin drove down to 3rd Street South, to Jane's Garden Café, her favorite brunch spot in Naples. Even though it was after noon, she ordered herself the Fabulous French Toast, which really was fabulous, along with a side of crispy bacon and a mimosa. When the food arrived a few minutes later, she dug right in, not caring what the people around her thought. She was starving, and Jane's had the best challah French toast around, served with berries and not-too-sweet maple syrup. Heaven.

Guin closed her eyes as she took another forkful. She then ate a bite of bacon and washed it down with a sip of her mimosa. She was feeling less anxious already.

When she was nearly done with her meal, her phone rang. She immediately grabbed it. It was the detective.

"Is Birdy okay?" she asked.

"He's fine," said the detective.

"How do you know?" asked Guin, suspiciously, eyeing the phone. "He checked out of the hospital, and I called over to the Ritz. There's no reservation under his name, or under Bettina's."

"They're using aliases."

"Of course," said Guin. Why didn't she think of that? "What names are they using?"

"It's on a need-to-know basis," he replied.

Guin felt her frustration rising.

"Well, I need to know."

"No, you don't," said the detective.

"But," she began. The detective cut her off.

"Ms. Jones, it is for your own good, and Mr. McMurtry's, that as few people as possible know his whereabouts."

Guin wanted to protest but couldn't think up a good reason.

"Fine. So, does that mean you're still trying to figure out who took a shot at him?"

The detective didn't reply.

Guin sighed.

"You going to Shelly and Steve's Monday?" she asked, changing the subject.

"Don't know," replied the detective. "I may be working late."

"Come for a little while," Guin said. "You'll need to eat at some point."

"Will you be there?" asked the detective.

"I will," said Guin. "And I know how much you enjoy Steve's brats."

Steve hailed from Wisconsin and always made sure to have a few bratwurst sausages on hand. Old habits died hard.

"Well, in that case," said the detective, a bit sarcastically, Guin thought.

"So, you'll be there?"

"I'll try," said the detective.

"Good enough. See you Monday at six," Guin replied. "And if you happen to hear from my fiancée, do be a dear and tell him to call me," she said, a little smile forming on her face.

"Anything else?" asked the detective.

"I'm good," Guin replied.

She smiled and ended the call. Then she finished her French toast and bacon, washing it down with the last bit of her mimosa. Ah. She signaled the server for her check and was back at her car a few minutes later.

She checked her phone one last time before starting the engine. Still no response from the Wilsons, Bettina, or Birdy.

Even though the detective had told her that Birdy was fine, she had a nagging feeling something was up. She put her phone on the passenger seat and started the car. She would just have to wait and see and hope Birdy called her.

Guin was flipping frantically through her closet. What does one wear on a yacht to have cocktails with a multimillionaire?

She texted Shelly.

"Help!" she wrote. "What do I wear to drinks on a yacht?"

"I'll be right over!" Shelly typed back.

"You don't need to come here," Guin replied.

"NP," Shelly wrote. "Got nothing better to do. :-)"

Guin was secretly relieved. Shelly had a great style sense and always knew what would look good on Guin. Guin had even told Shelly she should be a stylist or a personal shopper, but Shelly had just laughed. She much preferred making jewelry.

Less than half an hour later, Guin's doorbell rang. She hurried to the door.

"The doctor is in!" Shelly announced.

Guin smiled and led her back to the bedroom. Shelly was intimately familiar with Guin's walk-in closet, having helped Guin pick out outfits on several occasions.

"Let's see," she said, flipping through Guin's dresses. "How old is this guy?" she asked, turning to Guin.

"Around sixty, I think."

"You know anything about him? Any photos?"

"Nothing recent," said Guin. "He's a bit of a recluse. Ginny said to dress 'smart.'"

"Hmm…" said Shelly. "It's supposed to be a bit chilly this evening, so I'm thinking pants. Do you think he'd object to you wearing slacks?"

"No idea," said Guin. "Though I only have a couple pairs of dress pants."

"Let's see," said Shelly, searching for them.

Guin reached around her and pulled out a hanger with a pair of white cotton pants.

"I have these and a similar pair in navy," she said.

Shelly eyed them.

"What about a top?"

"Oh, I know!" said Guin. "I bought this cute blue-and-white-striped top, very nautical, a little while back and haven't even worn it."

"Show me," said Shelly.

Guin fished around in her closet until she found it.

"Whatcha think?" she asked.

"Perfect!" said Shelly.

"Which pants?" asked Guin.

"Definitely the white ones. Now go try everything on, so Aunt Shelly can evaluate."

Guin grinned and took the clothes into the bathroom. A couple minutes later, she walked out.

"Ta da! Does it work?"

Shelly gave her the once over.

"It needs some jewelry and heels. And I think you should wear your hair up, maybe in a French twist. But yes, it should be fine."

A little under an hour later, Guin was ready, thanks to Shelly's ministrations. And she had to admit, she looked good. Her hair was in a neat French twist, with a couple of curls charmingly framing her face. Her makeup looked natural, a little powder to hide her freckles, and a bit of rouge, eyeshadow, mascara, and matte lipstick. And her jewelry—a Tiffany heart necklace and matching bracelet, a Cartier tank watch (a gift from her mother), and a couple of rings—was understated yet smart.

"Perfect!" said Shelly.

Guin eyed herself in the full-length mirror.

"I haven't dressed like this in ages," she sighed.

"Well, it suits you," said Shelly. "We just need to find you some friends with yachts."

Guin smiled back at her.

"I'm waiting for you and Steve to get one."

Shelly snorted.

"Maybe a fishing boat."

Guin looked down at her watch.

"Gotta go!"

"Grab some heels!" called Shelly, scooting after Guin, who was hurrying to the front door.

"Got 'em!" said Guin, opening the front hall closet, where she kept most of her shoes.

As she was eyeing her options, she felt something furry brush against her legs.

"Oops, nearly forgot."

She turned and went into the kitchen, followed by the two cats.

"Hold your horses," said Guin.

She opened the pantry, grabbed the bag of cat food, and poured some into the two cat bowls.

Fauna continued to meow.

"Sorry, dude. That's what there is."

The cat gave her a withering look.

"Why can't you be like Flora?" said Guin, looking over at the multicolored cat, who was quietly nibbling on the dry food.

Fauna glared at her, then went to her bowl.

"Do you ever give them wet food?" Shelly asked.

"I do, but not at night," Guin replied.

She grabbed her bag and her keys and went back to the front hall closet.

"These," said Shelly, holding up a pair of white slingback pumps.

Guin slipped them on.

"Perfect," said Shelly, smiling.

"Wish me luck!" said Guin.

"Good luck!" said Shelly.

Then Guin raced down to the garage.

CHAPTER 29

Guin arrived at the marina where Digby's yacht was moored a little after five and whistled at the sight of his boat. She had only been on a yacht once before, years ago, with her ex. His company had rented it for an evening. This was altogether different. This whole ship belonged to just one person.

The thought of it momentarily intimidated Guin.

She looked around, wondering how to announce her presence. It wasn't as though there was a doorbell. There was, however, a walkway from the dock leading up to the boat.

She took a couple of steps and then called up.

"Hello? Anybody home?"

A male head appeared over the side of the yacht, then looked down.

"Are you Ms. Jones?"

The man looked much too young to be Digby Blyleven.

"I am," Guin replied.

"Come on up," called the man.

Guin made her way up the walkway. Or was it a gangplank? She'd have to look it up later. At the top she was met by the handsome young man who had addressed her.

"I'm Garrett Northway, Mr. Blyleven's personal assistant," he said, smiling and extending a hand.

Guin took it and smiled back.

"Guinivere Jones, reporter for the *Sanibel-Captiva Sun-Times*. But you probably already knew that."

"I did," he said, smiling. "Well, now that that's out of the way, can I get you a drink and give you the tour?"

Guin glanced around.

"Is Mr. Blyleven not available?" Guin asked.

"He's just finishing up a call and will be with you shortly. In the meantime, I am at your service."

For some reason, Garrett reminded Guin very much of her brother. She watched him as he made his way to the bar. Definitely Lance's type.

"So, drink?"

Guin had been spacing out.

"White wine spritzer?"

She didn't like to drink anything heavier when she was on the job.

"Coming right up," said Garrett. "Have a seat."

He had gone around to the other side of the bar and took out a bottle of chardonnay. He paused.

"Though, you know, I make the best margaritas this side of Key West."

Guin raised her eyebrows. She loved a good margarita.

Garrett saw her perk up.

"I shouldn't," Guin said. "I'm supposed to be working."

"One little margarita won't kill you. Trust me, you won't regret it."

Guin wasn't so sure but agreed. After all, she didn't want to seem rude.

Garrett reached over and grabbed a bottle of tequila, very good tequila, then proceeded to mix her margarita, like one of those people you see in bartender competitions, or Tom Cruise in *Cocktail*. Guin watched him, captivated.

"You a bartender in a previous life?" Guin asked.

Garrett smiled.

"During law school I did some bartending to help pay the bills."

"So, you're a lawyer?" Guin asked.

"Non-practicing," he replied.

Guin was dying to ask him questions, but she refrained.

"Here you go," he said, placing the margarita in front of her. "Let me know what you think."

Guin took a sip. Then another.

"Oh my God," she said, looking over at him. "This may the best margarita I've ever had."

Garrett grinned.

"You trying to get our guest here soused?" came a deep voice.

Guin turned to see a man, dressed as she imagined the captain of a yacht might look, coming towards them.

"Just treating her to a little island hospitality," replied Garrett.

He turned to Guin.

"Ms. Jones, may I present Mr. J. Douglas Blyleven."

"But you may call me Digby," said Digby, extending a hand.

"Pleased to meet you, Digby," said Guin. "And you may call me Guin."

"Guin," he said, and paused. "That's an unusual name."

"It's short for Guinivere."

Digby continued to regard her.

"My mother had a thing for Arthurian legends," Guin explained. "My older brother's Lancelot. And yes, I know."

Digby chuckled.

"And if that's not bad enough, my ex is named Arthur."

Digby and Garrett both smiled.

Good lord, what was in that margarita? Guin wondered. She never rambled so much.

"So, fair lady, what can I do for you?" Digby asked her.

"Well," said Guin, not sure how much Ginny had told him. She was dying to have another sip of that margarita but knew she had probably already had enough. "I was hoping to get some information about Natura's relationship with Birdy McMurtry."

There, she said it. She watched Digby's face, but he didn't seem annoyed.

"Ah, Birdy," said Digby, a bit wistfully.

Guin waited for him to continue.

"Have you been on one of his private tours?" he asked her.

"I have, yes," Guin replied.

"Marvelous, isn't he?"

"How long have you've known Birdy?" she asked him.

"How long has it been now, Garrett? Four years? Five?"

Garrett looked thoughtful.

"Just over four years now, I believe."

"And when did he start doing work for Natura?" Guin asked, looking from Digby to Garrett.

"Just over three years ago," Garrett replied.

"He played hard to get," said Digby. "But we convinced him," he added, a smile curving his lips. "He's been a big help to us."

"So you must have been upset when he asked to cancel his contract with Natura."

"Just a misunderstanding. That's all," said Digby, looking unphased. "Birdy needs Natura, and we need him."

Guin looked over at Garrett, who was making himself busy behind the bar.

"G and T, sir?" he said, offering Digby a lowball glass.

"Don't mind if I do," he replied, taking the drink. He took a sip. "Garrett, what would I do without you?"

Garrett smiled.

"And I see he fixed you one of his special margaritas,"

Digby said, looking at Guin's drink. "Not a tequila man myself, but I hear they're quite good."

Guin looked down at her drink.

"Very good," she said.

"Go on, drink up," Digby said.

Guin took a polite sip.

"I was just going to give Guin here a tour of the boat," said Garrett.

"Excellent idea," said Digby. "I need to make another call. Then we can continue our conversation, Guinivere."

He excused himself and Guin turned back to Garrett.

"Shall we?" he said, letting himself out from behind the bar.

Guin took another sip of her drink.

"You can bring it with you," Garrett said, smiling.

"I'd better not," she replied.

She placed the glass back on the bar and got up.

"This way," said Garrett.

Guin had to work to keep her jaw from dropping as Garrett showed her around Digby's yacht. She knew there were larger yachts out there, but Digby's boat was still quite impressive. There were two bedrooms, three if you counted the office, each with its own bathroom; an extra half-bath for guests; an indoor and outdoor dining area, as well as an indoor and outdoor living area; and a fully equipped kitchen.

"This is Mr. Blyleven's home away from home," explained Garrett.

"And where is home?" asked Guin.

She had done a search, several actually, on Digby, but there was very little information online about him. He had somehow managed to stay out of the public eye for the last ten years or so.

"He has a place in New York, one in the Caymans, and another in Monaco."

"Nice," said Guin. "And have you been to all three?"

"I have," Garrett replied.

"You have a favorite?"

"Personally, I love the flat in Monaco. It's the smallest of the three, but the views.... And there's Monaco, of course."

Of course, thought Guin. She had always wanted to go to Monaco.

"I'll just go see if Digby is done with his call," said Garrett, when he was done with the tour.

They were standing at the bow of the ship, in a cozy outdoor seating area.

"Wait right here," he instructed Guin.

Guin walked over to the rail and looked out. It was a beautiful evening, and the sunset cast a reddish glow over the marina.

"Beautiful, isn't it?" came a voice behind her. Digby. "I never get tired of Captiva sunsets."

"Do you spend much time on Captiva?" asked Guin.

"Not as much as I'd like," he replied.

"What brought you here this time?"

"Business."

"Anything to do with Birdy?"

It was growing dark out, and while the lights from the marina had come on, it was hard to see Digby's face.

"What is it you are after, Ms. Jones?"

His tone had turned a bit testy.

"I'm trying to find out who might want Birdy out of the way."

"And you think I had something to do with his being shot."

Guin was startled.

"Oh yes, I know all about the incident," Digby said.

Guin was dying to ask how. Had the detective spoken to Digby? Probably. Or maybe someone else had told him.

"So, did you have anything to do with it?" asked Guin. Clearly, the drink had given her courage, or made her stupid. "I understand Birdy was prepared to go public with some unsavory information about Natura if you didn't release him from his contract."

Digby waved a hand, dismissing the thought.

"He was bluffing. The relationship was far too lucrative to Birdy, and besides, he signed an NDA."

"Though those can be broken," Guin retorted.

"You haven't seen ours," said Digby. "Our lawyers are no match for Birdy."

"Still, you probably wouldn't want Natura's reputation called into question."

Digby sighed, as if this conversation was boring him.

"Natura's reputation is above reproach, and one disgruntled employee will not make a difference."

Guin wasn't so sure of that.

"Now, if you don't have any other questions, Ms. Jones..."

"Where were you the evening Birdy was shot?" Guin asked.

"Right here on the boat, as I am almost every evening."

"Anyone back that up?"

"Garrett, my chef, the people at the marina..."

Guin imagined they would all lie for Digby, if asked.

"Now I'm afraid, Ms. Jones, I really must ask you to excuse yourself. Garrett will see you out."

Garrett appeared out of nowhere and gestured for Guin to follow him.

"And do give my best to dear Birdy when you see him," called Digby. "I'd hate for anything else unpleasant to happen to him."

Guin felt a chill and shivered involuntarily.

"Ms. Jones?" said Garrett, leading her back towards the ramp from the boat to the dock.

"Thanks again for the drink," said Guin, as she was about to go down the walkway.

"My pleasure," replied Garrett. "Here's my card," he said, handing it to her. "If you have additional questions, feel free to reach out to me. Digby can be a bit prickly, especially when he hasn't eaten."

"I'm the same way," said Guin, smiling. "Had I known, I would have brought food. I make a mean chocolate chip cookie."

Garrett chuckled.

"Next time."

"Oh, one more thing," said Guin, turning.

Garrett gave her a questioning look.

"When do you depart?"

"That depends," he said.

Guin looked up at him, tilting her head.

"On Digby."

Guin waited for him to say more, but he didn't.

"Well, thanks again," said Guin.

"No problem," replied Garrett. "Have a good evening."

"You, too," said Guin.

She made her way down the ramp, past the dozens of boats moored at the marina, back to her little purple Mini, which suddenly seemed quite small.

CHAPTER 30

Guin arrived home a little while later and fixed herself a vegetable omelet with some multigrain toast for dinner. She finished eating and had plopped down on the sofa, planning on watching some corny romantic movie on the Hallmark Channel, or a cooking show, when her phone pinged. It was a text message from the detective. That was odd.

"Is Birdy with you?" read the text.

"No," she quickly typed back. "Why? What's up?"

Seconds later, her phone rang. It was the detective.

"We have a problem."

The detective explained that earlier that evening a woman, claiming to be Birdy's wife, had come to the hotel, asking to see Birdy.

"Wife?!" said Guin. "Did she give a name?"

"Yes, Guin Jones."

Guin opened her mouth to speak, but nothing came out.

"You still there?"

Guin nodded her head. A few seconds later, she spoke.

"It wasn't me."

The detective let out a huff of breath.

"I was in Naples this morning," Guin continued, "but not this evening. And you told me he was there under an assumed name and wouldn't tell me what it was," she said, indignantly. "So even if I wanted to see him, I wouldn't know who to ask for."

"I thought maybe you had figured it out," replied the detective.

"Well, I didn't," said Guin. "Besides, I'm supposed to be his fiancée, not his wife." She paused. "When did you say Birdy went missing?"

"Just a little while ago."

"Well, maybe he'll turn up later. Who said he was missing anyway?"

"Ms. Betteridge. She came back from having drinks and Birdy wasn't in his room. When she asked at the desk if anyone had seen Birdy go out, they said he had probably gone out with his wife."

"Well, it wasn't me. "Did the person at the hotel give you a description?" Guin asked.

"She said the woman was average height with reddish hair," replied the detective.

"Lots of women are average height and have reddish hair," Guin retorted.

"Yes, but how many of them give their name as Guin Jones?"

Guin didn't have a good response.

"So tell me again where you were earlier," said the detective.

"Seriously?" Guin replied.

"Just tell me," said the detective.

"I was conducting an interview."

"Who with?" asked the detective.

"J. Douglas Blyleven, aboard his yacht."

"And he can verify that?"

"He can," said Guin, "as can his assistant, Garrett Northway. They can both attest to the fact that I was on the boat, which was docked in Captiva, at the time of Birdy's disappearance."

The detective didn't say anything.

"If you don't believe me, you are welcome to come to the condo and search for him here."

The detective sighed.

"That won't be necessary."

"Is Bettina even sure Birdy is really missing?" Guin asked. "Maybe he was lonely or bored and went to meet someone. You should talk to that caterer, Rebecca, the one who catered the Wilsons' party in Birdy's honor. I know Birdy was kind of seeing her."

"Doesn't explain someone showing up at the hotel, claiming to be his wife, and giving them your name," said the detective.

"True."

Guin thought for a minute.

"So I'm assuming the person at the front desk called up to Birdy's room. Was he there?"

"According to the hotel, he was," said the detective.

"And they told him a Guin Jones was there to see him?"

"Presumably," said the detective.

"And they sent her up?"

"They did."

"Did they see either the woman or Birdy after that?" Guin asked.

"No," said the detective. "The reception area was supposedly very busy."

A dozen things went through Guin's mind, most of them not good, but she tried to think positively.

"For all we know, he could show up later tonight." Though she didn't really believe that. After all, if he had just stepped out for a bit, why hadn't he returned her messages or left a note for Bettina?

"I hope so, Ms. Jones," said the detective. "But if you happen to hear from him, give me a call."

"Will do," Guin said.

They ended the call and Guin immediately tried Birdy's number. It went straight to voicemail.

Guin was getting ready for bed when her phone rang. She rushed over to get it, hoping it was Birdy or the detective. It was neither.

"Where is he?" said Bettina.

"I assume you mean Birdy," Guin calmly replied.

"Of course I mean Birdy. Where is he? Is he hiding out at your place?"

Guin sighed.

"As I told the detective, I haven't seen or heard from Birdy since yesterday."

"The woman at the front desk said a Guin Jones, claiming to be Birdy's wife, had come to see him, and the description fit you."

"That description could fit many people," Guin replied, slightly irritated. "Have you tried calling his phone or texting him?"

"Do you think I'm stupid?" Bettina said. "Of course I did."

"Let me guess," said Guin. "He didn't reply."

"No, he did not."

"For what it's worth," said Guin, "I've been trying to reach him, too. No answer."

Guin could picture Bettina pacing around her suite at the Ritz.

"Look, it's possible he went out for dinner or something with this woman and will be back later," Guin told her. Though she didn't really believe that.

"It's almost 9:30," snapped Bettina.

"Which isn't really that late," said Guin. "There's a good chance he'll walk in the door any minute."

Though again, Guin didn't really believe that. But the last thing she needed was Bettina freaking out.

"I just can't believe he would have gone off without telling me," she huffed.

"Has he ever gone off on his own before?" Guin asked.

There was a momentary silence on the other end.

"Once or twice," said Bettina, begrudgingly.

"And both times he came back?"

"Yes," said Bettina.

"So, look, if he's not back by the time you get up tomorrow, follow up with Detective O'Loughlin. He'll know what to do."

"You're not covering for him, are you?" Bettina asked, suspiciously.

"I'm not. I promise," said Guin.

Guin could feel the other woman's anxiety. She was starting to feel pretty anxious herself.

"So do you have any idea who might have posed as Birdy's wife?" Guin asked.

"Other than you?" Bettina retorted.

"Yes, other than me," Guin replied. "Is there anyone you know of, anyone at all, a fan or admirer, who knew where Birdy was staying?"

"No one was supposed to know where Birdy was staying," snapped Bettina. "And even if they did, he was here under an assumed name."

"Is it possible you might have mentioned the name to someone? Or could someone have followed you from the hospital to the hotel?"

There was silence at the other end of the line. Finally, Bettina spoke.

"I don't think anyone followed us."

So had Bettina mentioned to someone that they would be staying at the Ritz under an assumed name?

"Look, it's late," Guin said, suddenly feeling quite tired. "Get some sleep. Maybe Birdy will turn up in the morning. If he hasn't, call the detective again."

"Fine," said Bettina. "But if you hear from him, tell him to get his ass back here."

Guin smiled, despite herself.

"I promise."

They ended the call. Guin got into bed and put her phone on top of her nightstand, leaving it on in case the detective or Birdy tried to reach her. She grabbed her book and started to read, glancing over at her phone every few minutes.

CHAPTER 31

It was nearly 7:30 by the time Guin got up Sunday morning.

"How did I sleep so late?" she wondered aloud.

Though to say she had slept was an overstatement. She had tossed and turned all night and had awakened every time her phone pinged. But it was never Birdy.

Upon seeing that Guin was awake, Fauna made her way to Guin's head and meowed.

"Give me a break, will ya? I just got up," she said, shooing the cat away.

Undeterred, Fauna continued to meow.

"Fine, I'll feed you. Tyrant."

She got out of bed and walked to the kitchen. She reached into the pantry, pulled out a can of cat food, and evenly divided the contents into the two cat bowls.

"Enjoy," she said to the cats, who had been keeping a close eye on her.

Then she went back into her bedroom, thought about crawling back into bed, shook her head, and went to her closet. She quickly threw on some clothes, splashed some cold water on her face, put her hair into a ponytail, grabbed her bag and her keys, and headed to the farmers market.

Guin made a beeline to Jimmy's Java as soon as she entered the market.

"God, that's good," she said, after taking a couple of sips of coffee.

The man working the booth smiled at her.

"You need more beans? We just roasted a fresh batch."

"Sure, why not?" she said.

She helped herself to a bag and gave the man some money. Then it was onto the next booth. By the time she was done, she had filled her cart with some bagels, some cheese, a bag of crab cakes, a variety of vegetables, and a *pain au chocolat* and a mocha eclair from Jean-Luc's.

Ris had said he would try to call her around nine, so she hadn't lingered at the market. As she was putting her purchases away, her phone rang. It was Ris.

"Hey!" she said, stopping what she was doing. "How are you?"

"Good!" said Ris. "How are you?"

"Not so good," said Guin.

"Oh?" he said. "What's up?"

"Birdy's gone missing, and Bettina and the detective think I kidnapped him."

"Did you?" asked Ris.

Guin made a face.

"No, I did not kidnap him."

"Well, that's a relief," said Ris.

"Thanks," said Guin. "But I'm worried."

"I'm sure he'll turn up," said Ris. "Knowing Birdy, he flew the coop to hang out with some bird."

He chuckled at his clever turn of phrase. Guin was not amused.

"Mmph," she said. "Anyway, how are *you*? And where are you?"

"I'm actually in Singapore for a few days."

"Nice," said Guin. "You giving a lecture there?"

"I am. I was asked last minute. And as I had a couple of days free, I said 'Why not?' Especially as they offered to pay all of my expenses."

"Nice," Guin said again.

"I just wish you were here with me," he said. "You should see the hotel they put me at."

"Is it fancy?"

"Very," said Ris. "I feel like some dignitary."

"Well, you're very important to me," Guin said, smiling.

"You would love it here," said Ris. "It's so clean."

"I'm sure," said Guin. "But I'll see you soon. Just a couple more weeks now. I can't wait to see Australia."

"You'll love it."

Guin was about to say something but her thought was interrupted by her phone beeping. She tried to ignore it but was worried it could be Birdy.

"Hey, Ris, I'm sorry to do this, but I'm getting a call. Can I call you back in a few? It may be important."

"Okay, I should be here."

"Thanks," she said. She immediately picked up the other call, hoping it hadn't gone into voicemail.

"Well, he's still not back, and he's not answering his cell," came Bettina's surly voice.

Guin sighed.

"Did you call the detective?"

"I did. He wasn't there."

"Did you leave a message?" asked Guin.

"I did."

Guin wasn't sure what else she could do.

"Have you heard from him?" Bettina asked.

"No," said Guin.

"Well, if you do, text me immediately."

"I will," said Guin. "I'll even call the detective right after

I get off the phone with you, to make sure he knows this is urgent."

"Thanks," said Bettina, begrudgingly.

She sounded tired. Guin wondered if she had gotten any sleep.

"Did you happen to think of anyone who may have known Birdy was staying at the Ritz?" Guin asked.

"No," said Bettina.

"Well, if you think of anything, anything at all, let me know."

Bettina didn't respond.

"I need to go," Guin said after several seconds had passed. "But I'll call or text you later if I hear anything."

"I have plans, so best to send me a text," Bettina replied.

Guin didn't know what else to say, so she said goodbye and ended the call. Then she phoned Ris back. Fortunately, he didn't have to rush off to someplace, so they were finally able to chat for more than a few minutes. Guin patiently listened as Ris told her all about his travels. It sounded like he was having a marvelous time. She was happy for him, but it made her own life seem quite boring.

She had just started to tell him about her Valentine's Day piece when she heard the beep of an incoming call.

"Hey Ris, I need to get this. Talk again in a couple of days?"

"I'll send you a text to arrange it," he said. "Hey Guin…"

She was anxious for the call not to go into voicemail, but she didn't want to cut him off.

"Yes?"

"I love you."

"I love you, too," she said. "Gotta go!"

She went to answer the other call, but it was too late. It had already gone to voicemail.

The call had been from the detective, asking if she had heard from Birdy. She had called him back and told him she had not. He told her to let him know if she did.

Her call done, she put her coffee in the microwave to heat it up and made some scrambled eggs to go with her *pain au chocolat*. When the eggs were ready, she slid them onto a plate and ate them standing up at the counter.

She looked out past the lanai, a half-dozen questions going through her head. Where was Birdy? Was he okay? And who was this woman claiming to be his wife? She had Googled the caterer, Rebecca, but she didn't fit the description the hotel had given the detective. Could it have been Briony? Though Briony was far from average height, and she doubted Birdy would go anywhere willingly with her. Though you never knew.

She sighed and continued to stare out at the golf course, absent-mindedly eating her eggs and *pain au chocolat*. It was a beautiful morning, not too hot, and she thought about going for a walk. But she had work to do. Even though it was Sunday.

She finished her breakfast and quickly washed her plate and fork. Then she poured herself a glass of water and headed to her office/bedroom.

She spent the next hour or so skimming articles about Natura and trying to dig up more information on Digby, but she couldn't find anything new. Frustrated, she called Craig. He was probably on some boat, fishing, as it was Sunday, but on the off chance he was around…

His voicemail picked up and Guin left a message.

"What am I missing?" she said, staring at her monitor.

She typed "J. Douglas Blyleven" into her search engine again and then clicked on Images. She scrolled through the photos and stopped at one featuring Digby with two people she recognized, Ginny and Joel. Well, that was hardly a surprise. They were old friends, according to Ginny. She continued to scroll. Then stopped again. That couple in the photo, it looked like Kathy and John Wilson. There was another man with them, a younger one she didn't recognize. She clicked on the link to go to the page where the photo was posted. As she did, her phone started to ring.

"Guin Jones," she said, picking up, not looking at the caller ID. Her eyes were still focused on her monitor.

"Guin, it's Craig. Everything okay?"

"No, everything is not okay," she said, tearing her eyes away from her monitor. "Birdy's been kidnapped, or at least we think he's been kidnapped. And I could use your help."

"I'm not sure what I can do, but shoot."

"You out fishing?"

"We just docked. I should be home in half an hour. You want to come over for lunch?"

Guin hesitated. She didn't want to impose.

"Come on over," Craig said. "Betty would love to see you."

"Well, if it's no trouble…" said Guin.

"No trouble at all. I'll just give Betty a shout, let her know you'll be joining us."

"Okay, but if you don't have enough food…"

"Are you kidding?" said Craig. "The way Betty cooks, there's food for an army."

Guin smiled.

"Okay. What time should I meet you over there?"

"Say half an hour, forty-five minutes?"

"Perfect," said Guin. "And thanks."

"No need to thank me. Happy to have you."

Guin ended the call and returned her attention to the page on her screen. The photo was, indeed, of Digby, and Kathy and John Wilson, and Dick Grayson, Natura's VP of Marketing. It was taken at some charity event.

She wanted to do a little more digging, but she really needed to take a shower and change if she was to have lunch with the Jeffers. She closed her browser and got up.

CHAPTER 32

Guin arrived at Craig and Betty's place forty-five minutes later.

"So good to see you, dear," said Betty, ushering her inside.

"Thank you for having me," said Guin.

"Betty's made her special chopped seafood salad," said Craig.

Guin walked over to the dining table. On it was a big salad bowl filled with lettuce, tomatoes, cucumber, shrimp, scallops, and squid, a plate with multigrain rolls, and a big pitcher of water.

"Looks great!" said Guin.

"Have a seat," said Craig, gesturing to the chair where Guin usually sat.

They sat and ate, making small talk, for the next ten minutes or so. Craig told Guin and Betty all about the morning's fishing excursion, and the women smiled indulgently.

When they were done, they brought the dishes into the kitchen.

"Well, I need to be heading off," said Betty, after stacking the plates next to the sink. "I'm playing mahjong with the ladies this afternoon."

"Have fun," said Guin.

"We always do," said Betty. "You two try not to get into

too much trouble while I'm out," she added with a twinkle.

Craig made a face, though he couldn't help smiling a bit when Betty gave him a kiss on the cheek.

"I'll take care of this stuff," he said.

"Thank you, dear," she said, smiling at him. "I'll be back later."

She grabbed her bag and her keys and waved goodbye. Guin waved back at her.

"Thanks for lunch!" she called.

"So someone claiming to be McMurtry's wife spirited him away from the Ritz?"

"Allegedly, yes," said Guin, after telling Craig what she knew.

She was leaning against a counter in Craig and Betty's kitchen as Craig did the washing up.

"Have the Naples police been notified?"

"I don't know," said Guin. "I know Detective O'Loughlin knows. Any ideas on how to find out who this mystery woman is?"

"Ms. Betteridge didn't have a guess?"

"She and the detective thought I had spirited Birdy away. But I was nowhere near the hotel when he was supposedly abducted."

"What time did Ms. Betteridge say she got back to the room?" Craig asked.

"I'm not sure," said Guin. "I think around eight."

"And there was no note or message from McMurtry, saying he'd gone out?"

"Not that I'm aware of," said Guin.

"What about his clothes and his wallet? Were they still there?"

"I forgot to ask," Guin replied. She could have kicked

herself. "I'll text Bettina and ask her."

She went to retrieve her phone.

"You don't have to text her this minute," said Craig. "Getting back to this mystery woman, any idea how she knew where to find McMurtry?"

"I asked Bettina that. She swears she didn't tell anyone."

"Hmm…" Craig said.

"Did the person at the desk see Birdy and the woman leave?"

"No," said Guin.

"Well, if you ask me, I think you and I should take a little trip down to Naples," said Craig.

"Now?" asked Guin.

"You got something better to do?"

Guin thought for a second.

"Not really."

"Then let's go. You mind driving? Betty's car's in the shop, so I let her take mine."

"No problem," said Guin. "As long as you don't mind driving in the Mini."

"I'll live," said Craig.

Craig was not a large man, but he was taller and broader than Guin.

"Let's go then," said Guin.

A few minutes later, they were headed to the Causeway.

They arrived at the Ritz-Carlton, Naples, a little over an hour later.

"Wow," said Guin, pulling into the driveway.

"You've never been?" Craig asked.

"Nope," she replied.

"Nice place, if you like that sort of thing."

Guin parked in front of the lobby and a valet scurried

around to open the door for her. She smiled at him.

"We shouldn't be long," she told the young man.

"You checking in?" he asked her.

"No, just meeting someone," she replied. "We shouldn't be more than an hour, if that."

"Okay," said the young man.

Craig was already out of the car and standing by the front door. Guin walked over to where he was standing, and they made their way inside.

Guin had texted Bettina before they left, letting her know that she and Craig were headed over, and Bettina said she would meet them. Guin texted her to let her know they had arrived.

They entered the lobby and looked around. A minute later, Guin spied Bettina heading straight for her. She was well put together but looked tired.

"Any news?" Guin asked her.

"None. I was hoping you might have some news for me," Bettina replied.

"Sorry, no," Guin said.

"We should go to the front desk," said Craig.

Bettina looked at Craig.

"Bettina, allow me to introduce my colleague, Craig Jeffers."

Bettina eyed him somewhat suspiciously.

"Craig is an award-winning crime reporter from Chicago," Guin explained.

"So, can you help us find him?" Bettina asked.

"I'm going to try," he replied. "What name was Mr. McMurtry using?"

Bettina glanced around.

"It's okay," said Guin. "I doubt anyone is listening."

"Arthur Jones," Bettina replied.

"*What*?!" said Guin, rather loudly.

A few people glanced their way.

"He said his name was Arthur Jones?" Guin asked, lowering her voice. "Where did he get that idea?"

Bettina shrugged.

Guin tried to regain her composure. Arthur Jones was the name of her ex-husband. No wonder the detective suspected her.

"Fine, let's go over to the front desk," Guin finally said.

The three of them headed over.

"Hi there," Guin said to the young woman standing behind the reception desk. "I'm hoping you can help me."

"I hope so, too," said the young woman, who smiled at Guin.

"Do you know who was working the front desk around 5 p.m. yesterday?" Guin asked her.

"That would be me," said the young woman.

Guin smiled and read the young woman's badge. It said her name was Callie.

"And have you ever seen me before, Callie?" Guin asked the young woman.

"No, ma'am," Callie replied.

"So you didn't see me here at the front desk, around five o'clock yesterday, asking to see a guest of yours, a Mr. Arthur Jones."

Callie looked confused.

"No ma'am. As I told you, I've never seen you before."

"Well, we were told that Mr. Jones had a visitor around five o'clock yesterday, claiming to be his wife."

Callie waited for her to continue.

"The only problem is, Mr. Jones doesn't have a wife," said Craig. "And the woman claiming to be his wife gave you a false name."

Callie looked distinctly nervous.

"I'm Guin Jones," said Guin. "The real Guin Jones."

"Oh gosh. I'm sorry, ma'am," said Callie, looking at her.

"That's okay, Callie," said Guin. "No one is blaming you. But could you help us out and tell us what you remember about this woman? What did she look like?"

Callie thought for a minute.

"Well," she said, scrunching her face a bit. "She was a little taller than you, and was, uh, kind of..."

"Was kind of?" asked Craig.

Callie blushed.

"Busty."

"What about her face?" Craig asked, ignoring Callie's discomfort.

"She was wearing sunglasses," said Callie. "So I couldn't see her eyes. And her hair was pulled back."

"Did you happen to notice the color of her hair?" Craig asked her.

"It was kind of reddish," Callie replied.

"And her complexion, would you describe it as fair or dark?" Craig asked.

"Kind of medium," said Callie.

"Was she young or old?" Craig continued.

Callie looked thoughtful.

"Did she look like she was in her twenties? Her thirties? Older?"

"At least in her thirties," said Callie. "Though, like I said, with her sunglasses on, it was a bit hard to tell."

"Did she have any kind of accent?" Craig asked.

Callie thought for a minute.

"Now that you mention it, she might have had a bit of an accent, but I couldn't place it."

"Anything else you noticed about the woman?" asked Guin. "Like what she was wearing?"

Again, Callie paused to think.

"She was wearing a blouse and a skirt. And she had on these hoop earrings."

"Sounds like a hooker to me," Craig whispered to Guin. He looked over at Bettina. "Could your client have requested some company while you were out, Ms. Betteridge?"

Bettina's face turned a shade of purple.

"Never! Bir—" She saw Guin shaking her head. "Arthur would never hire a—*company*," she hissed.

"You can't watch the man twenty-four-seven," Craig replied.

Bettina made a face.

Guin turned to her.

"Bettina, think. Is there anyone, anyone at all, that *Arthur* knows who matches that description?"

"No," Bettina said, firmly.

"You sure?" Craig asked.

"Yes."

Guin turned back to the young woman at the front desk.

"Thank you for your help, Callie. If there's anything else you can remember, could you contact me?"

She fished in her bag and pulled out her card case.

"Here's my card. You can call, text, or email me."

Callie took the card and looked at it.

"You're a reporter?"

"I am," said Guin.

Callie frowned.

"Don't worry. I won't tell anyone about your involvement," said Guin. Though Detective O'Loughlin no doubt already knew. "We just want to find Mr. Jones."

Callie looked relieved.

"Thanks," she said. "I'll let you know if I remember anything else."

"Thanks," said Guin.

Somewhere close by a cell phone started to ring. Bettina's, of course.

Craig and Guin watched as Bettina grabbed it.

"Hello?!" she said.

She looked over at Craig and Guin.

"Hold on a sec," Bettina said into her phone.

She shook her head, indicating it was not Birdy, then she turned back to her phone.

"Darling, can I phone you back in just a second? I'm just finishing up some business."

She paused.

"I'm at the Ritz in Naples. Promise, I'll call you right back. Ciao!"

She hung up.

Craig and Guin were looking at her.

"What?" she said, annoyed. "I can't take a phone call?"

"Who were you talking to?" Guin asked.

"A client," said Bettina.

"You told him you were staying at the Ritz in Naples," said Craig.

"So?" said Bettina.

Craig and Guin exchanged a look.

"By any chance were you speaking on the phone to anyone while you were checking in here yesterday?" Guin asked.

Bettina looked annoyed.

"If you want to find your client, Ms. Betteridge, I suggest you try to jog that memory of yours," said Craig.

"Fine," said Bettina.

Craig and Guin waited. Finally, a couple minutes later, after making several faces, Bettina spoke.

"I'm pretty sure I didn't speak to any clients when we were checking in."

"What about non-clients?" asked Craig. "Who were you having drinks with?"

"An old friend. Totally trustworthy." She paused. "The

only person I spoke with when I got here was Kathy. She wanted to know when I planned on picking up Birdy's things or if I would be sending someone to fetch them."

"Kathy?" asked Craig.

"Kathy Wilson," Bettina replied, giving them a look that said, *'What other Kathy did you think I could have meant?'*

"Bettina, did you tell Kathy Wilson where you and Birdy were staying?" Guin asked her.

"I may have mentioned it," she replied. "But you can't possibly think Kathy and John had anything to do with this. Birdy's like a son to them!"

"Did you tell them what name he was using?" asked Craig.

Bettina looked distinctly uncomfortable.

"No, but…"

"No, but what, Ms. Betteridge?"

Craig fixed her with a look that had Guin ready to confess, though she wasn't sure to what.

Bettina sighed.

"I was talking to her when we checked in. It's possible she heard me say the name Arthur Jones, though it's unlikely. And besides, Kathy would never harm Birdy—and she doesn't fit the description the receptionist gave."

"It's true," Guin said. "She looks nothing like the woman Callie described. Even if she wore a wig."

"Look, I need to call Giancarlo back," said Bettina. "If you'll excuse me?"

"Fine," said Guin, with a sigh.

Craig and Guin watched as Bettina walked away, speaking quite loudly into her phone. Craig shook his head.

"You young people and your phones."

"We're probably all guilty of talking like no one's listening," said Guin.

"Not me," said Craig.

"Fine, except for you," said Guin, with a grin.

She glanced around, then back at Craig.

"Now what?"

"I think we need to have a chat with Mrs. Wilson," said Craig.

"You heard the woman at the front desk's description of the woman claiming to be Birdy's wife," said Guin. "It couldn't possibly have been Kathy Wilson."

"Maybe not," said Craig. "But we should still have a chat with her."

"Okay, I'll give her a call," said Guin.

CHAPTER 33

Guin stood a little way away and called the Wilson house.

"Wilson residence," said a female voice, the same one who had answered before.

"Is Mrs. Wilson there?" asked Guin.

"She's not available," said the woman.

"Do you know when she'll be back?" asked Guin. "It's important that I speak with her."

"She and Mr. Wilson are away," said the woman.

"Do you know when they'll be back?" Guin asked.

"No," replied the woman.

"Well, could you take a message, in case they call?"

There was no reply.

"Please tell Mrs. Wilson that Guinivere Jones called, and that it's urgent she call me back."

"*Gwen of ear*?" asked the woman.

Guin sighed.

"Just tell her Guin called. G-U-I-N. She'll know who it is."

She gave the woman her mobile number.

"And who am I speaking with, please?" asked Guin.

"Catalina."

"Well, thanks for your help, Catalina."

Guin ended the call and turned to Craig.

"Any luck?" he asked her.

"No. The Wilsons are apparently out of town."

"You have her cell phone number?"

"I do."

She entered Kathy Wilson's number. The phone rang several times, then a female voice answered.

"Hello?"

"Mrs. Wilson—Kathy?"

"Speaking."

"Kathy, it's Guinivere Jones."

"Oh, hello Guinivere. Is everything okay?"

"No. Birdy's gone missing."

"Gone missing?"

"Yes, he left his hotel room yesterday late afternoon without telling anyone, and he hasn't been seen since. I was hoping he might have gone to see you and Mr. Wilson."

"Oh dear," said Mrs. Wilson. "I'm afraid I haven't heard from Birdy since he left the hospital. And Mr. Wilson and I are away."

"Well, if you do hear from him, could you call or text me? Bettina and I are worried about him."

"I'm sure he'll turn up eventually," said Mrs. Wilson, who didn't sound the least bit worried. "He's probably just suffering from cabin fever. You know Birdy. He's not happy unless he's climbing a tree."

Guin didn't know Birdy, but she didn't think he'd be foolish enough to go climb a tree while recovering from a gunshot wound.

"Okay," said Guin. "I hope you're right. But if you hear anything, anything at all, let me or Bettina or the police know."

"The police?"

"Yes. Bettina contacted Detective O'Loughlin at the Sanibel Police Department when she couldn't reach Birdy."

"That seems a bit dramatic. Though Bettina was always a bit of a drama queen."

Guin couldn't argue with that.

There was some kind of noise in the background, which Guin couldn't make out.

"Well, I need to go, dear. Do let me know if Birdy shows up."

"Will do," said Guin.

She ended the call and turned back to Craig.

"Well?" he asked.

Guin shook her head.

"She said she hasn't heard from him, but not to worry. Said he was probably suffering from cabin fever and snuck out to go climb a tree or something."

Craig raised his eyebrows.

"Not likely in his condition."

"That's what I told her," said Guin. "But she knows Birdy better than I do. Maybe he did do a runner. I know he wasn't happy about being cooped up at the hospital or at some fancy hotel."

"Let's assume he did check out, without telling anyone. Where did he go?" asked Craig.

"That's a very good question," said Guin.

She stopped and turned toward the elevators.

"I should have asked Bettina if Birdy took anything with him, or if anything was missing from the room."

She grabbed her phone back out and entered Bettina's number.

"Did you hear something?" came Bettina's harried voice.

"No, not yet. But I did speak with Kathy Wilson. She thinks Birdy's done a runner."

Bettina sighed.

"I thought that too, at first. But he wouldn't go this long without at least telling me that he was okay."

"Did he take his wallet and passport?"

"Unless he hid them somewhere in the room."

"And you told the detective that?"

There was silence on the other end of the line.

"I assume his phone's not there either," said Guin.

"I didn't see it on the dresser or the nightstand," Bettina replied.

"Maybe it's under the bed or in a drawer?" suggested Guin.

"If that was the case, I would have heard it, wouldn't I?" said Bettina, clearly annoyed.

"Not if it was buried under something or the ringer was turned off."

"Fine, I'll go look again. But don't you think the maids would have found it if it was under the bed?"

Guin wasn't going to argue with her.

"Just humor me and take another look. You want me and Craig to come up and help?"

"Fine. Come on up. Our rooms are on the Club level."

She gave Guin Birdy's room number.

"I need to get ready, so make it fast."

"Come on," Guin said to Craig.

"Where are we going?" he asked.

"Up to Birdy's room."

"I give up," said Guin, straightening up.

She had looked under both beds, the dresser, the couch, and anyplace the phone might have been that wasn't obvious.

"I told you," said Bettina. "It's not here."

"It was worth a shot," said Guin.

"Now, if you both will excuse me," said Bettina. "I have to get ready."

"Where're you off to?" asked Craig.

"I have dinner plans," she replied.

"Anyone we know?" asked Craig, regarding her.

Bettina turned and looked at him.

"What exactly are you implying?"

"Nothing. Just reporter's curiosity."

"Well, it's none of your business. Now, if you will excuse me?" she said, walking over to the door and opening it.

Guin and Craig exchanged looks, then headed toward the door.

"Hope you have a good dinner," Craig said, as they departed.

Bettina didn't respond, just slammed the door shut behind them.

"I don't think she likes us very much," Craig said, looking over at Guin, a bit of a smile on his face.

"Not one little bit," said Guin, returning his smile.

They headed back down to the lobby.

"Now what?" asked Guin.

"We head back to Sanibel," said Craig.

"That's it?"

"Guin, I know you're frustrated, but this is really a matter for the police."

"But the police aren't doing anything!"

"We don't know that," said Craig.

"Everyone thinks Birdy's just gone out for a walk or something."

"That's not true. O'Loughlin doesn't think that."

Guin made a huffing sound.

"What about the Naples police? Shouldn't they be conducting a search?" she asked Craig.

"Probably, but I'm sure the detective has contacts in the Naples police department."

"Fine," said Guin. "Let's go."

She took several steps and stopped.

"Birdy's things."

"What about them?" asked Craig.

"They're still at the Wilsons', waiting to be picked up."

She smiled up at Craig.

"Let me guess," he said. "You want to go pick them up."

"Well, Bettina doesn't seem in a rush to."

Craig sighed.

"Fine, if it will make you happy. But how do you know the housekeeper will just give you his stuff?"

"I'm his fiancée, remember?" she said, practically grinning now.

"I just hope you know what you're doing," said Craig.

"It'll be fine," said Guin.

"Well, you may want to let Bettina know, just in case she's headed to Sanibel later."

"Doubtful," said Guin. "But I'll text her, just in case."

She quickly sent Bettina a text, letting her know she and Craig would be picking up Birdy's things.

"All right. Let's go," she said.

CHAPTER 34

It was dark by the time Guin and Craig arrived at the Wilsons', and it didn't appear that anyone was home.

"Maybe I should come back tomorrow," said Guin.

"We're here," said Craig. "And didn't Mrs. Wilson say she has someone watching the place, a butler or maid or something?"

"Okay," said Guin.

She walked up the flight of stairs and rang the doorbell. No answer. She rang it again, then knocked on the door. She thought she heard something, but no one came to the door.

"I don't think anyone's there," she said, turning to Craig. "Or maybe they're having dinner."

"Hmm…" he replied, looking skeptical.

He rang the bell and pounded on the door.

"Anyone home?" he called.

Less than a minute later, the door was opened by a short, stocky man.

"Yes?!" the man said, clearly annoyed.

"Good evening," said Guin, smiling at the man. "I'm Guinivere Jones. I'm a friend of Mrs. Wilson's and Birdy McMurtry's. I'm here to pick up Birdy's things."

The man, who wasn't much taller than Guin, with dark wavy hair and an olive complexion, eyed her suspiciously.

"How you know Mr. Birdy?" he asked her.

"I'm his fiancée," said Guin.

The man looked down at her hand.

"Where your ring?"

"We only recently got engaged," Guin quickly explained. Which was sort of the truth.

"Mmph," replied the man, still eyeing her and Craig suspiciously.

"Ms. Betteridge was supposed to pick up his things, but she was unavoidably detained. So I offered to come get them."

The man continued to look at Guin.

"You can call her, if you like," Guin offered.

As if making a decision, the man opened the door all the way.

Craig and Guin stepped inside.

"You stay here," said the man. "I go get Mr. Birdy's things."

"Thank you, uh...?"

Guin was hoping to get the man's name, but he was already walking briskly away.

Craig took a couple steps and looked around.

"Nice place."

"It is," said Guin.

"Just the two of them live here?" he asked.

"Most of the time."

"Mmph," he replied, making a face.

As they were waiting for the man to return with Birdy's things, a woman poked her head out from the area leading to the kitchen. As soon as she saw Guin and Craig, though, she disappeared. Guin looked over at Craig. They took a couple steps toward where they had seen the woman but stopped at the sight of the man coming down the stairs with a large duffel bag.

A hissing sound came from the direction where the woman had been. The man, also hearing it, stopped and detoured to where the woman had appeared and disappeared, out of Guin's view. Guin quietly ran to near where the man had turned.

She could hear the man speaking with a woman, but she couldn't understand what they were saying. She moved a little closer but quickly moved back to where Craig was standing when she heard the man's footsteps.

He eyed her suspiciously, then placed the large duffel on the floor in front of her.

"Here," he said. "Mr. Birdy's things."

"That's everything?" asked Guin.

"*Si,*" grunted the man.

Birdy had presumably taken a small bag to the hospital, and then to the Ritz. Still it did not seem like a lot of stuff. Then again, someone who traveled as much as Birdy did probably traveled light.

"Well, thank you, Mister…"

"Tomas."

"Thank you, Mr. Tomas," said Guin.

"Just Tomas," said Tomas.

He held the front door open.

"I think that's our cue to leave," Guin whispered to Craig.

Craig picked up the duffel bag, and they left.

"*Buenas noches!*" called Craig, as Tomas slammed the door shut behind them.

They walked down the stairs, back to Guin's car. Guin crammed the duffel bag into the trunk, then got in.

"Well, he wasn't very friendly," she said to Craig, as she started the car.

"He's hiding something," said Craig. "And who was that woman?"

"I'm guessing it was the Wilsons' housekeeper, Catalina," said Guin.

"Why was she hiding then?" asked Craig.

"Maybe she's shy?" said Guin.

"Mmph," said Craig. "I'm telling you, something's not right."

Just then Guin's stomach let out a loud growl.

"Hungry?" he asked her.

Guin glanced at the clock on her dashboard.

"Oh my gosh, I totally lost track of time. Betty must be ready to kill me!"

"Nah," said Craig. "I let her know I'd be home late."

Guin's stomach growled again.

"Shh!" she commanded.

They pulled into Craig's driveway.

"Why don't you come in?" suggested Craig. "There's plenty of food."

"I don't want to intrude," said Guin. "I've already monopolized you."

"Come on," said Craig, getting out of the car. "You're practically family."

Guin's stomach rumbled again.

"If you're sure," she said. She was rather hungry.

Craig smiled at her as she followed him to the door. He took out his keys and opened it.

"Hello? Anybody home?" he called out.

Betty poked her head out of the kitchen.

"There you are!" she said. "You two eat?" she said, spying Guin lurking behind Craig.

"We were hoping you might have some leftovers on offer," said Craig.

"Well, it just so happens I have a whole roast chicken and a nice salad just waiting to be eaten."

"Have I ever told you you're amazing?" said Craig, going over to his wife and giving her a noisy kiss on the cheek.

Betty grinned, then shooed him away. Guin sighed.

Seeing how much the two of them cared about each other always made her a bit wistful. If only her marriage had been as happy.

"I had a feeling you two hadn't eaten when you sent me that message," Betty said. "I know how you get when you're working on a story."

She gave Craig a look that reminded Guin of the look her middle school teacher gave her when she forgot her homework.

"You know me so well," Craig said, going over to his wife and giving her another kiss on the cheek.

"I should hope so after over forty years," Betty replied, hustling them out of the kitchen and over to the table. "Have a seat," she commanded. "I'll be right back with the chicken and the salad."

"Can I help you with anything?" asked Guin.

"Tell you what, you can bring out the plates and silverware."

Guin dutifully followed Betty into the kitchen.

"The plates are over there," Betty said, pointing to a cabinet. "And the forks and knives are in there," she said, pointing to a drawer.

Guin obediently took out three plates and three forks and knives and placed everything on the dining table. Betty followed her out with the chicken, which she had cut into pieces and placed on a serving platter.

"There's a pitcher of filtered water in the fridge, if you want some," she told Guin.

Guin got the pitcher and brought it to the table.

"You didn't eat?" Guin asked, a bit surprised. Craig and Betty typically ate around six.

"I had a little snack. I had a feeling Craig would be home on the late side."

"My wife, the psychic," Craig said, smiling at her.

"Well, shall we eat?" Betty asked.

She pulled out her chair, then made a face.

"I forgot glasses."

"I'll go get them," said Craig.

Betty smiled at him as he went into the kitchen to retrieve them.

While they ate, Craig and Guin told Betty what they had been up to.

"What about Birdy's camera bag?" she had asked, when they had told her about retrieving Birdy's duffel bag.

"I assumed he had it with him," Guin replied.

"At the hospital?" said Betty.

Guin tried to remember if she had seen Birdy's camera bag in his hospital room. It was possible the Wilsons or Bettina had brought it to the hospital. Though what Birdy would do with it there, she didn't know. Still, considering it was probably his most important possession, she could see him asking for the bag.

"I don't remember seeing the bag at the hospital," Guin said. "But it could have been in the closet. I should text Bettina. Do you mind?"

"Go right ahead," said Betty. "Would you like some fruit or herbal tea?"

They had finished the chicken and salad and had cleared the table.

"No thank you," Guin replied, politely. "I should really get going. Let me just see if Bettina knows where Birdy's camera bag is."

She sent Bettina a text marked URGENT, asking if she knew whether Birdy had his camera bag, then waited for a reply. Several minutes went by. No reply.

"Go home and get some rest," said Craig. "You look beat."

"I feel beat," said Guin.

"Would you like a little chicken to take with you?" asked Betty.

Guin smiled at her.

"Thank you, but no." She yawned, quickly covering her mouth. "I should really get going. Fauna is probably starving."

She thanked them for feeding her, then said goodbye. Twenty minutes later, she was back at the condo.

"MEOW!" Fauna howled, as soon as Guin opened the front door. Both cats were waiting for her.

Guin sighed and gave them some food and fresh water.

"There," she said, looking down at them. (They had immediately lunged for the food as soon as it had hit the bowls.) "You're welcome."

She put the bag of cat food away, then headed to her bedroom/office. Even though it was late, and she was tired, she was determined to do a little work.

She checked her phone for messages, but there was no word from Bettina... or Birdy, or the detective. She sighed and sent fresh texts to Birdy and the detective, asking them to write her back or call her. She stared down at the phone, willing them to respond. After a minute went by with no replies, she put down her phone and booted up her computer.

CHAPTER 35

It was just after seven when Guin opened her eyes. She had been too restless to go to bed at her usual time. So she had wound up watching one of those mystery movies on the Hallmark Channel and hadn't fallen asleep until nearly midnight.

She yawned and looked at the foot of the bed, where both cats were still asleep, or pretending to be. She smiled and reached for her phone, turning it on. Then she padded down the short hallway to her bathroom.

There were no messages from the detective, or Bettina, or Birdy. She was hoping that at least Bettina would have written her back, but she was no doubt busy. As for the detective... Well, she knew better than to expect him to get back to her right away. Of course, the person she really wanted to hear from was Birdy. But there was still no sign of him.

She stared at her phone for several seconds, then put it down on her night table. She walked over to her computer and booted it up. She stared at the screen, then decided she needed coffee first.

She returned to her computer ten minutes later, a mug of fresh hot coffee in her hands. She sat down and pulled up her notes. She was reading through them when her phone started buzzing. It was a text from Shelly.

"You still coming to the BBQ tonight?"

Right. The barbeque.

"I'll be there!" Guin wrote her back. "Can I bring something?" Though she didn't feel like making anything.

"Nah, we're good," Shelly texted. "Just bring yourself."

"OK," typed Guin. "Gotta work. C u later."

"Bye," Shelly wrote.

Guin put her phone in the drawer, so she wouldn't be distracted. Then she immediately took it out. She wanted to be able to hear the notification if the detective or Birdy or Bettina contacted her.

Finally, a little before eleven, Guin received a text from Bettina.

"Pretty sure Birdy left his camera bag at the Wilsons'," it read.

Guin made a face.

"Only got a duffel bag," Guin wrote her back.

"You must have forgotten it," Bettina replied.

Guin made another face. If there had been a camera bag, she and Craig would surely have noticed it and taken it with them.

"Well it wasn't with the duffel bag," Guin texted her. "Can you call over there and find out what's up?"

Guin waited for a reply, but none came.

She went back to her computer. She had spent the morning going over her notes regarding who might wish to harm Birdy. While she had come across several people who might hold a grudge against him, she couldn't see any of them attempting to poison, shoot, and/or kidnap him. She sighed and put her head in her hands.

As she closed her eyes, she heard her phone buzz. It was another text from Bettina.

"Tomas says he doesn't have the camera bag. Says Birdy probably has it if you didn't take it."

Guin stared at her phone. The only bag she saw had been the large, green duffel bag.

"Well, I don't have it," typed Guin.

No reply, again.

"You hear from the police?" Guin texted her.

She waited for a reply, but none was forthcoming. Guin sighed and looked back at her monitor. Could Birdy have taken his camera bag? If Kathy Wilson's theory was true, Birdy very well may have.

Guin sent a text to Craig.

"You there?" she wrote.

No reply. Maybe he was out fishing.

Suddenly her mind flashed to Digby's yacht. Digby. She had forgotten about that photo she had found of Digby with the Wilsons. She did a search and found it again. The photo had been taken at a fundraiser on Sanibel, for some nonprofit called Healing Plants, Healing Bodies, which she had never heard of.

She picked up her phone and called Ginny's mobile. If the event had taken place on Sanibel, Ginny would know about it.

"Yes?" said Ginny.

"So, I'm looking at this photo, taken a few years ago, of Digby with John and Kathy Wilson, and the CMO of Natura, a guy named Dick Grayson. And I'm wondering if you recall the fundraiser they all attended, for some nonprofit called Healing Plants, Healing Bodies."

"Hmm…" said Ginny, thinking.

Guin waited.

"About three years ago, you say?" asked Ginny.

Guin went back to her monitor, to find the date on the page.

"Yes, it was just shy of three years ago, during the season."

Guin waited for Ginny to say something.

"Got it!" said Ginny. "Healing Plants, Healing Bodies is one of the charities that Kathy is involved with. She had a breast cancer scare a few years back, and she got very into alternative medicine."

"Is she on the board?" asked Guin.

"I don't know," said Ginny. "I just know she was very involved with them."

Guin made a note to check out the charity as soon as she got off the phone.

"Any idea what Digby and Dick Grayson were doing there?"

"Well, as Natura is in the business, as they say, Kathy had probably asked them to sponsor the fundraiser. Good publicity."

Especially with all the negative publicity Natura had been getting, thought Guin.

"So the Wilsons are friends with Digby?"

"I don't know if they're friends exactly," said Ginny.

They certainly looked chummy in that photo, thought Guin. But she didn't say anything.

"Well, thanks for your help, Ginny."

"You find out anything about our missing ornithologist?" she asked.

"Not yet," said Guin. "Kathy Wilson thinks he just snuck off somewhere. Went walkabout or something. But the man was recovering from a gunshot wound."

"Well, keep me posted," said Ginny. "And get me that review of the Paper Fig Kitchen."

Guin sighed.

"Will do."

She ended the call and went back to her monitor, staring at the photo of the Wilsons with Digby and Dick Grayson.

She typed "Natura John Wilson" into her search engine and was about to hit enter when her phone rang. She grabbed it, thinking it might be Birdy or the detective, but it was Craig.

"Oh, hi Craig."

"Don't sound so disappointed," Craig replied, chuckling.

"Sorry," said Guin. "I was hoping it was Birdy or the detective."

"Still no word?" asked Craig.

"No," said Guin.

"So how can I help?"

"Can you check with your contacts in the local police departments and see if anyone's heard anything about Birdy? Also, I found a photo of Digby Blyleven and Dick Grayson with the Wilsons. Turns out they're both involved with some charity called Healing Plants, Healing Bodies."

"You think there's a connection?"

"I don't know," said Guin. "I'm doing some research. But I never heard of this charity before. Have you?"

"Doesn't ring a bell. Anything else?"

"Yeah, Bettina finally got back to me. She says Birdy's camera bag isn't at the hotel. She actually accused me of having it or forgetting to get it from the Wilsons'."

Craig harrumphed.

"I may be a bit forgetful at times," Guin continued, "but I think I would have noticed if there had been a camera bag by the duffel."

Guin heard some noise in the background and Craig saying "okay" to someone.

"Hey Guin, I need to go," Craig said. "Can I get back to you later?

"Of course!" said Guin.

"Thanks," said Craig. "I'll check in with you after I get home."

Guin went back to her computer and typed in "Dick Grayson."

"Let's find out a bit more about you, boy wonder."

He was perfect. At least on paper.

That was Guin's take after going through Dick Grayson's LinkedIn profile and reading about him online.

Graduated cum laude from Vanderbilt. Captain of the lacrosse team. Served in the Marines, where he earned a marksmanship competition badge.

She paused. So he certainly had the skill to have shot Birdy.

She continued reading.

MBA from Harvard. Married with two children, a boy and a girl. Chief marketing officer at Natura for five years now. On the boards of several charities, including Healing Plants, Healing Bodies, whose address was a post office box on Sanibel.

She clicked on Images.

"Hold on," said Guin, pausing at a photo of a smiling Dick Grayson raising a glass of Champagne. The photo credit read "Briony Betteridge."

Guin quickly typed "Dick Grayson Briony Betteridge" into her search bar. There were at least a dozen photos of Dick Grayson, taken by Briony, and—yes!—there was even one of him with his arm around her, both of them smiling.

Of course, it could have been totally innocent.

"Yeah, right," said Guin.

Suddenly, a thought occurred to her. She typed "Dick Grayson Naples" into her search engine and hit "Enter."

According to her search, there were a dozen people with the name Richard Grayson who were living or had recently lived in Naples, Florida.

She went through the search results, looking to see if any of them could be Dick Grayson, the CMO of Natura.

"Ding, ding, ding!" she said, finding a listing that fit the bill.

One Richard Grayson, 40, had purchased a house in

downtown Naples two years ago, according to property tax records. It had to be him.

"So is Dick Grayson your mystery man, Briony?" Guin mused. And was he in Naples at the time of the Wilsons' party and Birdy's shooting?

Guin retrieved the guest list Kathy Wilson had sent her and slowly scanned it. How had she missed it before? There, about a third of the way down, was one Richard Grayson.

CHAPTER 36

Guin was fixing herself some lunch and going over everything in her head when she remembered she still had Birdy's duffel bag. She had put it in the guest room closet and went to retrieve it. She flicked on the light in the guest room, got the bag, and placed it on one of the twin beds. She felt a little funny about going through Birdy's things without his permission, but maybe there was something there that could help her find him.

She took a deep breath, exhaled, then opened the bag.

Birdy was clearly an experienced traveler. Everything was neatly rolled or folded, and there was nothing extraneous. She didn't find a toiletry kit, but he had probably taken it with him to the hospital and then the hotel.

She carefully took each item out of the bag and placed it on the bed, until the bag was empty. Then she scanned the contents. There didn't appear to be anything unusual. There were pants and shirts, socks and underwear, some pajama bottoms and a couple of t-shirts, a pair of dressier shoes, a jacket, and a sweater.

She felt around the inside of the bag, looking for a secret compartment, but she didn't find one. She checked the side pockets. Nothing there either.

She stared at the empty bag and the piles of clothing and sighed.

"Forgive me, Birdy, if I don't put everything back the way you like it," she said.

Then she began to place each item back in the bag. As she was picking up one of the button-down shirts to put it back, she felt something inside, like a very thin piece of cardboard. She put the shirt down and reached inside.

"Well, what do you know?" she said, extracting a manila envelope.

She held the envelope up to the light. There was no writing on either side, but there was definitely something inside. She opened the flap and carefully pulled out a folded piece of paper, hoping she wasn't contaminating evidence.

She unfolded the paper. On it, written in neat block letters, was a single sentence: SAY ANYTHING AND YOU'LL BE SORRY.

Say what and to whom? Guin wondered. Could the message writer be warning Birdy about saying something to the press or law enforcement about Natura? Could the note have come from the killer, or would-be killer?

Guin examined the note, holding it by the edges. The writing was neat. It could have been penned by a man or a woman.

She turned on the lamp next to the bed and held the piece of paper over it, looking for some sort of clue, a watermark, perhaps. But she didn't see anything.

She put the note back in the envelope and set it aside. Then she felt the rest of Birdy's things, in case there was another hidden note somewhere. But she didn't find anything.

Guin stared at the envelope. Had Birdy placed it in the shirt, or had someone else done it? She had no idea. Birdy hadn't mentioned the note, but that didn't mean anything.

She put the envelope back in the duffel bag, on top of his things. Then she reached into her back pocket for her phone and called the detective on his mobile.

"This better be good," said the detective.

"I found a note, hidden among Birdy's things."

"What kind of note?" asked the detective. "A ransom note?"

"No," said Guin. "It said, 'Say anything and you'll be sorry.' It's written in all caps."

"You touch the note?" asked the detective.

Guin winced. She knew she probably should have worn latex gloves (which she actually kept a stash of), but the damage was done.

"Yes, and the envelope."

The detective didn't say anything.

"You want it?" asked Guin. "I'm pretty busy today, but I could give it to you at Shelly and Steve's later."

"Fine," replied the detective, a few seconds later.

Guin smiled.

"I'll see you tonight."

The detective ended the call.

Her phone still in her hand, Guin called Craig.

"I found something, in Birdy's things," Guin blurted out as soon as Craig said hello. "A note."

"What does it say?" Craig asked.

"It says, 'Say anything and you'll be sorry.' And it's written in all caps."

"Hmm," said Craig. "Any idea who might have written it?"

"I have lots of ideas, but I doubt I could prove any of them. I'm also not sure if Birdy actually saw the note."

"Why's that?" asked Craig.

"I found it inside one of his button-down shirts, in a manila envelope, tucked in, like one of those pieces of cardboard you find when you send your shirts out to be laundered, or when they're new."

"Was the envelope sealed? Any writing on it?"

"It was unsealed, and no writing. The note was folded up neatly inside. I told the detective. I'm going to give it to him later."

"He'll probably have it checked for prints," said Craig.

"And will no doubt find a few of mine," Guin sighed.

"Don't beat yourself up about it," said Craig. "It happens. The important thing is you found something that may help the police find Birdy."

"I hope so. So, were you out fishing this morning?" Guin asked him.

"I was."

"You catch anything?"

"Nothing to write home about," he said. "But I did hear something interest."

"Oh?" said Guin.

Craig's fishing buddies included members of the Sanibel police department, the Lee County Sheriff's office, the local medical examiners' offices, and the Sanibel and Captiva fire departments.

"I asked, just in passing, if any of the guys had heard anything about a missing guy or a shooting over on West Gulf, and Joe, who works over at the Blue Dolphin Cottages, said he'd seen a police car parked over at Beach Access #6 the past few days and wondered what was up. Then Jimbo said he heard some guy got shot over by there."

"Did Joe or Jimbo happen to mention Birdy?" asked Guin.

"No," said Craig.

Guin was disappointed. Neither bit of information was very helpful.

"But," said Craig, "I did hear another interesting tidbit."

"Oh?" said Guin.

"Apparently there was some kind of disturbance

reported coming from Blyleven's yacht, not long after McMurtry disappeared from the Ritz."

Guin's eyebrows shot up.

"Do you think there could be a connection? Did the police search the boat?

"The disturbance was called in by people aboard two of the neighboring yachts. But when the police showed up to check it out, Blyleven's crew wouldn't let them board without a search warrant," Craig replied.

"Sounds suspicious to me," Guin said. "Who told you about this?"

"One of my sources. He was there."

Guin knew better than to ask Craig exactly who his source was.

"So, you think Digby could have kidnapped Birdy and is keeping him on his yacht?"

"It's possible," said Craig.

"And what about West Gulf drive? Beach Access #6 is right by the Wilsons'."

"Well, it is where Birdy got shot. Maybe they were following up," said Craig.

"They also could have been checking to see if he had gone back there, to get his things, before leaving town," mused Guin. "Though I'm not buying that Birdy went off without telling anyone. When I last saw him, he was in no condition to lug around a big, heavy bag, or even a camera bag."

She paused for a few seconds.

"So are the police going to get a search warrant and search Digby's yacht?"

"Don't know," said Craig.

Guin felt frustrated.

"Did the guys know or hear anything else?"

"Nothing pertaining to McMurtry," he replied.

"Well, let me know if you hear anything else," she said.

"Will do."

"Oh, I almost forgot," Guin said. "I did a little digging into Dick Grayson, and it turns out he has a place in Naples and appears to be quite chummy with one Briony Betteridge."

Craig whistled.

"I wonder if he's the married man she's been seeing. And," she added, "he was on the guest list for the Wilsons' party."

"You think the two of them had something to do with Birdy being poisoned?" Craig asked.

"They both had motive," Guin replied. "And Natura is a big distributor of mandrake root. It would be quite easy for Grayson to get some and then slip it into Birdy's food."

Though Guin wasn't sure how exactly he could have done that. But it was possible.

"Hmm..." said Craig.

"Anyway, I'm going to see the detective later. Maybe I can pry something out of him."

"Good luck with that."

Was that skepticism?

"Well, I should let you go," Guin said. "I'll follow up with you later."

Guin ended the call and went back to her computer. She had a while yet until she needed to head over to Shelly and Steve's place, and she wanted to add the new information to her notes.

She stared at her entry for Healing Plants, Healing Bodies. There wasn't much there. She typed "Healing Plants, Healing Bodies" into her search engine. There were thousands of results, but she didn't see any with a charity by that name. She added the word *charity* to the end of the phrase and hit "Enter" again. This time she found it.

She clicked on the link going to the charity's website. It looked like it had been designed in the 1990s, with lots of dated stock photos. She clicked on the About Us page. It contained the usual generic mission statement. She clicked on the Donate button. It took her to a form, where you could enter your credit card information. Next, she clicked on the Contact Us page. There was another form but no actual contact information—no address, or phone number, or name.

"Well, that wasn't very helpful," Guin said to Flora, who was lounging atop her desk. "Let's see what Charity Navigator has to say."

She went to the Charity Navigator site and typed in "Healing Plants, Healing Bodies." She scrolled through a list of nonprofits with similar names until she found it. It had a two-star rating, not very good, and it had supplied no information for the last couple of years.

"Hmm…" said Guin.

She scanned the entry. There, under Board Leadership, was the name J. Douglas Blyleven, and underneath it, listed as CEO, was John Wilson.

"Very interesting," said Guin.

She clicked on the CEO bio. There was a picture of Mr. Wilson, clearly taken many years before, and a summary of his various positions and interests. She started to read and immediately stopped.

"An angel investor, Mr. Wilson has helped several startups go on to achieve great success, including Natura Natraceuticals…"

She stared at the screen. So that explained the Natura connection. But could the Wilsons have had anything to do with Birdy's troubles? She shook her head. The Wilsons thought of Birdy like a son.

She continued working until a calendar reminder popped

up, telling her she needed to be at Shelly and Steve's shortly.

"Oops, time to go," she said, gently removing Fauna from her lap. She had fallen asleep there a while before.

Guin went to her closet to change. After staring at her clothes for several minutes, she pulled on a pair of skinny jeans and a flowy, long-sleeved top. Then she went into the bathroom, combed her hair, and applied a little makeup. As Steve's new boss would be there, she thought she should look a little nicer than usual.

She eyed herself in the mirror.

"Good enough," she said.

She grabbed her bag and her keys, slipped on a pair of heels, and headed out the door.

CHAPTER 37

Guin rang the doorbell a little after six and waited for someone to answer. A minute later, Steve opened the door.

"Hey," said Guin.

"Hey yourself," replied Steve, smiling at her. "Glad you could make it."

"Thanks for inviting me," she replied.

She followed him down the hall.

"Can I get you a beer?"

"That would be great," said Guin.

He led her out to the lanai, where a handful of people were milling around, drinking beer and chatting, including Shelly, who as soon as she spotted Guin came rushing over.

"There you are!" Shelly cried. "I was worried you wouldn't show."

"I'm here," said Guin, taking the beer Steve handed her and taking a sip.

She glanced around.

"He's not here yet," said Shelly.

"Who?" asked Guin, innocently.

"You know who," said Shelly. "The detective."

"He told me he might be a little late," Guin said.

"So, any word on Birdy?" Shelly asked in a loud whisper.

"No," said Guin, taking another sip of her beer. "It's like he vanished into thin air."

Just then the doorbell rang. Guin and Shelly both turned.

"I should get that," said Shelly. "You want to come with me and see who it is?"

She grinned at Guin, who didn't return the smile, then walked quickly to the front door. Guin following her at a discreet distance.

"Detective!" Shelly practically shouted, upon seeing him. "Come in, come in! We've been expecting you."

Guin rolled her eyes.

"Can I get you a beer?" she asked him, escorting him out to the lanai.

"I can only stay for a little while," he replied.

He spotted Guin and the two of them stood there, neither saying anything. Shelly looked from one to the other.

"I'll be right back with that beer," she told him.

The detective took a few more steps, until he was just a foot or so away from Guin.

"You look nice," he said.

"Thanks," said Guin.

They continued to stand there, awkwardly, for several seconds.

"Here you go," Shelly said, thrusting a beer at the detective.

"Thanks," he said.

"We need to talk," Guin said in a low voice.

"About?" asked the detective, taking a swig of his beer.

"You know what about," Guin replied.

The detective's face remained neutral.

Guin motioned him to the edge of the lanai.

"I think Birdy's been kidnapped, and Natura has something to do with it," she said in a low voice, leaning into him.

The detective eyed her but didn't say anything.

"I've been doing some digging," Guin continued, "into

Natura and some of its executives. Both the CEO and the CMO were in the area when Birdy was poisoned and shot at. And Birdy had told me before he disappeared that he had discovered something, something that made him want out of his contract with Natura, a very lucrative contract, by all accounts. But when he asked to be let go, they refused and threatened to sue him, or worse, if he went public with any of his accusations."

Guin reached into her bag.

"And here's the note I found."

She handed the envelope to the detective.

He held it at his side.

"Aren't you going to say something?"

"What would you like me to say, Ms. Jones?" asked the detective, looking at her.

They were standing very close together, and Guin could see flecks of amber in the detective's tawny-colored eyes. She felt herself growing warm.

"I'd like you to tell me what you know and if you've located Birdy. I heard the Lee County Sheriff's Office sent some cops over to investigate a disturbance aboard Digby Blyleven's yacht a couple hours after Birdy had disappeared, but the crew wouldn't let them board without a search warrant."

The detective raised an eyebrow.

"Well?" she said.

It was like they were having a staring contest.

Guin was about to speak when she eyed Shelly coming toward them.

"Come along, you two," she said. "We're about to eat."

She shooed them over to the big dining table. On it were platters of sausages, chicken, and fish, along with a big salad, garlic bread, and corn.

"Looks great, Shell," said Guin, eyeing the copious amounts of food.

Shelly introduced them to everyone, then indicated for them to sit. She had placed the detective next to Steve's boss and Guin a little way away. Guin had wanted to speak more with the detective, but she didn't get a chance until later.

"Would you excuse us?" asked Guin, after dessert—a platter of fruit and some cookies—had been served.

The detective had been chatting with Steve's boss, who, it turned out, was also a Red Sox fan.

Oh great, Guin had thought. Now I'll never get a word in. But she finally managed to pull the detective away.

"So, do you know where Birdy is or don't you?" Guin hissed.

The detective looked at her.

"No," he finally replied.

Guin was crestfallen. But then she thought she saw something flash across the detective's face.

"But you have an idea," she said.

"If I tell you, you have to promise not to go investigate. Deal?"

She made a face.

"This isn't a game, Ms. Jones. We're dealing with some very dangerous people."

"You mean Natura?" said Guin. "I covered much bigger companies when I was writing about business up in New York. Natura doesn't scare me."

Though none of the businesses she had covered had sent someone to take a shot at her, at least as far as she knew.

"It should," said the detective.

"So is Blyleven holding Birdy prisoner on his yacht?"

"You going to stop snooping?"

"It's not snooping. It's reporting. And it's my job."

The detective did not look happy.

"I've asked you once, Ms. Jones, now I'm telling you: Let the police handle this."

"Fine. Don't help me," said Guin. So much for getting the detective to reveal what he knew.

"I need to go," said the detective. "Please thank the Silvermans for me."

Guin looked at her watch.

"But it's not even 8:30. Where are you off to?"

"Work," he replied, tersely.

"I'll go with you," Guin said.

She took a few steps back towards the dining area.

"Shelly! Steve! The detective and I have to run. I'll call you tomorrow!"

Shelly came rushing over.

"You have to go?" she said, looking from one to the other.

"*I* need to go," said the detective. "Ms. Jones here will be staying."

"I will not," stated Guin.

Shelly looked from one to the other.

"I'll just leave you two to it," she said, sweetly. "Thanks for coming! You can let yourselves out."

CHAPTER 38

As soon as they had stepped outside and gone down the steps, Guin grabbed the detective's arm.

He looked down at her hand on his arm and Guin removed it.

"Please, detective. Just tell me something. I'll never forgive myself if something's happened to Birdy."

Guin gave him her best pitiful look. The detective sighed.

"We have a lead."

"To where Birdy is?" Guin asked.

"Yes," replied the detective.

Guin looked hopeful.

"But I don't want you going anywhere near the place."

"As long as you find Birdy," she said, trying to look compliant.

He eyed her suspiciously.

"I have to go. Good night, Ms. Jones."

"Aren't you going to walk me to my car?"

He stopped and looked at her.

"Would you like me to walk you to your car?"

Guin didn't know what had come over her, but she nodded her head.

"It's down the block."

The detective followed her to her car.

"Thanks for coming tonight," she said to him, as they

stood next to the Mini. "I'm sure you scored Steve some points with his boss."

The detective didn't say anything.

Guin took a step toward him.

A light breeze swept by, blowing some curls across Guin's face.

The detective reached over and moved them aside.

Guin could feel her heart beating faster. She looked up at him, her lips parting.

The next thing she knew, he was kissing her, and she was kissing him back. A minute later, or was it five? he took a step back.

"I have to go," he said, gruffly.

Guin stood there, a bit dazed. What had just happened?

"Okay," she said. "Good night, detective."

He turned and headed back down the block. Guin waited until he got to his car, then climbed into the Mini. As soon as he pulled out, she followed him.

He took a left onto Middle Gulf and headed west, taking it all the way to West Gulf Drive. Guin had a feeling she knew where he was going.

She continued to follow him, keeping a safe distance. Though she was worried he would spot the Mini. Fortunately, it was dark.

He parked his car in the lot for Beach Access #6 and got out. She watched as he headed down the Wilsons' driveway, then she slowly continued down West Gulf and took the spot next to his.

She made her way silently down the Wilsons' driveway, using only the meager light from her cell phone to illuminate the way.

She stopped halfway down, scanning for the detective. He was over by some trees, speaking with someone, probably a police officer. She moved a little closer, trying not to make any noise. She took another step, then her phone started to buzz.

"Shh!" she told it, desperately trying to silence it.

The detective and the man whipped around, and Guin saw that the man was pointing a gun right at her. Guin held up her hands.

"Don't shoot!" she said. "It's me, Guin, Guin Jones."

She looked over at the detective. She couldn't see his face in the dark, but she had a feeling he wasn't happy.

"You followed me?" he said, trying to control his anger. "After I told you to stay out of this?"

Guin could tell he was furious.

"You could have been killed."

"I'm sorry," she said.

"You can put the gun away, Rayburn" the detective told the other man. "As for you, Ms. Jones…"

"Sorry, Officer Rayburn," Guin said to the police officer.

He nodded in her direction.

Guin had met Officer Rayburn when she was investigating the murder of Veronica Swales.

"I told you to leave the detective work to the police," said the detective.

"And I told you I needed to find out what happened to Birdy."

The detective sighed.

"So you think he's in there?" asked Guin, looking up at the house.

The detective didn't reply.

Suddenly, Guin felt a slight breeze and heard what sounded like a sharp crack.

"Duck!" shouted the detective, throwing himself at Guin and shoving her to the ground.

Someone had taken a shot at them.

Officer Rayburn returned fire, though Guin had no idea

what or who he was firing at.

Seconds later, all was quiet.

"Are you okay?" asked the detective, helping Guin up.

"Just a little bruised," replied Guin. "Was someone shooting at us?"

"Yes," said Officer Rayburn, still holding his gun. "And he could still be out there. I don't think I hit him, or I would have heard something."

"Where's your car?" asked the detective.

"Next to yours," she replied.

He went over to her and took her by the arm.

"Let's go," he said.

"What about the gunman?" asked Guin.

"Officer Rayburn, will you cover us?"

Rayburn nodded.

When they got back to the parking area, the detective barked at her.

"I should have you arrested."

"For what?"

"Interfering with an investigation."

"So is Birdy at the Wilsons'?"

Guin looked at the detective, waiting for an answer. But the detective didn't reply.

"I want you to unlock that car, get in, and drive home," he said, still clasping her arm.

Guin turned so she was facing him. He was a head taller than her and much broader. In the dim light, he looked a bit menacing, but Guin wasn't afraid.

"Why won't you tell me what's going on?"

"I told you, I don't want you getting hurt," he replied, gruffly.

"Why?" Guin asked again, looking up into his eyes.

They stood there for several seconds.

"Sir?"

It was Officer Rayburn.

The detective let go of Guin's arm and took a step back.

"Goodnight, Ms. Jones. I trust you can find your way home?"

"I'm going," she said. "But you're not going to stop me from trying to find Birdy."

The detective turned and followed Officer Rayburn back toward the Wilson house.

"I think Birdy's at the Wilsons'," Guin said to Craig. She had called him as soon as she got back to the condo.

"You sure?" asked Craig.

"He's either there or on Digby's yacht."

"And you know this how?"

"Well, you were the one who mentioned the yacht, and I just followed the detective to the Wilsons' place, and—"

Craig cut her off.

"You followed the detective?"

"Yes," said Guin, "he met Officer Rayburn over there. Rayburn was clearly keeping an eye on the place. But before I could ask them what was going on, someone shot at us."

"Someone shot at you?" said Craig.

"Yes, but Officer Rayburn shot back, and no one got hurt."

"You could have been killed," said Craig.

"But I wasn't. And I need to get into that house."

"You really think that's wise?"

Guin made a face.

"I need to find out if Birdy is in there."

Craig sighed.

"Maybe you should leave the detective work to the detective."

"You sound just like him," said Guin, annoyed. Of all people, Craig should understand.

"Yeah, well, he has a point."

Guin rolled her eyes.

"Like that would have stopped you?"

Craig didn't reply.

"So, will you help me sneak into the Wilsons' place?"

Craig sighed.

"Can it wait until tomorrow? Betty wants me to come watch *The Great British Baking Show* with her."

Guin smiled.

"I love that show! Go, watch with Betty. Just don't tell me who wins. You watching the new one?"

"Yeah, though Betty's still upset about Mary Berry not being on."

"Understandable," said Guin. "Well, goodnight. Talk to you tomorrow."

The next morning, Guin woke up a little after six and decided to go to the beach. She sprang out of bed, went to the bathroom, got dressed, quickly gave the cats some food, threw some things in her fanny pack, grabbed her shelling bag and her keys, and headed out the door.

Despite the low tide, though, Blind Pass was a fail. There were barely any shells, or good shells, on the beach, and Guin felt frustrated.

"Not finding anything?" asked a familiar voice.

"Lenny!" said Guin, looking up. "I didn't see you there."

"Obviously," said Lenny. "Got a lot on your mind?"

"I do," said Guin. "I was hoping I'd come out here and find a Scotch bonnet, or a true tulip, or a nice, big horse conch to distract me. But no such luck."

"You should have been out here the other day. My friend Karen found a great big Scotch bonnet just over there," he said, pointing.

"Is that supposed to make me feel better?" asked Guin. "Because it doesn't."

"You're in a mood," said Lenny.

"Yeah, well," said Guin, looking down at the wrack line, willing the sea to disgorge a junonia, or some other good shell, and lay it right at her feet.

"You want to tell Uncle Lenny what's bugging you?"

Guin sighed.

"I'm worried about Birdy, you know, the ornithologist, the one I interviewed? He's gone missing, and I think the detective knows where he is, but he won't tell me anything."

"Hmm…" said Lenny.

"I have a hunch where he might be, but the detective and Craig don't want me to go snooping. They think it's too dangerous."

She left out the bit about someone shooting at her.

"I see…" said Lenny.

"I just want to make sure Birdy is okay. And if he is at the Wilsons'…"

She trailed off. Suddenly, an idea occurred to her. She smiled up at Lenny.

"I've gotta go. Thanks, Lenny!"

Lenny smiled back at her.

"Glad I could help," he said.

Guin turned and practically ran down the beach.

CHAPTER 39

Guin called Kathy Wilson's mobile as soon as she got home from the beach and waited for her to pick up. The phone rang at least five times, then it went to voicemail.

"Hey, Kathy," Guin said. "This is Guin Jones. I was hoping to speak with you, about a new piece I'm working on. Give me a call back as soon as you can at [she gave her number]. Thanks."

Next, she called Shelly.

"Hey, what's up?" Shelly asked. "You and the detective, you know…" she added, conspiratorially.

Guin felt her face turning red.

"No!" she said, a bit too adamantly.

"Uh-huh," said Shelly.

"It's not like that," Guin insisted.

"Whatever you say, girlfriend."

Guin gritted her teeth.

"ANYWAY," she said. "You game for a little sleuthing?"

"Ooh, what did you have in mind?"

Shelly was always up for a little sleuthing, especially if it involved snooping.

Guin smiled.

"I want to sneak into the Wilson place and see if Birdy is there."

"Why don't you just ring the doorbell and ask to see him?"

"Because I don't think he's necessarily there of his own free will."

"You think they've got him tied up in the basement?" asked Shelly.

"Something like that," said Guin.

"And you want to rescue him?"

"Something like that," said Guin.

"How romantic!" said Shelly.

"Romance has nothing to do with it," stated Guin.

"Whatever you say. So, how can I help?"

Guin explained her plan to Shelly. Shelly asked a few questions, which Guin tried to answer.

"So, we good?" Guin asked her, after going over what she needed Shelly to do one more time.

"Just text me when you're ready," said Shelly.

"Will do," said Guin. "Just don't tell Steve or anyone what we're up to."

"What if we're caught?" asked Shelly, a bit nervously.

"We won't be," said Guin. Though as she said it, she felt a little less sure.

Guin was doing research on the Paper Fig Kitchen when her phone rang.

"Hello?" she said.

"Guin, dear, it's Kathy Wilson. I just got your message."

"Hi Kathy," said Guin. "Thank you so much for getting back to me. Are you still away?"

"Yes, until Wednesday."

Good, thought Guin. That would give her enough time.

"You mentioned you wanted to talk to me, for an article?"

"Yes," said Guin. "I know you're involved with a number of charitable causes on the island, and I'm working on a piece for February, for around Valentine's Day, on local nonprofits and how people can share the love."

Guin hadn't actually been assigned such a piece, but she was sure Ginny would greenlight it if Guin asked her to. Or so she hoped.

"What a wonderful idea!" said Mrs. Wilson. "How can I help?"

"Well, I thought you and I could have a chat, in person, and I could pick your brain. But if you're away…"

"Could we get together this Friday? Would that give you enough time?"

More than enough, thought Guin.

"Friday is fine," Guin replied. "What time?"

"Why don't you come over for lunch? Catalina can whip something up. She's an excellent cook."

"Sounds great," said Guin. She paused. "So does Catalina live with you?"

"Oh no," said Mrs. Wilson. "She and her husband, Tomas, have a place in Fort Myers. They come to our place a few times a week. He takes care of our landscaping and does odd jobs for us, and Catalina cleans and cooks."

"Have they been looking after the place while you and John have been away?"

"Yes, why?"

"I just figured, a big place like yours, you might worry about it getting robbed."

Kathy Wilson laughed.

"On Sanibel? Very unlikely. In fact, don't tell anyone, but we often leave the side door unlocked as John is always forgetting his keys."

"Mum's the word," said Guin, grinning. "So, have you by any chance heard from Birdy?"

"As a matter of fact, I did," replied Mrs. Wilson.

That caught Guin off guard.

"You did?" asked Guin.

"Yes," said Mrs. Wilson. "You sound surprised."

"Did he call you?" asked Guin.

"No, he sent an email, letting us know he was fine."

"Did he say where he was?" asked Guin.

"No, but he said not to worry," replied Mrs. Wilson.

Guin made a face.

"I see," said Guin.

"I told you, Birdy can take of himself. He probably got to the Ritz, took one look around, and decided to bolt. Very much like Birdy."

But why had he waited so long to let people know if he was all right? wondered Guin.

"And when did you receive this email from him?" Guin asked her.

"Late last night," replied Mrs. Wilson.

"And did he say anything else?" Guin asked.

"No, but that's typical Birdy."

"I wonder why he didn't email me," Guin said.

"He's probably off in some jungle somewhere," said Mrs. Wilson. She paused. "You develop a little crush on him?" She chuckled.

Guin was about to say something, but Mrs. Wilson cut her off.

"It's okay. If I was younger, I'd probably have a crush on him, too. He's quite charming. You two made a very handsome couple. I had a feeling there might be something going on."

Guin groaned inwardly. She absolutely did not have a crush on Birdy.

"I'm just concerned about him," she said. "He hasn't returned any of my messages."

"Well, I'm sure he will, eventually," said Mrs. Wilson. "I need to go. Is there something else I can help you with?"

"No," said Guin. "Thanks for letting me know about Birdy. I'll see you Friday at noon."

"Wonderful," said Mrs. Wilson. "See you then."

They ended the call and Guin stared out the window. She wanted to believe Mrs. Wilson, that Birdy was okay, but her gut told her not to. Something just didn't feel right.

She picked up her phone and called Bettina's number. It rang several times before Bettina picked up.

"Yes?!"

Why did Bettina always sound annoyed? Guin was going to say something snarky, but she controlled herself.

"So, have you heard from Birdy?" Guin asked her.

"As a matter of fact, I received an email from him last night," Bettina replied.

Guin raised her eyebrows.

"Oh? What did the email say?"

"He said he was fine and not to worry."

"That was it?" asked Guin.

"Pretty much. But that's typical Birdy," Bettina replied.

"And you're not concerned?"

"I was, but, like I said, it's typical Birdy. At least he's all right."

"We don't know that," said Guin.

"What do you mean?" asked Bettina.

"I mean, he disappears while recovering from a gunshot wound, doesn't say anything to anyone, then sends a quick email, and everything's okay?"

"You don't know Birdy," said Bettina.

"No, I don't," said Guin. "But it sounds suspicious to me."

Bettina sighed.

"Look, Guin. I appreciate your concern, but Birdy is fine. You don't know him like I do. He'd rather camp out in a tent than stay in some big, fancy hotel. He probably took one look at this place and decided to bolt."

"And ran off without telling anyone?"

Bettina sighed again.

"I don't forgive him for giving us all a scare, but he said he's fine, and not to worry, and that he would write more soon."

Hmm… thought Guin. She was not at all convinced that Birdy was fine, but she didn't feel like arguing with Bettina.

"Well, if you say so…" Guin said.

"I do. And now I have an appointment to attend to. So, if there isn't anything else…"

"Did you try calling his phone?" Guin asked.

"He said in his note that he had horrible cell service," replied Bettina.

But he was able to send an email? Guin was definitely suspicious now. But Bettina either didn't care or didn't want to know if there was a problem.

"Well, if you hear from him again, would you let me know?" asked Guin.

"Sure," said Bettina. "Now I really must go."

She hung up and Guin stood there, gazing out her bedroom window at the golf course and the jungle-like greenery beyond. Something wasn't right.

Just then her phone pinged. She looked down. There was a new email message, from Birdy.

"I'm fine," said the message. "Had to get away. Sorry for worrying you."

Guin made a face. The timing of the email only made her more suspicious that something was up.

She sat down at her computer and opened the email on her browser. The email said it was from Birdy McMurtry, but when she hovered over the address, it was not the one she had for him. Of course, he could have multiple email addresses, but she doubted it.

She phoned Craig. Thankfully, he picked up.

"You find out anything?" she asked him.

"Not yet," he said. "But I'm assuming you have news?"

"I just spoke with Kathy Wilson and Bettina," said Guin. "They both got emails from Birdy last night, saying everything was fine."

"I'm guessing you don't believe that's the case, judging by your tone."

"No, I do not. Shortly after I spoke with them, I received an email, supposedly from Birdy, saying the same thing."

"Supposedly?"

"When I checked out the address, it wasn't the same address he gave me."

"Maybe he has more than one email address," said Craig. "Many people do."

"I thought of that, but I have a feeling."

"And what does your 'feeling' tell you?"

"That Birdy is in trouble."

"You tell the police about the emails?" asked Craig.

"Not yet," said Guin. "They'll probably say this proves that he's okay, and I know he's not."

Craig sighed.

"I know I shouldn't ask this but, what do you want me to do?"

Guin smiled. Despite his being supposedly retired, Craig still couldn't resist the opportunity to uncover a crime.

"As a matter of fact…" she said.

CHAPTER 40

"So, Shelly will go ring the doorbell and then distract whoever answers, that is if anyone's at home, and I'll sneak in the side door and search for Birdy," Guin explained to Craig.

"And I'm to keep an eye on the place and text you if I see anyone? That's your plan?" he asked, his tone betraying a certain amount of skepticism.

"Unless you have a better one," said Guin.

Craig sighed.

"And you're sure the Wilsons are away until Wednesday and this couple isn't actually staying there?"

"That's what Kathy Wilson said."

"I don't like it."

Guin held her breath. She needed Craig if this was going to work.

"However, I know there's probably nothing I can do to stop you..."

"Probably not," said Guin.

Craig furrowed his brow and sighed.

"I'll keep an eye out. But if you're not back out of that house in fifteen minutes, I'm calling the police. You got it?"

"Got it," said Guin, smiling.

"What time we going over there?" he asked.

"Nine o'clock tonight. Catalina and Tomas should be gone by then."

"And if not?" asked Craig.

"Like I said, Shelly will distract them while I sneak in the side door."

"I still don't like it. What if the police are still watching the place?"

"We'll avoid them," said Guin.

Craig made a noise that sounded like disapproval to Guin.

"No one's going to be there, Craig. Birdy's probably not even there. But I have to check."

"Fine," huffed Craig. "I still don't like it."

"I know," said Guin. "But a man's life may be in danger. So, I'll see you over at Beach Access #6 at nine?"

"Yeah," said Craig. "I just need to figure out what to tell Betty."

"I'm sure you'll think of something," said Guin. "And again, thank you."

Craig grumbled goodbye, then hung up.

Guin arrived at Shelly's place at eight and went over the plan with her again.

"I don't care what you tell them," said Guin. "Just make it sound convincing. And keep them occupied for as long as you can."

"What about the police?" asked Shelly. "Did you tell the detective what you're up to?"

"Absolutely not," said Guin. "They probably think Birdy is fine, thanks to those emails he supposedly sent. And the detective would tell me I was wasting my time, or, more likely, try to stop me."

Guin had told Shelly about the emails, and she agreed they sounded suspicious.

"What if someone shoots at us?"

Guin paused. She didn't have a good answer.

"I doubt that anyone will shoot at us," she finally said.

"I hope not. Steve would kill me."

Guin smiled.

Shelly had told Steve that Guin had been feeling blue, and that she was taking her out for dessert to cheer her up.

"Okay, so are we set?" asked Guin.

"Ready when you are!" said Shelly.

"Bye Steve!" Guin called.

"I'll be home around ten!" Shelly added.

There was no answer.

"He probably has his headphones on," said Shelly.

Guin took a deep breath, then she and Shelly headed out.

Shelly parked her car at Beach Access #6, Guin having left the Mini at Shelly and Steve's place. Craig arrived a few minutes later.

She went over the plan with the two of them one more time. Then they made their way down the Wilsons' driveway. Guin had brought a special flashlight that she used during sea turtle season, which emitted a soft, amber light. Craig positioned himself in a spot with a clear view of the front door and the side door, hidden from view. Then Shelly and Guin quietly walked to the house, which appeared to be dark, except for a light above the front door.

Guin went around the side and found the door Kathy Wilson had mentioned. She gently turned it and found it unlocked. She gave Shelly the okay sign with her flashlight, flicking it on and off twice. Then Shelly climbed the two short flights of steps to the front door and rang the doorbell as Guin quietly opened the side door and let herself in.

Shelly waited at the front door for someone to answer. When no one did, she rang the doorbell again. Then she knocked. Still no answer. She waited a couple more minutes, then climbed down the stairs and went to where Craig was positioned.

"Nobody home?" he asked.

"Doesn't appear to be," said Shelly. "I rang the doorbell twice, and knocked, but no one answered."

Craig made a face. He didn't like it.

Inside, Guin was feeling her way around. She had only seen the lower level of the Wilsons' house briefly, and not in the dark. She didn't dare turn on any lights, using only her sea turtle flashlight, which didn't give off much light. She moved around, as silently as she could, opening doors and peering inside, quietly calling Birdy's name. She felt a bit ridiculous, but she knew of no other way to prove that Birdy wasn't there.

She made her way quietly up the stairs to the main level, though she doubted Birdy was there. Still, she felt she had to check. She held her breath as she crossed in front of the front door and made her way to the guest room. She had checked the guest room on the lower level, as well as the storage area, and there had been no sign of Birdy. There was also no sign of him here, or in John Wilson's office, which had, at one time, been another bedroom.

She sighed and made her way, practically on tip-toe, up to the second floor, where the master bedroom and another guest room were located. Guin quickly went into the master and looked around, quietly calling Birdy's name. Again, nothing.

She went down the short hallway to the last guest room, the one Birdy used when he was visiting, and slowly opened the door.

"Birdy?" she called, barely above a whisper.

She shined the flashlight on the bed. There, seemingly asleep, was Birdy.

"Birdy!" she said, overcome with relief.

She quickly moved toward the bed, when a voice, somewhere in the dark, stopped her.

"Good evening, Guinivere. We've been expecting you."

Guin whirled around, shining the flashlight on the speaker.

"You!" she said.

Kathy Wilson smiled at her.

"You said you were away!" said Guin, accusingly.

"I was, until a little while ago. Your call had us change our plans."

Guin turned back to Birdy. She leaned over and gently touched the side of his head.

"Birdy, are you okay?" she asked, softly.

There was no response, and his head seemed cool and damp.

"What have you done to him?" asked Guin, turning back to face Mrs. Wilson.

"Nothing. Just a mild sedative," she replied.

Guin shone the flashlight on Birdy. He didn't move. And he looked awfully pale.

"Doesn't look mild to me."

"I guess you're just going to have to trust me," said Mrs. Wilson, who was sitting in a chair near the other side of the bed.

"Well, sedative or no, I'm getting Birdy out of here," Guin announced.

Mrs. Wilson chuckled.

"And how do you plan on doing that?"

Guin made a face. Birdy probably outweighed her by at least fifty pounds. But she had to try. She moved toward the bed.

"Stop right there," commanded Mrs. Wilson.

Guin ignored her.

"Birdy, it's Guin," she said, jostling him slightly.

"I said, Stop right there," Mrs. Wilson repeated.

"Or what?" asked Guin, turning to look at her.

"Or I will take this gun and shoot you," said Mrs. Wilson.

Guin looked down and noticed Mrs. Wilson was pointing a gun right at her.

"Did you shoot Birdy?"

"No," Mrs. Wilson replied.

Guin looked skeptical.

"That was a misunderstanding," said Mrs. Wilson, still holding the gun on Guin. "Tomas was only supposed to fire a warning shot, not actually hit him."

"He could have killed him!" said Guin.

"I have already spoken to Tomas about that. He was quite apologetic. As for you..."

"I don't believe you would really shoot me," said Guin.

"Oh?" said Mrs. Wilson, smiling in the dim light. "Care to test that theory? What do you think the police would say? You are trespassing on private property, my dear. You broke into my home, and no one would fault a little old lady for trying to protect herself from a thief."

"I'm no thief, and you're no little old lady," said Guin, acidly.

"Maybe not to you, but to the rest of the world..."

Guin suddenly felt helpless. She looked over at Birdy, but he was clearly not about to help her. Then she looked back at Mrs. Wilson.

"I'm calling the police," said Guin, reaching for her phone, which was tucked into her back pocket.

"I wouldn't do that if I were you," said Mrs. Wilson.

Guin tried to surreptitiously press the button to call the police when suddenly an arm shot out from behind her and grabbed her across the chest.

"Stop!" Guin cried out.

A second later, another arm reached around her other side, and she felt a cloth being placed over her nose and mouth.

"Noooo…" she cried. Then all was dark.

"I thought you'd never get out of that bathroom," Mrs. Wilson said to her husband.

"Sorry. Couldn't help it."

"Yes, well," said Mrs. Wilson. "Now we have two bodies to move."

They looked down at the bed, where Birdy and Guin were lying side by side.

"They do make rather a nice couple," said Mrs. Wilson. "A shame we'll never know."

"And risk him ruining us?" asked Mr. Wilson.

Mrs. Wilson sighed.

"You put the blankets in the trunk?"

"Everything's ready."

"Good. Now let's get these two out of here before anyone else shows up."

With great effort, the Wilsons hauled Birdy and Guin to the elevator, which was located just outside the guest room. Then they rode down to the lower level.

"Hmph," groaned Mr. Wilson, dragging Birdy's body out of the elevator.

"Be careful with him," admonished Mrs. Wilson.

"Fine, you try lifting him," said Mr. Wilson.

Mrs. Wilson made a face.

"We should have told Tomas to stay."

"The fewer people involved, the better," said Mr. Wilson.

"Yes, well…" Mrs. Wilson replied.

Mr. Wilson dragged Birdy to an SUV that was parked in the garage.

"Open the trunk," he told his wife.

"Just wiggle your foot in front of the sensor," she grunted in reply.

She was busy trying to drag Guin's prostrate form to the vehicle and was struggling.

"Here, let me help you with her," said Mr. Wilson, lowering Birdy to the ground.

Mrs. Wilson placed Guin on the floor (she hadn't gotten very far) and waited for her husband. He gently picked Guin up in his arms and carried her to the back of the SUV.

"Light as a baby," he said. "Shall we put her in the back seat?"

"Fine. Wherever. We'll just need to cover them."

"Open the back door for me," said Mr. Wilson.

His wife came over and opened the rear driver's side door.

Mr. Wilson carefully placed Guin inside. She stirred and made a muffled sound as he laid her down across the back seat.

"You think we need to give her more chloroform?" he asked his wife.

"How much did you give her?"

"I just poured some onto the cloth."

Mrs. Wilson looked over at Guin, who was passed out in the back seat.

"Better not risk it. Besides, we need to get them to the yacht."

"Whatever you say," said Mr. Wilson. "Give me a hand with Birdy."

They started to put him in the trunk, when Mrs. Wilson stopped.

"I have a better idea. Put him in the back seat, next to Ms. Jones."

They moved Guin over slightly, placing her upright, then sat Birdy next to her. Guin's head leaned against Birdy's shoulder.

"Let's go," said Mrs. Wilson. "But first…"

She disconnected the safety on the garage door.

"Now open it, carefully," she commanded her husband. "We don't want to make any noise."

Mr. Wilson bent down and slowly pulled up the garage door, grunting as he did so. When it was open all the way, he got in the car.

They slowly pulled out, not turning on the headlights.

"Good thing you had Tomas disconnect the sensor on the outdoor lights," said Mr. Wilson.

Mrs. Wilson did not reply.

They headed slowly down the driveway and turned onto West Gulf Drive. They were nearing Rabbit Road when they heard the sound of sirens.

"Floor it!" commanded Mrs. Wilson.

Mr. Wilson accelerated, but as he picked up speed, he was confronted with several sets of headlights coming right at him. He slammed on the brakes.

"What are you doing?!" shouted Mrs. Wilson.

"Trying not to get us killed!" he shouted back.

The headlights and the sirens came closer, stopping a few feet ahead of them.

"Come out with your hands up," came a voice over a bullhorn.

The Wilsons turned to each other.

"Put the car in reverse!" commanded Mrs. Wilson.

Mr. Wilson looked over at her.

"It's over, Kathy."

"No!" she shrieked. "It is NOT over," she said, giving him a hostile look. "Just shut up and let me do the talking."

A bright light shone into the window. There were

policemen stationed on either side of the vehicle, with guns pointed at them.

"Come out with your hands up," repeated the voice.

Mr. Wilson opened the door.

"Hands up over your head," commanded the officer by the driver's side door.

Mr. Wilson placed his hands over his head.

"You, too," said the officer, addressing Mrs. Wilson.

"You wouldn't shoot a little, old lady, would you?" asked Mrs. Wilson, sweetly.

The passenger side door of the SUV was jerked open.

"Hands up, Mrs. Wilson," ordered Detective O'Loughlin. "Now."

"No need to be rude," said Mrs. Wilson.

"Now slowly get out of the vehicle," commanded the detective.

"It's a bit steep. Could someone lend me a hand?" she asked.

The detective scowled.

"Officer Pettit, would you please help Mrs. Wilson down?"

Officer Pettit came over and helped Mrs. Wilson out of the SUV.

"Thank you, young man," she said, sweetly. "Now what is all this fuss about?"

"Search the vehicle," commanded the detective.

"There are two people in the backseat," said a female officer. "A man and a woman."

The detective went around to the back and shone his flashlight on the two forms, neither of which moved.

"Check to see if they're breathing," the detective commanded.

"Yes sir," said the female officer.

She gently checked Birdy and Guin.

"They're alive," she said.

"Of course they're alive!" chided Mrs. Wilson. "They just had a bit too much to drink at dinner, and we kindly offered to take them home. They must have passed out."

The detective remained stone-faced.

"See if you can wake them up," he said to the female officer.

"Yes sir."

She got into the SUV and gently nudged Guin.

"Miss? Miss, wake up. You okay?"

Guin mumbled something but didn't wake up.

"She's pretty out of it, sir."

"Try the other one," commanded the detective. "Officer Pettit, see if you can help Officer Rodriguez."

Officer Pettit went around to the other side of the SUV and opened the door. Then he gently nudged Birdy.

"Wake up, sir."

Nothing.

He nudged Birdy a little harder.

"Sir, wake up," said Officer Pettit.

But Birdy didn't move.

Officer Pettit shook his head.

"I told you, they just had too much to drink. Young people," said Mrs. Wilson, shaking her head. "Now, if there's anything else, officers?"

Just then a car pulled up behind the SUV and two figures ran out.

"Stop that car!" shouted Shelly, even though the SUV was already stopped. "Guin's in there!"

Craig quickly came up behind Shelly.

"Mr. Jeffers," said the detective, acknowledging him.

"Is Guin okay?" asked Craig, looking from the detective to Officers Pettit and Rodriguez.

"According to these folks here, Ms. Jones and her companion just had a little too much to drink at dinner," replied the detective.

Craig looked at the detective.

"I take it that is not the case," said the detective.

"The Wilsons tried to kidnap Guin and that ornithologist!" said Shelly, unable to contain herself.

"Is that so?" the detective asked Mr. Wilson.

"Nonsense!" said Mr. Wilson. "It's like my wife said. We were having a little dinner party, and Ms. Jones and Mr. McMurtry just had a little too much to drink."

"Yeah, right, and I'm the King of England," said Craig.

The detective's lips curled up slightly.

"I'll bet you my best fishing rod these two are responsible for McMurtry's disappearance," continued Craig.

"I see," said the detective. "Well, why don't we all go over to the Sanibel Police Department and have us a nice little chat?"

He looked over at Mr. and Mrs. Wilson.

"You two, please accompany Officers Pettit and Rodriguez."

The two officers escorted the Wilsons to their police vehicle.

"What about Guin? Is she okay?" asked Shelly, clearly worried.

The detective went around to the side of the SUV.

"Ms. Jones," he said, slightly shaking her. "Guin," he said, in a voice no one else could hear.

Guin smiled and shifted slightly but didn't wake up. The detective sighed.

"Officer Rayburn, get EMS on the phone and have them send a team over to the police department, pronto."

"Yes, sir."

"And how do you propose getting them over to the police department?" asked Craig.

"Officer Rayburn here will take them."

"Do you think it's safe to move them?" Craig asked.

"He'll drive the SUV," replied the detective.

"What about us?" asked Shelly. "Someone should stay with Guin."

The detective looked over at her.

"Ms. Jones will be fine, Mrs. Silverman."

"How do you know that?" asked Shelly.

She stood there, looking at him, her hands on her hips.

"I will personally see to it," replied the detective.

Shelly thought about it for several seconds.

"Well, okay. But I don't like it. I'm her best friend. I should stay with her."

"I'm sure Ms. Jones would appreciate that, but right now what she needs most is medical attention."

"Yes, well…" said Shelly, wavering.

"I will have someone contact you as soon as Ms. Jones has been checked out."

"They'd better," said Shelly.

"I wouldn't mind getting a call, too," said Craig.

"Of course," said the detective. "Now, if you would escort Mrs. Silverman home, or to wherever you two came from…"

"No problem," said Craig. "And thank you."

The detective gave Craig a curt nod, then called over to Officer Rayburn. A few minutes later, the detective, the other police car, and the SUV were on their way to the Sanibel Police Department.

CHAPTER 41

Birdy was taken to the hospital. As for Guin, the paramedics had been able to revive her at the Sanibel Police Department. They had wanted her to go to the hospital, too, but she had refused. Even though she had felt nauseous and dizzy, she just wanted to go home and snuggle with the cats. The detective had argued with her, but Guin insisted she would be better sleeping it off at home.

"Fine," said the detective. "But I'm taking you myself."

Guin had not objected.

They had exited the police department and were nearly down the stairs when Guin had stumbled. The detective had grabbed her, holding her close.

"You okay?" he said.

Guin could feel his breath in her ear. It was like a jolt of electricity.

She looked up at him.

"I think so," she replied.

They stood there for a few more seconds, then he helped her to his car.

The detective didn't say anything as they drove, which surprised Guin. She was sure he was going to chastise her for sneaking into the Wilsons'.

When they arrived at her condo, the detective suggested they take the elevator, but Guin said she'd rather walk up the stairs. When they got to her door, Guin fumbled in her bag for her keys. The detective gently took the bag from Guin's shaking hands, and a minute later they were inside.

Both cats were waiting for them. They looked up at Guin and the detective. Then Fauna started to meow.

"I should feed them," Guin said to the detective.

"I can do it," he replied. "You need to get to bed."

Guin smiled at him.

"There's a bag of dry food in the pantry. Give them each a scoop."

The detective nodded and Guin made her way to the bedroom, placing one hand along the wall to steady herself.

"Easy there," said the detective, coming over to help her.

"I'm fine," said Guin. Though she felt terrible.

The detective helped her over to the bed.

"You sure you're okay?" he asked, as she collapsed onto her pillows.

She looked up at him.

"I feel like hell, but I'll live," she said.

He continued to stand above her.

"Really detective, I'll be fine. As long as you feed the cats."

She smiled up at him.

The detective paused, then turned and went to the kitchen.

Guin quickly pulled off her shirt and bra and pulled on her nightshirt. She needed to brush her teeth, but she felt too tired to move.

The detective returned a minute later.

"You going to be okay?" he asked her.

"Yeah," said Guin. "Though you promise not to tell anyone if I don't brush my teeth?"

The detective smiled, or what passed for a smile on him.

"I promise."

She looked up at him.

"You can go, detective. Really, I'll be fine."

The detective hesitated.

She placed a hand on the detective's arm. It felt solid.

"Go. I'll call you in the morning."

He stood there for another minute, as if debating with himself, then turned to go.

"Are you going to arrest the Wilsons?" she called to him as he stood in the doorway.

He stopped and turned.

"We'll need testimony from you and Mr. McMurtry."

"I'd be happy to supply it, after I've gotten some sleep," she said, yawning.

"You sure you don't want me to stay?"

Guin smiled.

"That's very gallant of you, detective. But really, I'll be fine."

Though a part of her wanted the detective to stay with her.

"I'll call you as soon as I get up. Now go."

The detective mumbled something, then turned to go. This time Guin didn't call him back. As soon as she heard the front door close, she forced herself out of bed and headed to the bathroom. A few minutes later, she was fast asleep.

The next morning she woke up with a headache but felt much better. She made her way to the kitchen and brewed a pot of coffee. She would need it. After having a few sips of caffeine, she grabbed her phone and called the detective.

"You feeling better?" he asked her.

"Much," she said. "And I'm ready to file a report. When should I come over there?"

"Aren't you forgetting something?" said the detective.

Guin made a face. Was she forgetting something? She racked her brain, which hurt. Oh right, the Mini was still parked over by Shelly and Steve's.

"I can call a cab, or I guess I could ask Shelly to come get me."

Knowing Shelly, she had probably left a dozen text messages for her, asking if she was okay.

"Don't bother," said the detective. "I'll come get you. Can you be ready in half an hour?"

"Sure," said Guin. "But really, you don't have to get me, detective. I can get a ride."

"I'll be there at 8:15," he said. Then he ended the call.

Guin drank more of her coffee. Then she toasted herself some bread. When it was ready, she slathered it with butter and a little jam. Comfort food. She ate it standing up, staring out past the lanai. When she was done, she checked her messages. As predicted, there were several panicky texts from Shelly, along with one from Craig and another from Ris. There was also a voicemail, a text message, and an email from her mother, all of which she ignored.

She called Shelly's number.

"Oh my God, are you okay?" said Shelly, as soon as she answered. "I was so worried! I wanted to go with you to the police department, but the detective wouldn't let me."

Guin smiled.

"I'm fine."

"Thank God!" said Shelly.

"Hey, Shell, I can't really talk. I just wanted to let you know I was okay. Can I phone you later?"

"Sure," she said, though Guin could hear the disappointment in her voice. "You want me to bring your car over to your place?"

"Thanks, but you don't have to. I'll come pick it up later."

"Okay," said Shelly.

Guin ended the call and then entered Craig's number.

"You okay?" he asked her.

"I'm fine. Just have a slamming headache. The detective's coming to pick me up in a few. I just wanted to let you know I'm alive."

"Thank goodness for that," said Craig. "You had us pretty scared."

"I know, and I'm sorry."

She looked at the clock.

"Gotta go. I'll message you later."

She ended the call and opened the text from Ris.

"Miss you," he had written, adding the emoji blowing a kiss.

"Miss you, too," she wrote him back, with the same emoji, though her heart wasn't in it.

"You what?!"

Guin looked at the detective, incredulous.

The detective had picked her up and driven her over to the police department. Guin had a half-dozen questions she wanted to ask him, but she waited until they were seated in the detective's office. As soon as he had closed the door, however, she had him about the Wilsons.

"We had to let them go this morning," he explained. "But with your testimony and Mr. McMurtry's, the DA should have more than enough to convict, fancy lawyer or no."

Guin wasn't convinced. She had seen too many wealthy people get off, and she was sure the Wilsons would hire the best lawyer, or lawyers, money could buy. Already one had managed to extricate them from police custody.

"Speaking of Birdy," she said, turning her gaze back on

the detective, "have you heard anything? Is he going to be okay?"

"He should be released from the hospital later today," replied the detective.

"Today? Is he well enough?"

"Ms. Betteridge insisted. She hired a private nurse to look after him."

"Can I go see him?" Guin asked.

The detective regarded her.

"I just want to make sure he's all right."

"The doctors expect him to make a full recovery," replied the detective. "As long as he takes it easy."

"And isn't poisoned or shot at," Guin added.

The detective smirked.

"So where's Bettina taking him?"

"To the Ritz," replied the detective.

Guin raised an eyebrow.

"So, I assume you have some questions for me."

"Tell me everything you know about the Wilsons," began the detective. And she did.

The detective sat back in his chair, fingering the Carlton Fisk-autographed baseball he kept on his desk. He asked her several questions, jotting down her answers in his notebook. When Guin was done, he closed the notebook and leaned back in his chair.

"We suspected the Wilsons were somehow involved," he told Guin.

"Birdy must be devastated," she said. "They were like parents to him."

"Some parents. That company of theirs is bad news. Those supplements they sell…. They should be illegal."

He shook his head.

"They sold pills to kids, claiming they'd make them more alert. Instead, they made them sick."

"Will the FDA investigate?" Guin asked.

"Maybe," said the detective. "Natura was careful not to market their products as able to prevent or cure any diseases."

"But surely someone can do something? I mean, if their products were actually harming people."

The detective sighed.

"Good luck with that. These natural supplements companies are all the same. You know how many people have tried to sue companies like Natura?"

Guin had seen a few articles mentioning legal trouble, but…

"But surely, this is different?"

"I hope so," said the detective. "If Mr. McMurtry is willing to go public."

"He was before," said Guin.

"That was before he knew his friends were involved."

"What about Digby Blyleven? He's the CEO of Natura. Surely, he's involved, too."

"He and his assistant and that marketing guy of his are all being brought in for questioning. It's a good thing Jeffers called us when he did. Otherwise you and McMurtry might have been setting sail to God knows where on that yacht of his."

Guin gulped.

"They were going to take us to Digby's yacht and dump us somewhere?"

"That's what we suspect."

Guin felt a bit dizzy.

"You okay?" the detective asked.

"Just still a bit woozy," Guin replied.

"You want some coffee?"

"You trying to kill me?" Guin asked.

The coffee at the police department was terrible.

"I'll be okay," said Guin. "Thank you for rescuing me."

"Thank your friends," said the detective.

Guin would be sure to do that.

"So, can I see Birdy?"

"After we've spoken with him. That agent of his is insisting he be allowed to recuperate in peace for a day or two before we speak with him, but I'm going to drive over there later."

"Can I come with you? I promise I won't say a word."

The detective looked at her.

"Okay, maybe a few words, but I promise not to interrupt. I just want to see him, make sure he's okay."

The detective rubbed his face.

"Fine, but no interrupting."

"I promise," said Guin, holding up her hand in the Girl Scout salute.

CHAPTER 42

Guin accompanied the detective to the Ritz-Carlton in Naples that afternoon. Bettina had argued with the detective, telling him that Birdy was still quite weak, and was in no shape to entertain visitors, but Birdy had overruled her. The sooner this whole thing was over with, he had told her, the sooner he could be on his way to Australia and New Guinea. So she had agreed to let the detective (and Guin) come see him.

Bettina escorted them to Birdy's bedroom. Birdy was propped up in a king-sized bed. Nearby was a woman, no doubt the private nurse Bettina had hired.

Birdy looked like a cadaver, Guin thought. He was so thin and pale. She couldn't imagine him being able to go anywhere anytime soon.

The detective, to his credit, asked Birdy if he was sure he was up to being questioned. But Birdy told him he was fine. He just needed some water. He took a couple of sips, then gestured for the detective to have a seat.

The detective asked Bettina and the nurse to give them some privacy. Bettina made to object but stopped at a look from the detective. She scowled at Guin as she left.

Guin took a seat a little ways away. The detective shot her a warning look, then began to question Birdy.

Birdy told the detective about his work for Natura, and

of his discomfort upon learning about how the company was marketing some of the plants he'd been sourcing for them and promoting. He told him he had confronted Dick Grayson, the Chief Marketing Officer, but that Grayson had convinced him that Natura was on the up and up, that it was all a misunderstanding.

Then he had read in the paper about a teenage boy whose family was suing Natura. The boy was "addicted," his parents' term, to one of Natura's supplements and had wound up committing suicide. When Birdy read the name of the product supposedly responsible, he felt ill. It was one of the ones he promoted. He immediately went back to Grayson and told him he was done with Natura and threatened to go public with what he knew.

The detective asked him if he knew of the Wilsons' involvement with Natura and Birdy shook his head. He said he knew the Wilsons were friendly, or socialized, with the CEO, J. Douglas Blyleven, that they served on the board of some charity together, but he had no idea they were major investors in the company. Neither Bettina nor the Wilsons nor Dick Grayson had mentioned it, and frankly he hadn't looked into Natura too deeply. That was Bettina's job.

Regarding why he had left the Ritz shortly after they had checked in, and how he had wound up back at the Wilsons', he told the detective that the Wilsons' housekeeper, Catalina, had paid him a visit at the hotel shortly after he had arrived there. She was quite upset at the time and told him that Mr. Wilson had suffered a massive heart attack and that Mrs. Wilson had asked her and Tomas to bring Birdy, just as soon as they could.

So she was the woman posing as Birdy's wife, who had given Guin's name! It all made sense now, thought Guin. Kathy Wilson must have overheard Bettina checking in and sent Catalina and Tomas to the Ritz to lure Birdy back to

Sanibel, having her use Guin's name in case anyone questioned reception, to throw them off the trail.

It hadn't occurred to Birdy to question Catalina's story, he told the detective. Catalina looked so worried. And he knew John Wilson wasn't in the best of health. He didn't bring anything with him as he had assumed he would be back at the hotel later that evening, and Catalina seemed to be in a big hurry. Little did he know that shortly after he got in their car, he'd be drugged—and kept as a prisoner at the Wilsons'. Indeed, he had no idea where he was until he regained consciousness at the hospital early that morning.

Birdy started to cough, and Guin immediately got up and ran over to him.

"You okay?" she asked. "Can I get you some more water?"

Birdy smiled up at her.

"Please," he said. "Though I would kill for some Scotch."

"Water coming right up," said Guin.

She grabbed his empty glass and went into the bathroom to refill it.

"Here you go," she said, handing it back to him a minute later.

He took a few sips, then handed it back to her.

"Thanks."

Guin looked over at the detective, who was reviewing his notes.

"You have any more questions?" Guin asked him.

"Not for Mr. McMurtry," he said, closing his notebook. "But I'd like to speak with that agent of his."

The detective stood up and moved toward the door.

"Wait," Birdy called.

Guin and the detective turned.

"Guin…" Birdy said.

"You okay if I stay?" Guin asked the detective.

"Be my guest," replied the detective. "I think I can handle Ms. Betteridge."

Guin smiled.

"Just let me know when you're done."

The detective nodded, then left the room, closing the door behind him.

Birdy reached out a hand. Guin walked over and took it.

Birdy stayed at the Ritz for several more days, and Guin stopped by to see him a couple more times. Birdy would regale her with tales of his exploits, and Guin would smile indulgently. She could tell he loved what he did, and she wasn't bothered by the fact that he rarely asked her about her life.

Finally, nearly a week after he had checked in, he told Guin he was heading off to New Guinea and invited her to have dinner with him before he left. She had agreed.

As they waited for their coffee, Birdy leaned across the table and grabbed Guin's hands.

"Come with me, Guin."

Guin had to admit a small part of her was tempted.

"I mean it," Birdy said, gazing into her eyes.

"I know you do, but..."

"Most women I know would leap at the offer," Birdy told her.

Guin smiled. She knew Birdy wasn't being arrogant. Well, maybe a bit. That was just the way he was.

"I'm sorry, Birdy, but the answer is still no. Though... You could always join me and Ris for a drink in Sydney!" she said brightly, smiling at him.

Birdy sighed. He was headed to the rainforests of New

Guinea the next day to photograph the flame bowerbird, the male of which had bright orange and yellow plumage and a yellow-tipped black tail and performed a mesmerizing courtship dance to lure a mate. He would be stopping in Sydney afterward, right around the time Guin would be there with Ris.

"I hope Hartwick knows how lucky he is."

Guin wondered. She had spoken to Ris the night before, very briefly, after not hearing from him for several days. They had discussed their plans for their Australia rendezvous. She couldn't wait.

"Hello? You there?"

Birdy was looking at her.

"Sorry, my mind must have wandered," Guin replied.

She smiled at him.

The server came over with their coffees. Birdy took a sip of his and made a face.

"Can anyone around here make a decent cup of coffee?" he asked her. "Come with me, Guin. Please…"

He looked so earnest, she wanted to laugh, but she didn't.

She placed a hand atop his.

"I appreciate the offer, but I can't."

Just then a phone started buzzing, Birdy's.

He glanced at it and frowned.

"Bad news?" Guin asked.

Birdy looked at his phone.

"It's Bettina."

"Ah," said Guin. "Well, I should get going anyway."

Birdy insisted on paying. Then he walked Guin to her car.

"Maybe I will take you up on that drink," he said, as they stood next to the Mini. "As long as Hartwick pays. He owes me one."

Guin smiled.

"I'm sure he'd love to catch up with you."

Birdy leaned over and gave Guin a kiss on the cheek.

"Until we meet again then," he said.

"Until we meet again," said Guin.

Thanks to Guin's and Birdy's testimonies, the Wilsons were charged with attempted murder and kidnapping. However, they were out on bail. And Guin feared they might never serve time as they had hired one of the top defense attorneys in Florida.

Catalina and Tomas had also been arrested, but both had refused to talk. Guin was convinced the Wilsons were paying their legal bills as she doubted they could afford the high-priced lawyer who was representing them.

As for Natura, there was a class-action suit pending against the company, and Birdy had agreed to testify on the plaintiffs' behalf. However, their products were still being sold. And both Digby and Dick Grayson swore they had had nothing to do with Birdy's poisoning, shooting, or kidnapping. Guin and the detective highly doubted both claims. But there was nothing they could do, though Guin had sent a former colleague of hers, who now worked at Bloomberg, her dirt on Natura. And he said he'd take a closer look at the company.

As for her mother's visit, it hadn't gone as badly as Guin had feared. Her brother Lance had flown down last minute for a few days, so she didn't have to deal with her mother on her own the entire time. And her mother and stepfather had enjoyed their time in Naples, from brunch at Jane's Garden Café, to tea at Brambles English Tea Room (though her mother loudly whispered that it didn't hold a candle to Claridge's, at which Guin and Lance had rolled their eyes), to dinner at the French Brasserie Rustique, as well as the activities Guin had suggested—which included a visit to the Baker Museum and the Naples Botanical Garden. They spent a single day on Sanibel and Captiva, which her mother deemed "quaint." But that was fine by Guin.

Her mother was now back up north, and Guin was getting ready to fly to Australia, when she received a call from her real estate agent, Polly Fahnestock.

"Hey, Poll, what's up?" Guin asked her.

"I know you're going away for two weeks," Polly said. "But you have to come look at this cottage over by West Gulf that just came on the market. It's perfect!"

Guin was skeptical.

"I'm leaving in two days, Polly."

"What are you doing right now?" she asked her.

"Is this place really that great?"

"Trust me," said Polly.

Guin made a face.

"Fine. What time should I meet you?"

"Now?"

"What's the address?" Guin asked.

Polly gave it to her.

"Fine, I'll see you there in 20 minutes."

"Perfect," said Polly.

The flight to Sydney had taken forever. Guin had flown from Fort Myers to Dallas, then from Dallas to Sydney. It had taken a day, and she was exhausted. Thank God for Business Class. On the flight to Dallas, she had kept thinking about the cottage near West Gulf Drive Polly had shown her. It really was perfect. But, as she told Polly, now was not the best time to make an offer.

Polly had told her to think about it, and Guin had. But

she wanted to discuss it with Ris first. That would not be a fun conversation. But she truly felt this place could be the one, with a little bit of work.

She emerged from the long flight from Dallas to Sydney disheveled and made straight for the bathroom, wanting to freshen up before she saw Ris, who would be meeting her outside the baggage claim area.

She splashed some cold water on her face and brushed her teeth and her hair, but she still felt like she looked like something the cat had dragged in. Not that either of her cats had ever dragged in anything.

She sighed as she looked at her reflection. Then she made her way to passport control, then onto baggage claim and customs, finally exiting into the arrivals' hall. She glanced around, looking for Ris.

"Guin!"

She turned and saw him moving toward her. Oh my God, she thought. How could he possibly look any better than he already did? But he did. She suddenly felt incredibly self-conscious. But before she could think too much, he picked her up and swung her around, causing her to laugh and feel all warm inside.

"God, I've missed you," he said, kissing her.

"I've missed you, too," Guin said, looking up at him, her cheeks flushed.

"Come," he said, taking her hand.

"My luggage?" Guin replied, smiling up at him.

He smiled sheepishly.

"Sorry," he said.

He grabbed the handle of Guin's suitcase in one hand and the handle of her carry-on in the other and headed toward the exit.

"Hey, wait up!" said Guin.

Ris was nearly a foot taller than Guin, with longer legs,

and Guin was worried about losing him in the crowded airport.

He stopped and waited for her to catch up.

"Where are we going?" she asked him.

"To my place."

"Can I take a nap when I get there?" she asked him.

"Maybe," he said, a twinkle in his eye.

She smiled back at him, then followed him out of the airport.

"Oh my God!" said Guin, staring out the window of the apartment. "That's the Sydney Opera House!"

Ris smiled.

"It is."

Guin looked around.

"This place is amazing. How on earth did you find it?"

"It belongs to a friend," he replied.

"Must be a good friend," said Guin. "Where's he now?"

"She's in Hong Kong on business."

Guin noted the "she" and felt a stab of unease.

"Well, very nice of her to lend you her place."

"You'll have to meet Ling when she comes to Florida."

"Does she come to Florida often?" Guin asked.

"Occasionally," Ris replied.

Guin immediately imagined a beautiful Chinese woman with shiny, long black hair laughing at Ris's bad jokes and made a face.

"Something wrong?" Ris asked her, noticing her expression.

"Sorry, just jetlagged," Guin replied, then yawned.

"I know you want to sleep, but the best cure for jetlag is activity."

Guin wasn't so sure about that.

"Trust me," he said.

"Fine," Guin replied.

Her stomach let out a loud gurgle.

Ris smiled.

"First order of business, food."

At the mention of the word *food*, Guin's stomach let out another gurgle. Ris laughed.

"Come, I'm taking you out for breakfast."

"Fine," said Guin, too tired and hungry to argue.

Ris smiled and took her to his favorite neighborhood bistro, just a few blocks away. Guin ordered a cappuccino, which came in a giant bowl, and the Belgian waffles and bacon, all of which were delicious.

"See," said Ris, when they were done. "I bet you're feeling better already."

"Yeah, yeah, yeah," said Guin, taking a last sip of her coffee. "So now what?"

"Now, I take you on the tour."

They spent the rest of the morning exploring Kirribilli, the area they were staying in, just across from downtown Sydney. Then Ris insisted they take a boat ride around Sydney harbor. Guin was exhausted by the time they got back to the flat around four.

"Can I go to bed now?" she asked.

"Not yet. There's still the surprise."

"Surprise?" she asked. "Can't it wait? I'm exhausted."

"Come on, you can make it. Besides, if you want to beat jet lag, you have to stay up until when you'd normally go to bed."

Guin groaned.

"You can put your feet up for a little while, but we need to head out at six."

"You going to tell me where we're going?"

"I told you, it's a surprise."

Guin rolled her eyes.

"Well, I'm going to take a shower," she announced. "Unless you have an objection?"

Ris smiled and told her to enjoy.

"Go get dressed. We need to head out soon."

Guin had been lounging in a pair of sweats and a big t-shirt after her shower.

She went into the bedroom and put on a dress. Then she put on some makeup. Normally, she wouldn't bother, but she felt that after her long trip, and day, she needed to add a little color to her face.

"Okay, I'm ready," she announced 15 minutes later.

She spun around in her dress.

Ris smiled at her.

"You look great. No one would ever know you were jetlagged," he said, looking dashing in a pair of chinos and a polo shirt.

"Yeah, right," said Guin.

"Shall we?" he said, offering her his arm.

"Do I have a choice?" she replied, taking it.

He laughed.

"Not really."

They arrived at the restaurant and Guin had to admit, the views were spectacular. The place was on the water, and you could see the Sydney Harbor Bridge and the business district.

"Is this the surprise?" she asked, as they stood on the deck, overlooking a large swimming pool.

"Nope. You're going to have to wait a little while longer."

As they stood there, looking out onto the water, she thought she heard someone calling Ris's name.

"Ris, you dog!"

She turned around. It couldn't be.

"And Guin! Looking as beautiful as ever."

Birdy took her hand and kissed it.

Guin felt herself blushing.

"Watch it, McMurtry," Ris growled, though Guin could tell he wasn't serious.

"Is this the surprise?" Guin asked, looking from one man to the other.

"It is!" said Ris. "Birdy's only in town a couple of days, and we thought…"

"Come," said Birdy. "I reserved a table for us and ordered some Champagne. I have some big news to share."

"And I have some big news, too," said Ris, giving Guin's shoulder a squeeze.

EPILOGUE

Birdy's big news was that he had won an award, a very prestigious award, he informed them, from National Geographic. And he had been hired to host a new documentary series on exotic birds, which would be airing on the National Geographic Channel.

"That's fabulous!" Guin said. And she meant it.

Birdy beamed.

"I've always wanted to host one of those nature shows."

"You'll be terrific," Guin told him.

"Well done," Ris added.

Birdy preened.

He also had some other news he thought Guin would be interested in.

"They set a trial date for the Wilsons."

"And?" Guin said, leaning forward.

"And there is a very good chance they will be going to jail in the near future."

"Good," said Guin. But she could tell by the expression on Birdy's face that he didn't take pleasure in the news. "I'm sorry," she added. "I know you were close."

He waved her away.

"They're going to get what they deserve. I spoke with the prosecutor. Thanks to my testimony, they have a pretty good case against them." He shook his head and took a sip of Champagne. "I just...."

Guin put a hand on top of his.

"You did the right thing."

"I know," said Birdy. "It still hurts."

"What about Natura?"

"The class action suit is proceeding, with my help. They have good lawyers, so it will take a while, but I have a feeling this time they won't be so lucky."

"Good," Guin said, again.

Ris cleared his throat.

Guin had almost forgotten about him.

"Didn't mean to hog the spotlight," said Birdy. "What's your big news, old man?"

"I've been invited to take over the chairmanship of the Marine & Ecological Sciences department at Florida Gulf Coast University."

"What?!" said Guin, staring at him.

Ris smiled.

"The current chair announced he would be retiring at the end of the school year and suggested I apply for the position. It's a big job, with a lot of responsibility, but I feel I'm up to it. The only catch is I need to fly back and do a series of interviews."

"Congratulations!" Birdy said, slapping Ris on the back.

"What about your trip, your lectures and things?" Guin asked him, somewhat stunned by the news.

"I'll have to cancel some things, but I can't pass up this opportunity. And it's only for a couple of weeks."

"Wow," Guin said, words failing her.

"I'm arranging the interviews to coincide with the Shell Show," he continued. "I figured they could use some help. Then I'll fly to Japan for a couple of weeks."

"And then?" asked Guin.

"Then I'll be home for good."

"But your trip?" Guin repeated. "Won't you miss seeing all those places you had talked about?"

Ris looked over at her and took her hands in his.

"The only thing I've missed since being here is you."

"Get a room," Birdy said, making a face.

He then picked up the Champagne bottle and refilled everyone's glass.

"A toast!" he said, raising his glass. "To people getting what they deserve—and to Guin!"

"To Guin," Ris said, raising his glass to her. "Thank you for coming all this way to see me."

Guin felt herself blushing. She took a sip of the Champagne.

"Cheers!" she said.

They clinked glasses and drank.

As they lay there in bed later that evening, Guin looked over at Ris. He had fallen asleep shortly after they had celebrated their reunion. She hadn't told him about the house. Hadn't wanted to. But now he would be coming back to Sanibel in a couple of weeks.

She gently touched his face. He even looked handsome when he slept. At her touch, he stirred.

"I didn't mean to wake you," Guin said.

He smiled up at her.

"Can't sleep?"

She shook her head.

"Come here," he said, pulling her close. "I know just the thing to tire you out."

"Oh you do, do you?" she said, allowing him to pull her on top of him.

"Um-hm," he said, kissing her softly, then rolling her over.

She kissed him back and sighed. A little while later, she was fast asleep.

"I can't believe I only have two more days in Australia," Guin said, as she stared out toward the ocean.

They had gone to a beach resort in Noosa, located to the north of Sydney, in Queensland, for a long weekend. Ris had rented a cottage right on the beach, and it had been heavenly.

In the distance, a phone rang.

"Is that your phone?" Ris asked.

"Hmm?" Guin answered.

"Your phone, it's been ringing nonstop."

Guin felt a bit panicky. Oh God, could something have happened to her mother, or Philip?

She ran to get her phone, but it had gone to voicemail, and she had been having problems accessing her voicemail messages in Australia. A few seconds later, she received a text. It was from Ginny.

"URGENT," read the text. "Suzy Seashell was just arrested. I need you back here, stat."

To be continued...

Look for Book Five in the Sanibel Island Mystery series, *Shell Shocked*, November 2019.

Acknowledgments

First, I'd like to thank you for reading this book. If you enjoyed it, please consider reviewing it or leaving a rating on Amazon and/or Goodreads.

Next, I'd like to thank my first readers: Amanda, Robin, Linda, and Sue (aka Mom), who made sure BIRDY was as good as (or better than) my previous books and were terrific at spotting typos and correcting errors. BIRDY is a better book because of the four of you.

Sadly, my beloved proofreader and stepfather, John, who was an expert on comma placement, as well as a bird watcher, passed away before I finished the book. But John, if you're out there somewhere, I hope you know I thought about you every day as I was writing this book. I miss you.

I'd also like to thank my incredibly talented cover designer, Kristin Bryant. I love this cover. And thank you to Polgarus Studio for making my books look as professional on the inside as they are on the outside.

Lastly, thank you to my wonderful, supportive husband, Kenny, who has always believed in me. I love you.

About the Sanibel Island Mystery series

To learn more about the Sanibel Island Mystery series, visit the website at http://www.SanibelIslandMysteries.com and "like" the Sanibel Island Mysteries Facebook page at https://www.facebook.com/SanibelIslandMysteries/.